CARRY-ON

CHRIS BELDEN

To Charles Peck —
Foster
For old times.
"All work & No play make
Jack a dull boy..."
All The best!

RAIN MOUNTAIN PRESS
NEW YORK CITY
- 2011 -

First Printing January 2012

Carry-on © 2012 by Chris Belden

ISBN: 978-0-9834783-4-8

Rain Mountain Press
www.rainmountainpress.com

Cover design and illustration by David Cole Wheeler.
Cover photograph, "Spirit Lake (Mount St. Helens)," by
Hieronymus Jones.

Text Layout:
David G. Barnett - Fat Cat Graphic Design
www.fatcatgraphic design.com

PRINTED BY
Publishers Graphics
Carol Stream, IL

Published in the good ol' U.S of A. by Rain Mountain Press, a small publisher with no ties to any corporation whatsoever, and thus barely surviving in the harsh world of publishing, so please tell your friends to support them and other small presses that are holding on, by the proverbial skin of their teeth, in an economy gone completely insane.

This book is a work of fiction, except in certain instances, when the author, as is his right as a creative person, has exploited certain real-life events for his own imaginative enjoyment and, hopefully, those of his readers. That said, none of the characters in this novel are real, not even the protagonist, who, admittedly, does share a few traits with the author.

Acknowledgments

The author wishes to express sincere thanks to the Renegades: Rob Cook, Marc DePalo, Stephanie Dickinson, Gil Fagiani, Mary Hebert, Andrew Kaufman, and Russ Siller.

With extra thanks to Stephanie and Rob, who so generously supported the writing and publication of this novel.

Last, but certainly not least, thanks to Melissa DeMeo and Francesca Belden, neither of whom can be blamed for this.

A portion of this novel previously appeared in *Skidrow Penthouse*.

Marriage is the unsuccessful attempt to make something lasting out of an incident.

—Albert Einstein

When I got to know her better, that is to say when she left me, no further explanation was necessary.

—*The Confessions of Zeno*, by Italo Svevo

There is so much hurt in the world. You have to evade and evade.

—Tennessee Williams

CHAPTER ONE: TURBULENCE

…Breathe.

You head down the long walkway, a slight tunneled descent, footsteps silent on thin carpeting, the air thick and warm, your fellow passengers clustered at the aircraft door like doomed cows boarding a truck—you need to breathe here, while you can, before you're sealed inside—*breathe*—your shoulder grown weary now from the weight of the carry-on bag, its contents growing heavier with each cowardly step you take—*C'mon, c'mon,* you think as ahead of you an old fart, decrepit, a thousand years old, with stiff bony hands, tries desperately to collapse the ingeniously designed handle on his little suitcase-on-wheels—Can I help? you ask, and he smiles yellow teeth, allows you to lift the bag over the gap, a transporting moment, stepping from land to something else entirely, something other—Thank you, young man—and here is the stewardess to greet you, Good morning, she says—ILSE, her name tag shouts in capital letters—and is that a twinkle in her eye? is it for you? can she possibly know it's your birthday? as you quickly thrust your left hand into your pocket, hiding your wedding band—Hi, you say, and she nods pleasantly—then a mumbled Oh crap as you enter the aisle which is now backed up with passengers attempting to stuff their baggage and hats and folded jackets and what-all into the overhead compartments— heave, push, groan, finagle—C'mon, c'mon, my shoulder is killing me, and oh how your arms itch, your forearms, the red lines up and down, don't scratch them, let them scab, don't even think about it—*breathe*—glance at your ticket, 34-F, window seat, you like the window seat, always have, ever since you were a child, but you'll never arrive there at this rate because some fool with a floppy designer bag can't manage to shut the overhead bin, the bag is just too damn big, its handles keep spilling out, it's like wrassling an octopus, the guy sweating now, red-faced, the wife in her seat looking up at him, humiliated—Typical, why on earth did I have to marry this schmuck who can't even store a bag properly?—his face redder and redder, one beat away from myocardial infarction—but look, who's this? ILSE, come to the rescue, squeezing past you with a polite Excuse me (*squeeze me?*), her alabaster elbow electrically brushing your arm—tingle tingle—oh the talent it requires to look good in that awful polyester uniform—she reaches up and like a magician makes the big floppy bag handles disappear, poof, slam, all there is to it, and now you are able to move on, to row 34, but first another smile from ILSE as she steps aside to let you pass—hand in pocket!— if only you had something to say to her, something appropriately witty, but you do not, you are shy, even afraid, so you find your row, flip open the overhead, oh-so-carefully hoist the carry-on up and in, touching it lightly, illogically, as if to make sure it will not get up and walk away, then, ignoring the small voice that keeps asking *Why?* you slam the bin shut, crabwalk past the empty aisle (34-D) and middle (34-E) seats to your own, 34-F, the window seat, and sit down, sigh.

Breathe.

Breathe.

Close your eyes.

As if from far away you can hear the thumpthumpthump of your heart mingled with the familiar sounds of air travel: the hiss of air conditioner nodules, the muted crash of baggage being stored below, the anxious murmur of passengers as they find their seats, stow their bags, buckle their seat belts. And the smells: air freshener, musty fabric, microwaved airline food, and the cold, freon-tinged aroma of packaged air that tickles the edges of your nostrils.

Please God, you say to yourself, let these two seats next to me remain vacant. A six hour flight, I need room to stretch out. *Please…*

Hullo, young man.

An elderly couple, retirees from the looks of them, he in a

shiny silver and red warm-up suit, she in a pant suit of stretchy blue material found nowhere in nature. From the safety of the aisle this extravagantly wrinkled, shrink-wrapped woman examines you closely for any sign of terrorist affiliation. A friend of a friend of her cousin Eunice was on board that plane that blew up over Scotland. Or was it Pittsburgh? You look a little scruffy, perhaps, but no hint of middle eastern blood. Hell, you don't even like the food, it gives you the runs. Apparently you've passed the test because she is unloading several glossy magazines onto her seat. *People. Good Housekeeping. Us.* Don't say a word, just smile and turn away, or else you'll be looking at snapshots of the grandkids all the way to Portland.

Her husband, at least seventy, is attempting to manhandle their faux designer bag into the overhead. The thing seems to weigh a ton. Does he see your bag there? Is he going to crush it? You leap to your feet, Here, lemme help you with that, sir, practically knocking the old geezer out of the way, you take hold of the bag—Christ, what's in here, a cinderblock?—and maneuver it into the bin so that yours is safe and sound. You touch it to make sure. From inside you might have heard a sigh but you slam the door before anyone else catches on. There we are, no problem.

Thanks a bunch, the old fella says as you slide yourself back to the window seat, followed closely by the missus, who, being a martyr of the old school, has noisily volunteered for the middle seat. Are you sure? asks the hubby, who is approximately half her size. She does not answer, but plops herself into the seat and proceeds to shift and re-shift her ample posterior, left cheek up, right cheek up, left, right, left right left right until, realizing it is of no use, there is no comfort to be found here, and with a sigh perfected over decades of practice to achieve maximum dramatic effect, she finally settles herself, only to turn to her husband and stage whisper, WE SHOULDA GONE FIRST CLASS. These words, uttered in an outer borough quack, hang in the air like a fart, wrinkling her husband's veiny nose. The poor old bastard needs a cocktail.

You turn your attention to the workers out on the tarmac. What must it be like to toil amongst these huge machines all day and night, like herding great iron dinosaurs, exposed to the elements, wearing sturdy cotton coveralls and those industrial strength earmuff noise reducers? Not so bad, maybe, on a lovely July morning like this, but what about February? The cold, the rain, the wind.

Uh oh. You have the distinct feeling that your neighbor is eyeballing you. You can actually sense her psychic tendrils slithering over the armrest, which she has boldly and decisively commandeered, directly into your space. Sure enough, the old woman is taking another careful inventory. Hmm, she thinks. Thirties, WASPy, jeans, unkempt hair, unshaven, wedding band (white gold)...scratch marks on forearms. What could that be about? A drug addict?! You have an urge, sudden and powerful, to turn to her and confess everything, but you turn instead toward the window, watch the workers feed luggage onto the conveyor belt. Please don't talk to me, please don't talk to me, please don't talk to me...

You shut your eyes again. So tired, but you cannot turn off your mind. It's like a radio receiver, picking up snippets of conversation from throughout the cabin:

...all I'm saying is you might've thought about me before you decided that...a one bedroom in the Village oh brother that'll run you about...he killed her of course he did it's open and shut as far as I'm concerned...why does it bother me so much that Jack didn't invite me to his pool party?...I want to live by myself...

Finally, the attendants pull shut the heavy door and the airplane is towed away from the gate. Everything has gone off without a hitch. You feel like a fugitive escaped through a dragnet.

Breathe.

The flight is jam-packed, a veritable sea of heads. You feel a twinge of anxiety. All these lungs, so little air. Breathe. As the plane rolls toward the runway, the wing, the starboard wing jutting out from directly below your window, it wobbles, the wing wobbles enough to make you wonder: just how are those humongous slabs of metal attached to the body of the aircraft? Are there enough nuts and bolts in the world to keep such a thing connected? Should it be wobbling like that? Should it?

As the plane rolls along the tarmac—so dainty, with those tiny little wheels, like a sumo wrestler en pointe—the flight attendants explain the complex ins and outs of seatbelt mechanics, the proper application of oxygen masks, the exact location of flotation cushions, blah blah blah. ILSE is way up front, a mile away she seems, her arms pale and thin and downy as she calmly mimes the movements expected of you should the aircraft suddenly plummet out of the sky toward the cold hard earth. She is, for now anyway, the most beautiful woman you have ever seen, with that wheatfield blonde hair and the way she smiled at you as you boarded—those narrow, knowing lips and straight white teeth.

After a brief wait on line the pilot soberly announces that we've been cleared for take-off, and with tremendous deliberation the silvery nose of the aircraft swivels and aims itself down the long runway, the engines whine to life, the world begins to shiver and shake as the plane lurches forward, gaining speed at a ridiculous rate, the plastic seats and bins and even the ceiling all vibrating now as if in an earthquake, the strips of green grass whizzing past your window, WELCOME TO NEW YORK spelled out in huge white letters, you can feel the jet's wheels bumping roughly over cracks in the runway—and then, the transcendent moment when, ignoring all laws of logic, the megaton 757 lifts its nose off the ground and heaves itself into the air, leaving the earth behind, the world dropping away like the floor of the Hell Hole at Coney Island, and the G force pushes your ass into your seat as this mammoth tin can full of human beings, hundreds of them, slices through the air toward the sun.

Airborne!

Then the plane suddenly dips to starboard, forcing you to take in and hold your breath, the wing pointing down at the gray water off Long Island Sound as it banks hard toward the south, then west, so that all of a sudden you feel as vulnerable as a frog on a duck's back, with only the distressingly thin wall of the cabin stopping you from rolling down the long cold wing, over its glinting edge and into the drink.

This sort of situation brings out the amateur philosopher in you. Man should not fly. It is unnatural and arrogant. Every crash, every blood-drenched collision, every horrifying plunge out of the sky into a mountainside or ocean or corn field is inevitable and appropriate...

Then, just as suddenly, the wing rises, the airplane levels off, the seat belt lights go off with a cheery DING, and ILSE slinks past en route to the kitchenette—all is right with the world. You can breathe.

She's different, you've noticed, this ILSE, from the other attendants, with their shellacked hair and powdered cheeks—they look like they should be lying in coffins, but not ILSE, no sir, her hair is long and soft and pulled back into a casual ponytail, a few golden strands falling over her forehead, and she wears just a hint of eyeliner. As she passes row 34 she smiles, if not directly at you, then vaguely in your direction, a conspiratorial smile, as if to say she is keeping an eye on you, she knows who and where you are, then she disappears into the back.

Gazing forward now over the tops of heads you catch sight of several Asian men wearing startling orange robes, one of whom stands chatting with his friends across the aisle. He chuckles loudly, tilting his closely shaved head back and revealing huge gleaming teeth. Do you think he ever has panic attacks? What the hell does he know that you don't know?

As the airplane levels off at a cruising altitude of 32,000 feet—that's more than six miles in the air!—you open a book, a guide to the Pacific Northwest. It is packed with information printed in a ludicrously small font, plus page after page of crude maps and lists. Hotels, motels, campgrounds, restaurants listed by price range. Too much information! You don't care about youth hostels or where to rent a moped. You're too old for that.

Read on, anyway. Relax.

Did you know that Portland was founded in 1843 by two fellows named Asa Lovejoy and William Overton, who had been trekking down the Willamette River? That Overton borrowed twenty-five cents from Lovejoy so they could both make a claim, then sold his claim to Francis Pettygrove for fifty dollars worth of supplies? Not the smartest move, as it turned out, but who could know? Pettygrove and Lovejoy then flipped a coin to see who would name the new frontier town. Pettygrove, of Portland,

Maine, won the toss, and named the place after his home town. At that time, there was little there but river, trees, and Mount Hood sulking fifty miles away.

And now you're asking yourself: what have *you* done with your life, mister? Are there any streets named after *you*?

Your agitation sets your arms to itching something terrible, but you must resist. Scratching will only open the wounds. Think of something else.

The flight attendants are inching their way down the aisle with the beverage cart. ILSE is cheerful and flirty, all smiles from twenty rows ahead. What will happen when she reaches row 34? You will ask for apple juice, she will nod—excellent choice, she'll think—and as you take the clear plastic cup from her, her small soft hand will touch yours for a fraction of a second longer than necessary. When you look to her for a further sign she will subtly wink, and after she has wheeled the cart to the next row you will discover a message on your cocktail napkin: DINNER IN PORTLAND?

Something to drink, sir?

ILSE. The genuine article. Her eyes appear to be looking deep inside of you, amused. Brown. With flecks of red. Her skin as smooth as a baby's ass. You would like to reach out and–

Sir?

App...

The A skids across your uvula on its way out through your suddenly parched lips.

Apple juice, please.

Your neighbors have already been served. She drinks a diet cola, he sips a powerful blend of whiskey and soda, you can smell it from here. Both remain amazingly oblivious to the sparks that scorch the air between you and the flight attendant.

During an interminable moment when ILSE awaits more ice cubes, you take the opportunity to imagine your date with her in Portland. After dinner, you are of course invited back to her cozy apartment. Red wine, music, soft kisses. Fast forward: naked, her skin rosy smooth, she writhes astride you while breathlessly reciting the procedure for in-flight emergencies...

Here you go, sir.

She has leaned her luscious torso forward, her pert bosom inches away from the whiskey drinker's wide eyes, and so you reach out nonchalantly for the cup, anticipating that oh-so-brief but juicily intimate moment of touch. When it fails to arrive, when she hands the beverage over to you as if to her brother, which is to say *platonically*, you are unprepared, and fail to grasp the cup any better than you have the situation, and the goddam thing slips right through your fingers to land smack on your neighbor's tray table, where it miraculously remains upright, but the apple juice bursts like lava from a volcano onto the woman's outfit. Oh! she exclaims and, involuntarily flexing her left arm, she knocks over the cup of diet cola, which gushes into the lap of her unsuspecting husband. Ah! he cries, though he expertly manages to hold onto his whiskey and soda, from which he takes an immediate, greedy sip.

I'm so sorry, you say, but the woman does not hear you, so consumed is she with drying herself and her husband. As you look on helplessly she grabs fresh napkins from ILSE and frantically blotters up the liquid. Meanwhile, ILSE seems amused by this bit of slapstick, a sly, barely polite smile erupting on her face. She is radiant. Your eyes meet for a moment, and she shrugs, a gesture so generous and understanding you are nearly brought to tears.

I'm really very sorry, you repeat, and your neighbor is surprisingly understanding. Don't sweat it, honey, she says. I been waiting years for this vacation and I won't let a little juice spurl it. With that she rolls the damp napkins into a ball and hands it over to ILSE, who then delivers fresh beverages to all, though this time your juice is passed hand to hand, from aisle seat to middle to window, like a hot dog at a baseball game. Thank you, you say, and then she is gone.

As you turn to watch ILSE make her lovely way down the aisle, the airplane suddenly lurches, wobbles, each jolt sending a spasm through your system. Your lower bowel goes ice cold. The seat belt light flashes on and the captain announces that we are experiencing some turbulence, we should be out of this shortly. The plane dips again, just enough to force a taste of bile into your throat. You should probably close your eyes, or stare straight ahead, or even try to read, but no, you are perversely drawn to the window and the sight of the starboard wing trembling under the strain of a powerful head wind. Just as you are recalling a popular adventure film you recently saw in which a bomb nearly sends a jet very much like this one hurtling out of the sky, there is a flash of bright orange to your left. A fire? No, just the formerly jolly Tibetan monk scrambling back to his seat from the rest room. You find the expression of terror on his face profoundly unsettling. Meanwhile, ILSE is still pouring drinks, oblivious of the disturbance as she calmly hands a cup of seltzer to a grateful passenger. Cool as can be. But you keep flashing to the image of a 757 snapping in two like a bread stick, or the wing dropping off into nowhere, leaving a huge gaping gash in the fuselage through which all the passengers tumble like peanuts from a can, falling falling falling through the unspeakably cold air, through white fluffy clouds that tickle like feathers, only to emerge a mile above some farmland, some vast field of soybeans that gets bigger and bigger as, picking up velocity now, you plummet toward its furrowed rows. Would you die of fright before you hit the ground?

Then, as if turning into the last, well-lubricated straightaway of an old rollercoaster, the airplane returns to its stable, seemingly unmoving state. You can let go of the armrest now.

Breathe. Shut your eyes. Try to sleep.

You are so tired. But your arms are tingling with the rapid growth of regenerating flesh, your mind racing with sounds and images pulled from the last few weeks. The flash of a face. Foul words. Bleeding wounds.

Where to start?

The way Sara lay there beside him on that morning? Her skin golden in the sunlight spilling through the windows, the hairs on her arms like fragile spider legs, her chest rising and falling. Like a child, so vulnerable, warmth emanating from her as she dreamed her dreams. The way he watched her. How was he to know? For years he'd been waking up next to this woman, and every morning this was what he saw. Lying on her right side, facing him, her right hand curled next to her face, with Dilsey nestled into the space between her bent knees and chest. He touched Sara's hand, her soft, warm palm. Dilsey opened her green eyes, lifted her head and yawned, but Sara, his wife, did not stir.

15

He swallowed his annoyance—where did she get such a talent for sleep? In cars, on airplanes, trains, she could nod off like a switch had been pulled while he sat there fighting off a barrage of thoughts—and climbed from bed, waded through the heat-blurred apartment—no air conditioning; Sara always said it smelled of death—and paused in the kitchen to pour some dry food into Dilsey's bowl, then continued on to the bathroom.

He had not slept well. Again. It was partly due to the heat wave, but for months now he'd been waking up in the middle of the night with his stomach in knots and his mind racing from one seemingly frivolous topic to the next—all while Sara slept soundly beside him. Last night's obsession: a press release, due this week, for a new book entitled *REBOUND: How to Survive Divorce in the 90s.* As he tossed and turned, the book's insipid cover kept flashing over the bed like a hologram: bright yellow, the title in thick black letters, and a crude, cartoonish illustration of a broken heart taped together with a bandaid. He could write a release for this book with both hands tied behind his back, and yet, for some reason, he had put it off for days. This was not good. Work was slow, this was his only assignment all week, and it meant money.

For hours he lay there obsessing, rehearsing the press release's bleak opening paragraph—divorce statistics, custody battles, the fear of sexually transmitted diseases—while the rhythm of Sara's calm breathing mocked him. She had arrived home late again, having gone out with Corinne, and he was barely awake when she crawled into bed beside him. Are you asleep? she'd asked, and he pretended to snore softly. Did she kiss him goodnight before rolling over onto her other side? He couldn't remember. She'd been staying out late a lot lately, having drinks with Corinne or other co-workers at the firm, or going to business-related parties to which he was never invited. And last week she spent four days in Los Angeles working out of the firm's west coast office.

What's in LA? he'd asked testily.

A client.

Who?

Francis Dunleavy.

Who's Francis Dunleavy?

A client.

I know that.

A musician. He can't make it to New York so I have to go out there.

Where will you stay?

The Chateau Marmont.

Can I come?

Relax. It's just a few days.

I'll stay out of your way.

Long pause, then: Maybe next time, sweetie. I'm sorry. I just need some space right now, okay?

Space. She needed space. He could relate, as there was so little space in this apartment, though it was larger than most. Two sizable rooms at either end—the bedroom overlooking the street, the living room looking onto a small, trash-cluttered courtyard— plus the kitchen and a spare room in between. The windowless bathroom, where he now sat reading last Sunday's New York Times Book Review while waiting for his tortured bowels to budge, was off the living room, miles away, it seemed, from his sleeping wife. A big place, sure, all his friends were envious, but he sometimes felt as though the walls were closing in. Yeah, he needed space too, space not cluttered with all these beauty aids spilling off the bathroom shelf, or the miles of clothes hung on metal racks in the spare room, or the shoes that littered the floors like the huge carcasses of brightly colored insects. Space to move around his own goddam apartment without feeling as though he were in a department store warehouse.

After scanning a review of a new biography of the young actor Boyd Hart—poorly researched...ineptly written... shallow and sensationalistic—and squeezing out a few, minnow-like turds, he returned to the bedroom. Over the years, it had become his responsibility to wake Sara up for work. She hated to get up, and would ignore or sleep through any alarm. Sometimes, if he was in a good mood, he might lie softly on top of her, easing her into consciousness with playful kisses on her face and neck. She could be so soft and warm in the morning, still wrapped in the fluffy blanket of sleep's ether. With a cracked voice she would beg for more rest, but he'd be relentless with the kisses until she finally wrapped an arm around him and squeezed. He could lie like this for hours, cocoon-like, if only she didn't have to go to work. Sometimes, if he was very lucky, he was able to coax her into a brief, exhilarating fuck before she got up to shower.

Lately, however, he had grown resentful about his duties, especially on those mornings after Sara had been out late. On these occasions he would resort to a more military style of wake-up. Up and at 'em! he might holler upon entering the bedroom, sometimes using Dilsey as a reluctant prop, dropping her onto Sara's stomach or back. Goddammit! Sara would mutter, shocked out of a sound sleep. I hate it when you do that. Rise and shine! he'd say with a smile. Your job awaits! Get a move on! *Today is the first day of the rest of your life!*

Recently, Martin had told him that he had a sadistic streak that was counter-productive to a healthy relationship, so this morning—despite serious temptation to wrench Sara from the kind of deep, restful sleep he'd been denied—he opted for a more balanced approach. He sat on the edge of the bed, placed a hand on her hip, and gently shook her. As he did so, he looked closely at her face. Sara was not what most people would call a beautiful woman, not in the classical, fashion magazine sense anyway, but there were times when she shared with such women the same glow, the same radiance that signaled a confidence in their ability to attract. He had smugly watched, on several occasions, as bold, handsome men tried to impress her in bars or at parties only to be snubbed in favor of her husband, at whom these men would stare in envy. This, however, was not one of those magical moments when Sara radiated beauty. She lay on her back, mouth slightly open. Her breathing came in shallow rasps. One cheek was red from lying on a crease in the pillow. She seemed animal-like, primitive, incompletely formed. He hated to think it, but his wife was ugly, and the thought made him embarrassed and ashamed.

Hey. Wake up.

Sara groaned and rolled over onto her side, facing away from him. It's so hot, she said. She sounded like she was under water.

Yeah. It's gonna be in the 90s again.

I'm taking the day off, she said.

18

Really?

Just give me another hour, okay?

Was this good? Did this mean she wanted to spend the day with him? Had she missed him in LA and on all those nights spent drinking with Corinne? He leaned over and kissed her hair. It smelled of smoke and scotch and cotton. All of a sudden he desired her. Perhaps later on they would have sex, a long sweaty afternoon fuck, followed by one of those perfect post-coital naps during which one dreams of absolutely nothing.

He made his way through the obstacle course in the spare room—those damn metal racks crowded with bright summer clothes, piles of platform shoes, a mountain of underwear destined for the dry cleaner—through the kitchen and into the living room. Still in his boxers, he knelt on the hardwood floor in the middle of the room, sat back on his ankles, then slowly bent forward until his forehead touched the floor. The Child's Pose.

He had been practicing yoga for several months now, ever since he'd experienced his first bona fide panic attack. It had been a morning much like this one, though not as hot, and he was fixing oatmeal for himself and Sara while she showered, when the radio newscaster casually mentioned that it was film actor Boyd Hart's thirtieth birthday. Thirty, he thought at the time. Thirty. Almost three years younger than me. A millionaire movie star, sleeping with beautiful starlets, drinking mai-tais at hipster clubs, his face splashed on magazine covers all over the world. Thirty. And suddenly he found he couldn't breathe. Thousands of thoughts and images began to flash through his consciousness, as if some demon inside his head were madly switching channels from one to the next. All the wrong moves he'd made in his life, all the bonehead decisions, all the opportunities squandered. The novel he'd never completed. The steady job he'd recently—rashly?—quit to go freelance. Never writing for the college newspaper. Dropping out of pre-law to be an English major. Not making a move on Mary Sue O'Hearn after the senior prom. Christ! He grew dizzy, sweat was pouring out of him. He barely resisted the urge to throw himself against a wall. His chest felt wrapped up, there was no room inside his ribcage for his lungs to expand. He paced furiously around the apartment, living room to kitchen to spare room to bedroom and back again, the sound of Sara humming in the shower providing a weird, infuriating soundtrack. Poor Dilsey got in his way and he kicked her. He needed to breathe.

Breathe.

It took him all that day to recover his equilibrium, and soon after, at Sara's urging, he began seeing a therapist.

Your system is being overloaded, Martin told him right off the bat. You're depressing your feelings, and you're starting to short out.

It all made sense, but why had he made so little progress since then? It takes time, Martin always said, so damn calmly. Meanwhile, there were more attacks, some even worse than the first. He lived in fear of them.

Breathe, he told himself as he attempted to achieve the satisfying Downward Dog position, a sort of upside down V, feet and hands flat on the floor, arms and legs straight, ass thrust into the air. Breathe. Empty your mind. He pictured a clear blue sky. Every stray thought—what to eat for breakfast, the little rivulet of sweat rolling down his spine, what to eat for lunch, what he'd like to do to Sara if she were in the Downward Dog position—was a cloud to be blown away from the blue sky in his mind. Breathe. He slid his right foot up between his hands, stretching his left leg out behind him. Breathe. Stretch. There was a new movie he wanted to see. No. Breathe. Stretch. Who was in it? Meryl Streep? Which movie did she win the Academy Award for? No no no! Breathe! See the blue sky. The empty blue sky. *Blue Sky.* That was Jessica Lange. He'd always had a thing for her, ever since King Kong. Those teeth. Those crooked, sexy teeth. Is she still with Sam Shepard? Breathe! Stretch! Back to the Downward Dog. Ass way up, back straight. Breathe. Looking back between his legs he saw his desk and chair in the corner of the room. *No!* Breathe! Stretch! *REBOUND* is the most invaluable guide to recovery for the recently divorced since...since...since what?

Shit.

This went on for forty five minutes or so, during which time he attempted with varying degrees of success the Triangle Pose, the Proud Warrior, and the Shoulder Stand, among many others, all while cataloguing in his mind the films of Jessica Lange, with a long pause at the bathtub scene in *Frances*—if his memory served him correctly, you could see her bush. By the time he finished, the blue sky in his mind was overcast with black rain clouds, and he lay perspiring on the floor in the Relaxation Pose, also known as the Corpse Pose. The apartment was growing steamier by the minute, signaling another brutally hot day. But it felt good to sweat, to exert himself a little. He spent far too much time sitting at his desk, lying around reading books, or watching television. Downstairs, in the kitchen of DeMeo's Trattoria, the chef must have started on the lunchtime marinara, for a heavy garlic aroma, so thick it was nearly visible, wafted in through the window. Over this, like mercury sliding across water, splashed the sound of children shouting and laughing at the playground down the street.

Fuck the heat, he thought. This is going to be a glorious day.

Before taking a shower he checked on Sara. She still lay on her side with Dilsey curled against her belly. He scratched between the cat's soft black ears and she began to purr, while Sara kept on sleeping.

《《—》》

Pardon me. Are you a writer?

It's the woman next to you. 34-E. She has a knowing smile on her face, as if she's been reading over your shoulder.

No, you tell her. Not really.

It's a lie of sorts. After all, you do earn your living—barely—by writing, but are you a Writer? There is the unfinished novel, but then everyone has one of those.

The reason I ask, she says, our son is a writer, and he writes in a notebook just like that one.

Really?

He's always scribbling away, like you just now, even when we're all out for dinner or on the bus he has that darn notebook with him.

That's a sure sign of a writer, I guess.

He's very talented. But then I would say so, wouldn't I? I'm

21

his mother! She laughs, or honks, then continues: But you're not a writer? You look kind of like a writer, if you don't mind my saying so. It's a compliment.

Thank you.

So that's some kind of diary then.

Sort of.

Because I keep a diary myself, just to keep my life in some kind of order. Otherwise it's just a muddle, meaningless—the unexamined life and all that—but if I put it in order, one thing after another, I find it sort of starts to make sense. Or at least it does to me. For years I've done it. It helps.

Yes.

Sometimes I look at my old diaries and I can see better where I was and what I was doing, you know? Things that at the time had no pattern suddenly make perfect sense. It's like a map you can look at after you've taken a long trip, you can see the roads you took and how you got there and why it took so long or why you got lost or why it all turned out okay. It's interesting, don't you think?

You give her a blank look. You want to tell her that yes, it is interesting, that she's on to something, but it's just so difficult to talk to people.

An announcement: the in-flight movie will commence in five minutes. As the flight attendants start handing out headsets and collecting fees, your neighbor turns to her husband and confers. You say a prayer that she will elect to watch the movie.

Do you know what this movie is about? she asks you.

I think it's about a high school football coach, you tell her, and you wince—this woman will not be interested in a movie about football. You decide to spice it up for her. And he falls in love with a woman, you say, and he has to choose between her and his work. It's sort of a love story.

She looks vaguely interested. Who's in it?

I think it's Boyd Hart.

Oh, I like him. And who's the woman?

I'm not sure. I've never actually seen it, but I read about it.

She confers some more with her husband, who takes out his wallet. Success! ILSE arrives with a bag of headsets.

It's a love story, right? the woman asks as she hands over her cash.

ILSE smiles. I haven't seen it, she says. Her eyes move to you like prison yard spotlights. She holds out a headset. You shake your head no. She nods—in approval?—and moves on.

The airplane is equipped with several monitors that hang from the ceiling above the aisle, each with the tint and contrast set slightly differently. This creates an interesting effect. Six Boyd Harts, each with a different skin tone, stretching off toward first class. Even without the sound, the story is easy to follow, and you find yourself being sucked in.

Hart plays a young high school science teacher who is elected to helm the school football team when the beloved old coach keels over from a heart attack during a mid-season practice. The team is rated poorly but has been on a roll lately and actually has a shot at a play-off berth. After a disastrous first game as coach, Boyd Hart starts to bone up on strategy, daily visiting the ailing old coach in the hospital, and eventually dedicates himself fully to improving the team. This comes at a cost, however: he is alienating the beautiful English teacher with whom he's in love. The team starts winning games, but the beautiful English teacher is tempted by the handsome but somewhat dull and predictable History teacher, who has long harbored feelings for her. Even more trouble arrives when the star quarterback is caught using marijuana and is suspended from school. Will the team be able to win the crucial last game of the regular season and make the play-offs? Will the second string quarterback, who has an alcoholic father and no mother and five younger siblings to look after, rise to the occasion and play a great game? Will the beautiful English teacher put aside her needs for a few weeks to accommodate the hopes and dreams of the man she loves?

More turbulence. Christ. The seat belt sign dings on, a disembodied voice tells you to remain seated. The effect of the turbulence is more pronounced here toward the rear of the cabin. It's like being in the back of a van on an icy road. Shimmy shimmy. The wing shudders. Bangs and thumps from overhead as the contents of the storage bins shift. What's that squeaking sound? A loose screw in the fuselage? You look around to see if anyone else notices. The couple next to you are calmly engrossed in the film—Boyd Hart and the beautiful English teacher having a heart to heart in the empty stands of the football stadium. You remember news reports of that flight to Hawaii a few years back. You saw the photos. A big chunk of the cabin roof was wrenched off. Everyone survived except one stewardess who was plucked from the cabin like a piece of chocolate, never to be seen again.

From close by, behind you or perhaps above you somewhere, you hear a soft, pleading voice. Why? Why?

As suddenly as it began, the shaking stops. Your neighbor loudly clucks her tongue. You open your eyes to see Boyd Hart and the beautiful English teacher quarreling. You try to read their lips. Certain words jump at you: please, last chance, game, love. The beautiful English teacher stands up and exits the stands. Boyd Hart walks out to the middle of the football field, lit up by night game floodlights, and thrusts his arms into the air. You hear screams emanating from the woman's headset.

Time for a piss. Nerves. You unbuckle your seat belt, rise into a crouch. Excuse me. Neither of your neighbors makes a move to get out of their seats. Sorry, you mutter as you squeeze between their knees and seat backs.

You can do that, the old man says with a grin, because you're so skinny. His breath reeks of whiskey.

All three lavatories are occupied, but there is no line. You wait in the open space behind the last row of seats. It feels good to be standing. You stretch toward the ceiling, then bend over to touch your toes. Breathe. If only you could touch your knees with your nose.

My, but you're limber.

You straighten up to see ILSE emerging from the rest room. She is smiling and her teeth are perfect. You feel your face go warm. Quickly, you hide your left hand in your pocket.

Yoga, you tell her.

I've always wanted to try that, she says. This job is murder on my sacroiliac.

I bet it is.

What a witty reply, you think. You really are an idiot.

34-F? she asks.

That's right.

ILSE tilts her head, smiles. And your *name* is…?

Oh! Uh…

You want to be careful here.

Caleb, you tell her. Caleb.

Hello, Caleb Caleb, she says. I'm ILSE.

I know.

An awkward pause here. To make matters worse, your bladder is ready to explode.

Excuse me, you say, and ILSE smiles again, so that when you shut the door behind you, and in the split second before the fluorescent bulb sputters to life, you see her white white teeth flashing in the darkness.

ILSE, you whisper.

You remember that night flight back from the west coast, years ago, just after you were married, three or four in the morning, everyone asleep, you sneaked into the lav together, fumbled with buttons and zippers, Jesus, the frenzy of it, the pounding, the sucking, the warm wetness, and the stifled laughter afterwards as you crept back to your seats.

Someone pulls at the door. Can't they read? Occupied! you shout. You haven't even peed yet. So difficult with an erection. C'mon, c'mon. Finally, you manage it, splashing on the silvery metal toilet. When you were a kid you expected when flushing an airplane commode to catch a glimpse of clouds through the open drain, and even now, as you press the FLUSH button, you watch closely as the stainless steel trap door falls away, only to see— and, as always, you are not sure whether to be disappointed or relieved—the foul darkness of the septic tank.

Wash your hands thoroughly now. Airplanes are veritable petri dishes. You examine your face in the mirror. Bags under your eyes. A few gray whiskers. You're getting older by the second.

You pause for a moment with your hand on the door latch. What if ILSE is still out there? What will you say to her?

Another tug at the door from outside. Someone must really have to go. You take a deep breath and open the door to find the relieved face of the old man from 34-D.

Gotta pee like you read about in books, he says as he clambers past you into the lav.

No sign of ILSE. Relieved and disappointed, you make your way up the aisle. While you're up you might as well check on your carry-on bag. What is that sound? Oh shit! The carry-on lies squished beneath the couple's larger, heavier bag. You quickly rearrange their luggage so it does not crush your own.

Sorry, sorry, you mutter.

Everyone is watching you. At least that's what it feels like. As a matter of fact, they are engrossed in the movie—Boyd Hart on the sidelines, the team on the gridiron, the beautiful English teacher in the stands. So why does the hair on the back of your neck tingle?

Right behind ya, buddy.

The old fella stands at your elbow in a state of post-urination bliss.

'scuse me, he says. Gotta see how this game turns out.

Back in your seat now a strange calm settles over you. A quilt of farmland on the rolling plains far below. A black river snaking its way through a gorge. A mountain range rising, cradling small towns in its valleys. You get the same feeling you get when passing through small towns on a train. People live down there, people with families and jobs and cars and television sets, people who laugh and cry and fight and have sex every once in a while. People, like you, who wake up in the middle of the night with razor sharp thoughts tearing at the lining of their bellies. People who are terrified.

«««—»»»

After showering and a shave he returned to the bedroom, naked, half aroused, determined to coax his wife into some morning sex. It felt good to walk around the apartment in nature's own, in the heat. He liked how his semi-erect penis felt as it swayed, heavier than usual, like a hammer in a carpenter's belt or a gun in a holster.

Wake up, mon cheri.

She still lay in the fetal position, facing the window. Dilsey pricked up her ears and, as he lay down, leapt from the bed with an annoyed meow. Sara's cotton nightgown, the one he'd given her last Christmas, had bunched up at her waist. He maneuvered his knees behind hers, his face in her hair, and rubbed against her bare ass.

Wakey wakey. Somebody wants to say hello.

Sara groaned and slid her rear end away from him. Undeterred, he scooted forward.

Me so horny.

There had been a time, it seemed so long ago, when Sara would have laughed at this, when she would have reached around and grabbed his cock and positioned it between her thighs. But this morning she just groaned and rolled onto her back. Not a good sign. He went instantly slack. Sara's eyes, he could see now, were red and wet. She stared at the ceiling, where years ago she had arranged glow in the dark stars, on the day they moved in. How many years now? Five?

She folded her hands across her chest. Her lower lip quivered.

Oh no, he thought. His mouth went dry, his stomach felt like a bowling ball in a paper sack. *No.*

What is it? he whispered.

I... She swallowed hard. I...

She was stuttering. Not once in all the years he'd known her had she stuttered, with the exception of the day he had proposed, when she had a difficult time with what eventually emerged as a Yes.

I want...

It was like standing in front of a firing squad. He knew what was coming, he knew it would hurt like hell, and while he wanted desperately to run away, there was no point—the guns were loaded and cocked, aim was taken. All he could do was puff madly on his last cigarette and wait to be blown away.

I want to...

She turned her head to look straight at him now, an act of courage that touched him deeply. Oh hell, he thought as his very own gusher pooled in the space behind his eyeballs.

I want to live by myself.

These are some of the thoughts that coursed through his mind in that split second:

27

I am all alone in the universe and some day I am going to die.

I will never again have the opportunity to ejaculate into this woman—maybe *any* woman.

The kitty litter requires changing.

Is she fucking someone else?

Breathe.

Fine. No more arguments about the Macy's bill.

REBOUND is the most invaluable guide for the recently divorced since... since ...

It is 10:04 a.m., according to the glowing blue numbers on the bedside alarm clock.

My nose is running.

What would Martin tell me to do?

If I had a knife handy I would stab her in the heart.

Breathe.

I love you.

I hate you.

I want to die.

Then he wept. He wept like a baby for the better part of an hour. Where do all those tears come from? Is there some reservoir in the back of our heads? Not since he was an infant, alone and hungry and frightened in his crib, had he bellowed like this. Sara held him, also sobbing, and when he was finally finished, when no more tears would come, it was very strange, but he felt lighter, almost euphoric, and he felt closer to her than he had been in a long time.

Then she opened her mouth:

I love you, I really do, she said, you're the most perfect man in the world, the best I've ever known, there's just something wrong with me, it isn't you, it's *me*, I'm just so confused, I don't know what makes me happy, I don't know what I want, or need, maybe I can't be happy with a man like you, a man as good as you, maybe that's my problem, I don't know, but listen to me, I do know you'll find someone else, I just know it, someone who will appreciate you, someone who wants you...

Was all this supposed to make him feel better?

...someone who will do all the things you want to do, who'll be there for you, who'll—

If I'm so fucking perfect, he said, why are you leaving me?

I don't know—like I said, there's something wrong with me, I think I drain the life out of the men I love, it's happened before, with Tony, with Johnny, they changed.

And I've changed too?

You used to be so full of life, remember? But now, I don't know, it's like you don't care, it's like—

So it *is* me.

No! It's *us*! It's... Oh, I don't know, I can't explain it properly.

He felt another eruption coming on. The look on her face when he started crying again was one of complete horror, as if she had stabbed him and only now realized how much blood is inside a person. She did not hold him this time. She sat up against the headboard and watched, muttering, I'm sorry, so sorry, I wish I felt different...

When this round of tears was over, after what seemed like hours, there was the inevitable question to ask, and it turned his insides to stone. He could not look at her, he was too afraid he would detect a lie.

Is there...

Across the street, an old woman leaned out her window, elbows on a blue pillow. Her hair was as white as paper.

Is there someone...

It was like shitting an arrowhead.

Is there someone else?

There was a terrible pause, then Sara said, There's no one else in my life.

He sighed audibly.

In fact, she went on, what I think I need right now is to be on my own.

The old lady across the way waved to a friend on the street below. Did you go see Joey? the friend hollered up. The old woman nodded yes. So how'd he look? the friend asked. The old lady shrugged and said, He looked *dead*. How do you *think* he looked?

Let's get outta here, he said. I can't breathe in this place.

They took a long walk around the Village, barely speaking,

29

like two people who happened to be walking in the same direction. The air was moist and saturated with car fumes, the white hot sky reflecting off the pavement around Washington Square Park. There were the usual drug peddlers at the park entrance, blocking their way. Smoke, smoke, they muttered. He wanted to slug one of them. Wouldn't it feel great to smash his fist into a nose, to hear the crunch of bone and cartilage, to see the wide, unbelieving eyes? Wouldn't it feel just wonderful?

To make matters worse, looking around the park, it seemed that everyone was holding hands, couple after couple, all varieties of them, men and women, men and men, women and women, black and white and brown and yellow, all so goddam happy, so pleased with themselves, having just had or about to have enthusiastic, mutually orgasmic sex, all full of hope for their entwined futures.

He sat on a bench and tried to compose himself. It could be worse. He could have a terrible, fatal disease. Colon cancer. Lou Gehrig's Disease. Ebola. Sara sat next to him, but he refused to look at her. He would not give her the satisfaction. On the bench opposite them a beautiful young college student in cut-off jeans sat on her boyfriend's lap. She bit his earlobe and giggled as he reached a hand up her t-shirt. That did it. The tears came in torrents. The students stared but he didn't care. Let them watch.

Sara put a hand on his back. It'll be okay. You're better off without me.

Shut up, he hissed. *Just stop it.* The words seemed to uncoil from his mouth and slap her in the face.

She looked away.

They sat there for a long time, sweating in the heat, saying nothing, until he felt the need to move. Without a word, he got up and headed out of the park. He could sense Sara two steps behind, like a nurse waiting for him to collapse, as they aimlessly wandered through the Village.

They ended up at a movie, of all things. *Code Red*, the new Boyd Hart thriller. Maybe it'll get your mind off things for a while, Sara said as they stood outside the theater. He was skeptical, but he couldn't think of anything better. At least the place would be air conditioned.

The movie was about a band of terrorists who plant a bomb on a commercial airliner. The bomb was set to explode when the plane lowers its altitude below 10,000 feet. There were all kinds of fist fights and shoot-outs between Boyd Hart and the ethnically diverse villains, and one very tense mid-air refueling.

Amid all the slick, jet-paced excitement he nearly did forget his troubles, at least until the denouement: Boyd Hart, all jaw and gleaming blue eyes, landed the airplane safely and collapsed into the arms of a flaxen-haired stewardess. They kissed, the music swelled, and he began to blubber.

Home, he cried. Home.

When they got back he lay in bed while Sara made some business calls. He must have fallen asleep because the next thing he knew the room was dark, and Sara was sitting beside him.

So are you staying somewhere else tonight? he asked. He still had his clothes on. He was unable to move. His muscles ached terribly, as if he'd moved a piano up three flights of stairs.

No. We'll sort it out later, okay?

He was so grateful he nearly started bawling again.

She disappeared for a while, then crawled into bed beside him, wearing her soft cotton nightshirt. She rolled out her arm and he rested his head against her shoulder. He thought: this is the last time I will ever sleep with this woman.

He lay awake for a long time, with his head nestled into the crook of Sara's shoulder and Dilsey stretched out contentedly in the narrow divide between their torsos. And with random constellations of stars still faintly glowing overhead, he at last fell into a deep and dreamless sleep.

«««—»»»

The in-flight movie has ended happily: Boyd Hart on his players' shoulders, a freeze framed kiss with the beautiful English teacher on the fifty yard line.

That was really very good, your neighbor announces to her husband as a treacly pop song oozes from her headset. That Boyd Hart is so handsome.

Mmmm, her husband replies.

31

The atmosphere on board has become one of restlessness, with passengers rushing to the rest rooms, standing and stretching in the aisles, chattering loudly. The monks erupt in laughter, which makes you uneasy.

The aircraft, you now notice, has slowly, almost imperceptibly, begun its descent. Oh, my ears ache, the woman next to you says as thick clouds rise and sweep past the window. More turbulence. You hold onto the arm rests and shut your eyes. You hope there are no other airplanes lurking within these clouds, small private jets piloted by amateurs flying blind through the fluffy whiteness. You open your eyes and gaze out the window, searching for that fast approaching wing light or the wide eye of a cockpit window. But all you see is whiteness until, descending now from the clouds, the airplane ceases its shaking and glides smoothly beneath an endless ceiling of soft gray.

ILSE stops by to remind you to straighten your seat back. You smile, but she is gone.

Below, everything is green: trees, fields and lawns, ponds and lakes. Black roads wind through forests toward flowerlike arrangements of subdivisions. These soon give way to warehouses and shopping malls and a many-laned expressway. You can make out cars now and people and a white dog running across a parking lot. At this altitude you get a fine idea of how fast this baby is flying. It's almost impossible to believe that, upon touching down in a few moments, there will be no casualties.

The pilot instructs the flight attendants to take their seats. Somewhere behind you ILSE is strapping herself in for yet another routine landing, while you dig your toes into the floor and clutch your knees and hold your breath in anticipation of that frightening but at the same time reassuring thud of rubber on cement. And in the split second before that moment, as the fourteen tons of iron hover dramatically above the runway, you remember the way your wife would clutch your hand, her palm soft and moist, her eyes full of fear and the need for reassurance, and now, as the jet bounces lightly on the tarmac, and the reverse engines begin to grind and howl, and the scratches on your arms begin to burn, one little tear forms in the corner of your eye, and you quickly wipe it away, lest anybody see.

CHAPTER TWO: HOW WE MET

It was at the party of a mutual acquaintance, a young actress who later went on to star in her own television situation comedy. Her name doesn't matter, she was gorgeous and she has long forgotten us.

Alphabet City, Avenue B, back when that neighborhood still stood for a sense of danger and excitement and potential riot. Open drug sales on the corner, bodegas with little more than beer and cereal on the shelves, men passed out in doorways with their trousers around their ankles. Apartments were cheap and filthy and accessible only by crooked stairs with warped metal edges.

The party was populated by beautiful, untouchable people, all crowded into a tiny studio with a sloping floor. Dance music, all bass and thump, so loud we could see it moving the smoke around above our heads. The occasional shriek of laughter, mostly from a woman with black lipstick and a studded tongue.

Later I would tell Caleb I was feeling anti-social that night. Pre-menstrual maybe, or just suffering the effects of hastily eaten chicken lo mein while cramming for a contract law exam. Whatever it was, I apparently felt the need to consume more beer than usual while wandering the cramped space between the so-called kitchen and the closet-sized bathroom, smiling, offering a few half-hearted hellos to the three or four people I knew.

He was standing in a corner, upstage as it were, observing. This is what Caleb did at parties—still does. Observe. Not above it all, just separate. Sometimes—a lot, lately—he tries to figure out what drew me to him. Perhaps I felt sorry for him, though he wasn't bad looking. How would I describe him to a police sketch artist? Average height, short brown hair, blue eyes, full lips, straight nose—all in all, a reasonably intelligent, modestly handsome face. As I approached from his blind side he was tapping his foot to the music in such a metronomically precise way that he must have somehow felt *inside* the beat, a little too safe and secure. Maybe, more than anything, I wanted to burst his bubble.

No room to dance, I said, raising my voice over the music. He was surprised that someone was speaking to him, someone out of nowhere, a complete stranger in a dress with spaghetti straps and freckles on her shoulders. Oh God, he thought, please help me not make a fool of myself. (I know what he thought because he told me later.)

I can't dance to this stuff anyway, he confessed. He tipped his beer to his lips, but it was empty, and probably had been for a while. Nevertheless, he pretended to drink, and I liked him for that.

Rock and roll or nothing, eh? I said, smiling my best smile. My hair was short in those days, and my smile was more real, uncorrupted by business and money and the law. I'm Sara, I said.

He introduced himself, and we shook hands. Weeks later, in bed, he told me my hand was soft and warm, that first time we touched, and that it, my hand, also had a special quality, a non-hand quality, like it had been places, seen things, and remembered them. No one had ever said anything about my hands like that.

I asked if he was alone and he said yes. He barely even knew the hostess, he told me. She was temping at the office where he worked, a publishing house in mid-town, and she'd left an invitation on his desk while he was at lunch. I normally wouldn't have come, he said, but I went to a movie in the neighborhood, and I was thirsty. So we talked a while about the movie he'd seen, and the book I was reading at the time, neither of which I remember, and I was intelligent and funny enough, and so was he.

Why wouldn't you have come? I asked.

What?

The party. You said you wouldn't have come normally.

By this time I could barely hear the music. It was as though he and I were sealed off from the rest of the room. There was us, and there was the throbbing, rumbling creature that was everyone else.

I don't like crowds, he said. In fact, I was just about to sneak out when you came over. He waited a beat, then added, I'm glad I stayed that extra minute.

I leaned close to hear him better, and I could smell him. A sweet, bready smell, like cinnamon raisin toast. It was all I could do not to bury my nose in his neck.

Just then a tall, rail-thin man with several safety pins dangling from his eyebrows pushed past us. Evidently, the party was shifting into a new gear, one that favored leather trousers and studded body parts.

I think that's a sign, Caleb said.

I think maybe you're right, I said. As it is, I'm going to have a hell of a time getting up for work in the morning.

We left together without saying a word to anyone, and I accepted his offer to escort me to Houston Street, where I could catch a cab. As we descended the five flights of stairs, he walked ahead of me, and I remembered what my grandmother once told me—that a true gentleman walks ahead of a lady while descending stairs, and behind her while ascending, just in case the lady should slip and fall.

Where do you live? he asked.

Upper West Side. You?

Brooklyn.

Long way home.

Tonight it will be.

It was a warm, late spring night, the sky a shiny dome of reflected city fluorescence. We passed a group of dark men selling crack to pale kids in cars, but I was not afraid. There was a slight breeze, and it stirred up that sweet scent of his. Somewhere nearby, I was certain, a song was being written.

When we reached Houston Street: Well, Sara, I enjoyed meeting you.

As a vacant cab passed by: Me too.

As another vacant cab passed by: Listen, would you like to get together sometime? Dinner, maybe?

As yet another cab slowed, the driver leaning over, waiting for the outstretched hand: Yes, I'd like that. I'll call you.

I pulled a pen from my purse and wrote his number on a

receipt. I did not offer my own number. The last time I'd done that, the guy had called me up three times a day for a month.

As I finally hailed a cab: Talk to you soon.

As he watched me climb in: Goodnight, Sara.

As I drove off, I turned and watched him standing on the sidewalk. He didn't move until after we turned a corner. All the way home I smelled the sweet aroma of cinnamon toast.

CHAPTER THREE:
THE PERFECT POST CARD

Look at you. Driving the wrong way. East, instead of west. Headed home? Meanwhile, Portland is a good twenty miles behind you by now. You turn off at the next exit, re-enter the expressway on the other side.

It's the rain, you tell yourself—thick, steady curtains of it that blur everything—plus clouds of fog that hover low over the ground like tear gas. Stay in the far right lane, fifty miles per hour, hands at ten and two o'clock, steady as she goes. Driving feels so foreign after all these years of not owning a car. Perhaps you should have opted for a mid-size instead of this death trap, just a sheet of tin foil between you and the dangerous elements of the universe. You felt very clever at the car rental office when you declined insurance coverage.

Are you sure? the inordinately concerned young man behind the counter had asked. But if you're in an accident, he explained, you'll be responsible for any damage done to the vehicle.

You have to laugh thinking about it. Accident? If there's an accident in this thing you won't be alive to pay anything.

Somewhere to your right, behind all that rain, flows the tumultuous Columbia River. On the left, just barely visible, steep gorge walls carved by nature over millions of years. A sixteen-wheeler closes in on you from behind and screams past in a flood of rainwater, and you could swear you hear something move around in the trunk where you put your luggage.

Breathe.

You think of ILSE, standing there at the airplane exit as you disembarked. Her smile, her twinkling eyes, and the way she said it—Stay limber, Caleb Caleb—in a voice so chipper and sincere it brings a sharp sting to your eyes even now. You wanted so badly to talk to her, to tell her something important, but all you could manage was, You too. And before you could add a word, before you could even say her name, her face had turned its beam on the next passenger, and you were gone.

The rain thins to a steady but manageable drizzle as you near the city limits. There are more exits here, leading to strip malls and housing developments, and traffic has picked up considerably. You round a long curve on the far end of a pretzel-like interchange, and the rain stops falling altogether, and it's as if this has happened just for you, because here is a clear view of the Willamette River, and, just on the other side, downtown Portland.

With its smattering of skyscrapers and buzzing expressways, Portland is a far cry from the settlement founded by Mr Lovejoy and Mr Overton, but still there is a charm to this river town, with its low, rusty bridges and downstream smoke stacks, and as you cross Morrisson Bridge you feel as though you can manage this place. Everything seems miniature, everything moves slowly. The streets are clean, the buildings old and charming, the motorists polite.

On the west side of town, just past an old minor league baseball stadium, you find the Orenthal Hotel. It's more like a *mo*tel, really, with two stories of outdoor-accessed rooms set somewhat awkwardly into a residential neighborhood that slopes up to the city park, but you are undeterred, as the Orenthal is top rated in your guidebook's Comfortable-But-Inexpensive section.

In the office you hand over a wad of cash to the clerk, a double-chinned woman who appears rooted to her chair behind the counter.

What's this green stuff? she jokes. Her name tag reads GLORIA. Last person to use cash here, she says, was Lewis and Clark.

I prefer not to leave any paper trails, you say, making sure to smile.

Please fill this out, Gloria says, sliding a check-in form across the counter.

How's business? you ask. (NAME: Shepard, Samuel.)

Tonight it's great. Michael Bolton's singing at the stadium. Who? (ADDRESS: NYC.)

Just the world's sexiest man, Gloria says. You're not here to see him?

I don't like music. (OCCUPATION: Author.)

Gloria stares at you as though you have two noses. For a moment you wonder if she will even give you the room key. Just in case, you flash her an I'm-only-kidding smile. She carefully sets the key on the counter, making sure not to touch you.

Room 231, she says. Second floor on the far right.

Thanks a bunch, Gloria. And enjoy the show.

When you're gone, Gloria probably turns to Eureka, the black girl who cleans the office, and says, I betcha he's here to see the show. I betcha anything he's queer.

Room 231. Blood red carpet, immaculate bathroom, television. A pine table and matching chair near the window. Over the double bed hangs a painting of geese in flight. The first thing you do is slide the carry-on bag under the bed. It has become increasingly heavy over the course of the day. You stand, move around the room, then crouch to look at the bag from various angles. As safe as anywhere, you decide. You take a long leak, change your shirt, sit for a moment at the table. Here we are. Out the window you can see the stadium and, not far beyond, the city's few skyscrapers. In the far distance, there is the faint suggestion of Mount Hood, unreal, like a painting on a theatrical backdrop. The sky is one clean tone of gray. You don't know a soul here.

Your chest is tight. Breathe. The scratches on your arms begin to burn. You rap your fingers on the tabletop to drown it all out.

A young couple passes by the window. Identical hair styles— short on top and sides, long in back—and matching paunches. They are holding hands. You hear them enter the room next door. A door slams, muffled voices, then music. A man singing, full-throated, bombastic. Your stomach growls. You haven't eaten anything since the rubbery airline waffles.

When a ma-a-an loves a wo-man...

You grab the guidebook, keys, your notebook, and run like hell to the car.

Well, he told Martin, It's all over. She dropped the bomb on me.

Martin's office was in mid-town, on the thirteenth floor of a tall modern apartment building, in a space intended as a one bedroom apartment.

He—Caleb, that is—lay on the couch—a standard domestic couch, with thick foam cushions and brightly patterned fabric, more the kind of couch one would find in a suburban living room than a psychoanalyst's office—with his hands folded across his chest, like a corpse in a coffin, staring up at a framed print of Wyeth's *Christina's World* on the wall. Over the past nine months he had grown so accustomed to this view that he sometimes felt he was in that field himself, staring longingly at the house upon the hill.

What bomb is that? Martin asked, his deep, God-like voice emanating from several feet behind the head of the couch.

She wants a separation.

He nearly gagged on the word. It was the first time he had actually uttered it out loud. Three days now since Sara had made the announcement and he had told no one. He was still living with her, sleeping on the sofa, half-heartedly searching for a cheap sublet, refusing to answer the telephone.

When did this happen? Martin asked in a tone that, disturbingly, betrayed not one ounce of surprise.

Friday. Friday morning at 10:04 AM. She…She just woke up and announced that she wants to be alone.

Out on Broadway, the scream of an ambulance ricocheted off the face of the opposite building and, like a stray bullet, through Martin's window.

What does that mean, *she announced*? Martin asked, his tone harder now, disapproving.

Well, she announced she wants a separation.

And you said what?

I…

He scoured his memory for what he considered a suitable answer, but he could find none.

I said nothing.

So your wife decided on her own that both of you ought to split up, and you said *what?*

Was this a trick question? Sweat was forming on Caleb's forehead.

I said nothing.

I see.

Martin was out of his sight, of course, but there was no problem picturing him there in his throne-like swivel chair, his plump white fingers forming a steeple which he tapped against his pursed lips. When Caleb had first met Martin, he'd been impressed by the therapist's no nonsense approach. Martin even *looked* like a therapist: turtleneck shirt under herringbone jacket, rimless spectacles, fastidiously trimmed beard. During the initial consultation they had sat face to face and ever since then Caleb had not been able to shake the image of Martin taking in—and appearing to *understand*—not just everything he said but also what lay beneath and between the words spoken: the bright eyes, the large, nodding head, and those hands—as pale and wrinkle-free as a baby's—joining and unjoining in front of his gray-whiskered chin. This guy *gets* it! Martin had subsequently suggested that Caleb lie on the couch during their sessions, an arrangement that took some getting used to. There was something a little too Biblical about conversing with someone he could not see, someone who, moreover, seemed often to be reading his thoughts. Then there were the distractions—the Wyeth print, the water mark on the ceiling, the view of the building across the way. Sometimes a man practiced singing opera in the apartment above. But eventually he'd grown accustomed to lying on the couch, and learned to gauge Martin's understanding of him by listening closely to the therapist's intonation—the way he said *wife* just now, or his brittle *I see.*

And how do you *feel* about your wife *unilaterally* deciding that you should separate? Martin asked, all six syllables of *unilaterally* thudding at his head like jabs from a heavyweight.

How do I *feel?* I guess I'm pissed.

That would be the right feeling! Martin shouted. And Martin hardly ever shouted. Sara decided *on her own*—out of the blue, as far as you can tell—that your marriage—a union of *two people*—should no longer be! That's outrageous! That's *enraging*!

Somewhere deep down inside Caleb was a tiny version of himself leaping up and down in response to this speech, shouting RIGHT ON! and FUCKING A!—he could almost feel this mini self butting up against the inside of his ribcage—but on the exterior he remained cool and detached and increasingly anxious, and all of a sudden he had to take a vicious piss.

«« — »»

Here comes your order of chicken and broccoli with garlic sauce. Look good, the waiter enthuses as he sets down the dish.

The Lucky Dragon looks like any Chinese restaurant anywhere: one potted ficus tree, mirrored walls, oppressive fluorescent lighting. It's late for lunch, and there are few customers, but they are all Chinese, which is a good sign. You sit by the window, gazing out at the empty street. Portland's Chinatown has an eerie, post-neutron bomb sort of atmosphere. Just the occasional passerby, the buildings are mostly warehouses, seemingly deserted, with no windows and thick metal doors.

You wolf down the chicken and broccoli. The same thing you always get. It tastes the way it always tastes. This makes you feel secure. Suddenly, you remember today is your birthday. Thirty-three. It has a terrible ring to it. Keep eating. And remember to breathe. You stare out the window. The street is so empty. The car is around the corner in a parking lot. You should have accepted the collision coverage, at least.

Breathe.

Just as you finish your lunch the sun crashes through the heavy clouds and bathes the street in a vivid yellow light. The world suddenly appears sharp and clear. Thirty-three isn't so bad, your mother said. You're old enough to have learned from your mistakes, but young enough to have your health.

What bullshit.

By the time you pay your bill and receive change the sun has been swallowed up by the clouds again. You wander the curiously empty downtown streets for a while, gazing in shop windows, taking note of the small differences one finds among cities—the width of sidewalks, the positioning of traffic lights, the shape and color of newspaper boxes and trash receptacles. You feel as though you've been transported to a slightly out of kilter parallel universe.

On a side street you come upon The Hippie Hall Of Fame, a small storefront operation dedicated to The History Of The National Hippie Movement In The Latter Half Of The 20th Century. There are a few other tourists gathered on the sidewalk, reading from interactive video displays set into the windows. HAVE YOUR PHOTO TAKEN WITH WAVY GRAVY!! declares a video monitor displaying a photo of the Woodstock hero. For twenty-five cents, according to another display, Jerry Garcia will hear your confession and dispense Pearls Of Pure Hippie Wisdom from a small speaker.

You try the door. Locked. From inside you hear Janis Joplin belting out "A Piece of My Heart." There are no hours of operation posted, but there is a red buzzer marked FREE CONDOMS, and, just below it, a crudely installed dispenser. Thinking of ILSE you press the buzzer firmly and wait. After a moment you push again, at which point the door swings open and a tall, prodigiously bearded man with a red satin bandanna and paisley trousers tells you they're plumb outta rubbers, sorry. That's a very popular button, he adds.

Completely understandable, you say. Then you ask if he has any post cards for sale.

Pardon?

You know—post cards. Hippie post cards.

He looks at you as though you are some sort of insane blasphemer, then turns his attention to the people behind you. Two teenage boys with long blue hair and a girl with—count them—six studs in her nose. He invites them in for a *concert*. All RIGHT! they shout and disappear inside, leaving you alone on the sidewalk. From behind the door you hear the opening shuffle of "Truckin'."

A few blocks away you discover another museum, this one dedicated to advertising. En route you are once again struck by how empty the streets are, but then you remember this is a holiday weekend. Independence Day. Everyone has gone home early. Normally the both of you would have gone somewhere, maybe to your mother's, or upstate, but here you are instead, all alone in a strange city. Breathe.

At the museum's front desk sits a fashion model waiting to be discovered. Perfect skin, green eyes, blonde hair you want to reach out and stroke. Look at you. Stunned. She takes your money and hands you a pass but you are unable to process such mundane activities while in the direct blaze of her eyes. Her lips: plump, soft, ever-so-slightly moist.

Any questions? she asks.

Her little speech—something about a special exhibit—ended about thirty seconds ago and you have been standing there gawking ever since. Is this guy on drugs? she wonders. Booze? Only last month she had to call security when some wino kept coming into the museum demanding to see an exhibit of old television commercials for hard liquor.

Sir?

Of course you have questions, but none of them could be considered even remotely appropriate, so you shake your suddenly very heavy head No and, clutching your pass in your hand like a child at the circus, you stagger toward the exhibits.

The History of Advertising is deadly dull, a parade of quaint, yellowy magazine ads full of promises—the BEST! the FINEST! the LONGEST-LASTING!—so you head past displays of famous props—shellacked burgers, huge boxes of anti-indigestion tablets, a large grape once inhabited by an actor—to a small, dark, deserted room at the far end of the small museum. It is like a chapel in here, with wooden benches and, at the spot where an altar might be, a large television set. Old commercials are playing non-stop—scratchy, bleached-out ads that you recall from childhood, ads you find unexpectedly moving. Beer ads, car ads, ads for floor cleansers and dishwashing liquids and toilet paper—images lodged somewhere in the shadowy recesses of your memory, right next to your teddy bear and soft blue blanket. There's the Marlboro Man! Mr. Clean! The old weeping Indian by the side of the road! The ads are interminable, some of them lasting sixty seconds, epic slices of your comfortable childhood in the midwest, where your biggest fear wasn't about how much money you made, or whether your wife loved you, or the certainty in your mind that you will someday develop testicular cancer, but: Will I make it home before the streetlights turn on? On your way out, you feel as though a fist has wrapped itself around your heart, so that you don't even notice the model lift her eyes then lower them quickly as you pass, and you are just barely aware of driving back to the hotel, negotiating some knotty traffic too, all the while humming the gentle Benson & Hedges theme: la lalala lala lala...

You don't snap out of it until you've entered Room 231 and checked on the status of the carry-on bag. Still there. Okay. You lie on the bed, stare at the ceiling. Voices from somewhere below you. Breathe.

I need a drink, you say to a crack in the ceiling, then jump from the bed.

Selecting the appropriate drinking establishment, you've always said, is a tricky business, roughly analogous to finding a mate. First there is the matter of physical attraction. Neon signs, you've found, are especially enticing, particularly if the sign is antique. If the sign is painted, however—and posted, say, over the door or on the window—the lettering must be attractive and clever. And of course there is the matter of the name. Who is not intrigued by a person with an exotic or unusual moniker? Lola, Siobhan, Siri, or...ILSE. It's the same with bars. Finally, and most importantly, there is personality. Exteriors can be deceiving, and this can lead to disappointment, if not heartache. There was the terrible night you entered a neon-lit saloon called The Blue Insult only to find wall to wall carpeting, fake wood paneling and no jukebox. You were out the door faster than you could say Pabst Blue Ribbon.

Bubba's Sulky Lounge. This looks promising. A corner tavern, a heavy, rust-laden neon sign buzzing above the doorway. Through the large plate glass window you see an endless bar, simple wood tables and chairs, a sawdust-covered slatboard floor. Bebop curls like smoke from under the door.

You enter, take a stool at the bar. Initials carved into its surface, great gashes scratched by drunks and lovers. Along the back wall are a dozen beer taps, lined up like the Rockettes with one knee each in the air. Ales and stouts and pilsners and porters and wheat beers…

What'll ya have?

The barkeep is a white-haired gentleman with a soft red face and a belly that droops significantly over his belt buckle.

That's what I'm trying to decide, you say.

I find it helps, Bubba says, if you can first identify your mood.

My mood?

Yes sir. For instance, are you melancholy? Then I would suggest a deep-flavored porter. Are you joyous? For that I'd recommend a bright pale ale. However, if you're angry, a bitter might do.

Do you have any grief beer?

The barkeep smiles. That would be our special today.

As Bubba lovingly fills a pint glass with a rich, dark golden brew, you glance around the place. There are not many other patrons here, just a few groups of two or three scattered among the tables. The air is thick with cigarette smoke and the smell of peanuts.

There you go, sir. One pint of grief beer. That'll be three bones.

You hand over the cash, then take a long, luxurious sip. Mmm. You have to hand it to Bubba. The man knows of what he speaks.

Death in the family?

You could say that.

Sorry to hear of it. Let me know if you need anything else.

《《《—》》》

So, Martin said, what did you do when Sara dropped this *bomb* on you?

Oh God, he thought. He was remembering that morning. His back still ached from all that sobbing.

I just crumbled, he said. I wept like a baby for two days straight.

So you cried.

Yeah.

All right. That's good. And did you say anything to her?

I said... He wished he had an answer that made him seem strong. I said nothing, really.

Nothing.

I just wept. What was I going to say? She was so determined. I mean, she knows I'm not happy about this—that much is clear, at least—but I just didn't have it in me to debate her on the subject. I *wept*.

Okay. So how do you feel toward her?

That question. Martin was always asking it. How do you *feel*? How do *you* feel? *How* do you feel?

Angry, he said.

Does she know that?

She must.

Did you tell her?

Not in so many words.

Then how would she know?

It's obvious.

Is it?

Tap tap tap went the pencil on Martin's legal pad.

What would you say to her now, the therapist asked, if she were here? To communicate to her how you really *feel*?

I don't know.

Well, give it a shot. Just pretend she's here, but she's not going to talk back. She's not going to debate the subject. Let her have it.

Okay. Uh...

This was like being forced to sing in public.

Uh... This isn't fair, Sara. Uh... I have a right to be in on this decision. It takes two people to get married, it takes two people to split up...

Okay. That's a start.

But Martin—the world is full of people who unilaterally, as you put it, dump their spouses. It happens all the time.

That may be true, but what interests me right now is how you *feel*. Sara will undoubtedly do whatever she pleases—that's her pattern—but it would behoove you to let her know how you *feel*

47

about all this. Otherwise, you are simply cooperating with her, you see. Now, however this turns out, whether she has her way or not, do you really want to accept it without letting her know exactly where you stand?

I guess not.

Tell me honestly. Do you want to split up with Sara?

No!

Okay. So what are you going to do about it?

He was stymied. He saw Sara's face, the determination in her eyes, her voice.

I don't know.

Sara may know, on some level, how angry you are, Martin said, but for your own peace of mind you absolutely must communicate to her how you *feel*. Otherwise, you're sitting on your *own* bomb. A time bomb.

A long pause, then Caleb said, Okay.

Do you have any idea how angry you are?

Probably not.

Have you considered counseling?

You mean, for the both of us?

That's right.

Well, it crossed my mind, but I don't think she'd go for it.

No?

She's made up her mind.

How about *you*? Would *you* get something out of seeing a couples counselor?

I think it might be helpful, yeah.

I'd be happy to refer you to someone. How's that sound?

Okay.

Meanwhile, in the time we have left, I really think we should work on getting in touch with this *anger* you're avoiding.

De we have to?

The thing is, you *tell* me you're angry, but I don't feel it from you, and neither, I'm sure, does Sara. Which, by the way, suits her just fine.

This was one of Martin's most sure-fire strategies: to remind his patient that a certain behavior plays right into the hands of the enemy.

So, Martin continued, why do you think you're avoiding the feeling?

I guess I'm afraid to feel it.

And why is that?

Because I might lose control?

Is that an answer or a question?

An answer?

Martin chuckled. And how would you lose control? Don't think about this too much. Just tell me what leaps to mind.

Violence.

Violence?

Yeah. Violence.

Tell me about it.

I don't know. I yell. I throw things. Break things.

What things?

Chairs. Lamps. Tables.

What else?

He remembered how, even as a child, he never fought with anyone. If he became angry he would simply start to cry. One day Jonny Kline pushed him all over the playground, one shove at a time, taunting him every step of the way, just to see what he would do, but he never shoved back, he just broke into tears.

Sorry, he said now as the tears rolled down his cheeks. I didn't think I had any of these left.

That's fine. You need a release. Every one of those tears, I expect, is loaded with anger. Maybe next time you can turn those into words. Think about that.

Martin paused, then added, Our time is up.

In the waiting room sat Martin's next patient, a young woman with short, almost golden hair and dark eyes. Caleb saw her every week on his way out and they had developed a ritual of quick nods and smiles. Because he'd been crying just now he tried not to look at her for more than half a second. She smiled and said hello. Hey, he replied, forcing a grin onto his face, then he rushed into the bathroom. After taking a long, noisy piss and washing his face he emerged to find her gone. As he waited for the elevator he wondered who this woman was and what kind of life she led. What did she do for a living? Did she have a lover? Were her parents still alive? Was she ever happy with herself? And as happened every week, once the elevator arrived and he stepped on, he promptly forgot about her.

«« — »»

The grief beer is going straight to your head. So many memories banging around in there, like knives inside a paper bag. A neighborhood newspaper lies nearby on the bar counter. Out of curiosity you check the APTS FOR RENT section of the classifieds. 900 sq ft 1 BR in turn of cent home $650. Studio w/ sep kit in prewar bldg $300. 2 BR w/ terr & FP $700. Etc. Picture yourself in a 900 square foot apartment, the charming antique furniture and red velvet curtains, jazz on the stereo, an open bottle of red wine on the coffee table, and ILSE, in a silk kimono, smiling at some witty remark you've made just as you are inserting your—

Care for another?

Bubba is leaning toward you, elbows on the counter. A more jovial beer this time maybe?

You decline for the time being, and ask where you might purchase some post cards. Bubba points out the window at the Dandy Drugs store across the street. Be right back, you say.

Inside Dandy Drugs you find a spinning rack of post cards— 5 for $1—some so old their colors have faded. You snap up five and a bottle of aloe for the scratches on your arms.

Where ya from? the elderly lady behind the counter asks as she rings up the total.

New York City, you proudly tell her.

Really? Manhattan?

Yes.

I used to live on Perry Street, she says, wearing a preposterous smile. In the West Village.

Uh huh, you mumble, remembering Dr. Leakey's office, the red door. That's a lovely street, you say.

I miss it sometimes, the woman says wistfully, remembering something herself.

I've just been thinking about maybe moving out here, you tell her. Rents are so much cheaper.

50

It's different, she says, though you're not sure if she means it as a good thing or a bad thing. You wait for her to elaborate, but she just stands there, her grin now taking on a grotesque, almost sardonic quality. Behind her, colorful boxes of condoms hang like little Christmas gifts from hooks on the wall.

I'll take a box of those, too, you say, pointing to a bright green box.

The twelve pack?

Yep.

She pops the box into a brown bag, quiet now, maybe thinking of Perry Street. Have a nice visit, she says as you exit.

Back at Bubba's you decide on an angry beer, in honor of Martin, and while you wait you rub the cool aloe onto your arms, the red scabs turning pink beneath the lotion.

You spread the post cards on the counter—bridges over the Willamette, Mount Hood, the botanical garden. It has long been a goal of yours to compose the perfect post card.

Dear Miles,
Got lost en route to Portland & even now, having found a
fleabag motel & appropriate saloon, am still lost.

The angry beer arrives, a best bitter. It goes down fine on top of the last beer, but it cannot wipe out the taste of rising anxiety. Bubba stands at the corner of the bar, washing mugs in soapy water, rinsing them, setting them out to dry. It's the Friday of a holiday weekend. Tonight the place will be jumping.

The beer here is cheap & good. Portland is an
otherworldly green beneath gray, w/old brick apt. houses
& flowers in every window. Rent: 900 sq. ft. for $650!
Let's move here & open a record store. In a day or so I
head west to the coast, then north. Then what?
Best,

How's that angry beer?

Hits the spot. Thanks.

The bar clock reads six but your body says it's nine. See ya later, mac, Bubba says as you head for the door. He's probably glad to see you go. Guys like you bring down the energy of a place. He wants groups of people, customers who talk and laugh and slap each other on the back. Not some poor depressed slob of a tourist who just sits there scribbling in a notebook. And what's with those marks on your arms? Looks like you wrassled a tiger.

Hope things look up for ya, Bubba adds after the door closes.

You're a bit drunk; your head feels as though it's full of tissue paper. The sun has appeared again, its bright light glaring off the puddles in the street. Here's a fast food Mexican joint, Healthy Hector's. Bean burrito, rice, a Coke to keep you awake. You sit at a window booth and watch as the sun moves in and out of clouds, like a lamp being turned on and off.

«««—»»»

Martin was right, he thought as he made his way to the subway. He went over all the things he needed to say to Sara, hoping he'd be able to remember them later, when she came home from work. Then it occurred to him that he didn't have to wait. Sara's office was nearby. Why not march over there right now, while the iron was hot, and read her the riot act?

It was yet another viciously hot day. The glass skyscrapers seemed to undulate. People's faces glistened with sweat and irritation. On Fifty-fifth Street a group of tourists crowded into their air-conditioned bus. On Sixth Avenue an unconscious man lay half-submerged in a plaza fountain. Outside the Museum of Modern Art a woman dragged her twin sons, maybe five years old, down the sidewalk as they wailed for ice cream cones.

When he passed the Abacus Press office he remembered the press release that was now overdue. *Rebound*. He hadn't even started it. Never had he been this late with an assignment. And they probably wouldn't send him anything else until he turned this one in. He promised himself to do it when he got home. For now all he could think about was Sara and what he needed to say to her.

Her office was on the twenty-third floor of the Asterisk Building. He had visited dozens of times, happily emerging from the marble-walled elevators to be waved through by Eugene the receptionist, and walking the narrow corridors between the cramped, book-lined offices of Sara's colleagues, many of whom knew him by name and would call out to him as he walked by. Today the elevator was crowded and as it rapidly rose he felt a little nauseous. Eugene—shaved head, impossibly long eyelashes, red silk shirt—was overwhelmed by phone calls and waved him through. Does Eugene know anything? he wondered. The whole office probably knows. Making his way down the hall, past large framed prints of O'Keeffe and Mapplethorpe flowers, he kept his eyes straight ahead so as not to make contact with anyone in their office. No one called out to him, not even Corinne, whose office was next door to Sara's, and with whom he had always enjoyed a breezy, unthreatening relationship. Corinne *definitely* knew. She'd been out with Sara Thursday night, the night before the bomb dropped, no doubt discussing strategy. As he passed her cluttered office he glanced inside. Corinne sat at her desk, telephone glued to her ear, eyes screwed shut in deep thought. He said nothing and moved on.

Sara's office was long and narrow, with a floor-to-ceiling window at the far end that overlooked St. Patrick's Cathedral. She sat at her desk, absorbed in a report she held in her hands. He stood in the doorway and watched her. She wore a sleeveless blouse that showed off her smooth, freckled shoulders and arms. Her hair was informally swept back behind her ears. He remembered another day long ago when he'd showed up unexpectedly. What're you up to? she had asked when he locked the door. He pinned her against the desk and pulled up her skirt. What if someone knocks? she asked. But he said nothing, he just kissed her, hard and wet, as she leaned back and wrapped her legs around him. When she came she had that look in her eyes that said she did not know exactly where she was.

Hello, he said.

When she looked up from the report there was a trace of shock on her face, which quickly transposed into surprise, then settled into a smile.

Oh, hi.

I was in the neighborhood.

Come in. She stood and approached him. He nearly expected her to skip over to him, as she always did, wrap her arms around him, and kiss him. This time, however, she stopped several feet away.

What's up? she asked.

Awkwardly, like a colleague, he sat in one of the three chairs situated between door and desk.

I wanted to say something.

Okay. She sat opposite him. What is it?

She was wearing a short black skirt. Her hands fidgeted on her bare knees. He wanted to reach out, take those hands, and break them.

I think we should see a counselor. A couples counselor.

He explained how Martin was going to supply him with a reference, and emphasized how important it was that they do this. She listened patiently, betraying no emotion.

I don't know, she said when he was done. I don't want to be put in a position where I'm being ganged up on.

Listen, he said, trying to contain himself, you decided all this shit on your own, okay? I've been totally left out of the fucking loop.

Honey—

Shut up. This is important to me. It's the least you can do.

He could see in her eyes that she knew exactly what was going on here: he'd just been to therapy, he was pumped up, he would never be so demanding otherwise.

All right, she said. I'll try it. Once, anyway.

Good. Thank you. He was beginning to calm down a bit. He looked her in the eye and said, Sara. I love you. I'm not going to give you up without a fight.

He felt as though he was in a play, a terrible play, and no one in the audience would ever believe him.

Sara did not respond. She had a lot of work to get back to. She'd talk to him later. Thanks for coming by.

On the elevator, dropping fast, he replayed the scene. The way she'd spoken to him, the look in her eye—she was determined, she was not going to budge.

They had not once touched each other.

The people in Healthy Hector's are starting to stare. You wonder what expressions must pass over your face as you recall this terrible business. You wouldn't be surprised to learn you've been making noises, little groans of pain, like a man having a nightmare. You apply more aloe to your itching arms, watched intently by the girl behind the counter, then leave.

The sky has clouded up again, and a fine, cool drizzle floats like mist in the air. You step from one pool of streetlamp light to the next, spending as little time as possible in the dark spaces in between. You pass a repertory cinema. *Shot in the Head*, starring Boyd Hart in his first big role, back when he was the darling of independent film. You tried to see it once when it was originally released, but it was sold out.

The theater is old and run-down in a charming sort of way. Lumpy seats, the odor of dust and decay, but also a beautiful deep crimson curtain and on the ceiling tiny lights arranged like stars. You spot the Big Dipper and the belt of Orion. (Maybe you should consult an astronomy book, you told her. Nah, she said, pasting another star to the bedroom ceiling. I'm creating my own special universe.) How many nights? How many nights of lying beside each other in the dark under those stars?

The place is filling up now. A young crowd, film buffs, mostly in pairs or larger groups. In front of you sits a young couple, the man talking too much and too animatedly, you can tell from the woman's face. A first date. He works at Powell's, though he's really a writer, a novelist, and is about half-way through his second book, the first having so far gone unaccepted by the corrupt publishers back east, though he's received some encouragement from a small press in Santa Fe. His date nods politely, searching her teeth with her tongue for a sliver of popcorn husk. Then, right in the middle of a heavily detailed synopsis of his masterpiece—a modern version of the Lindbergh kidnapping case in which a deranged loner makes off with the baby of a pop star resembling Madonna—the man says, Hey, how about I kiss you? and leans toward the woman with lips puckered. No! she exclaims, recoiling, thrusting up a hand to shield her face. Oh, he says, sorry, I just thought... She shakes her head vigorously and says, I'm just not ready for that, and he nods, pretending to understand, it's no big deal, but his lips are pursed into a thin line of rage that has you a little afraid for his date. Anyway, he says, and he nonchalantly resumes his plot synopsis while the woman bites her lip and glances hopefully at her watch, until—Thank God, she thinks—the lights begin to dim.

James McCoy—played by a very youthful Boyd Hart—lies in a hospital room with a bullet in his head, recalling events that led to his being shot. Months ago he discovered that his beautiful live-in girlfriend was having an affair with another man, and, being more curious than angry, James took to following her around, spying on her as she met with his rival at various locations around what appears to be Los Angeles. James does not seem at all upset that his beautiful girlfriend is betraying him. In fact, this knowledge seems to excite him. He takes photographs of the lovers as they eat and drink in restaurants, and he follows them to the man's house and videotapes them through the window as they have energetic sex. When he is alone, he spends a lot of time looking at the photos and videotapes, getting all worked up, so that when his beautiful girlfriend comes home he wants to make love with her. Over time, the beautiful girlfriend notices a change in James, and is pleased. He is more attentive, more affectionate, more aggressive sexually—in short, everything she'd been missing. One day, when James follows her to her latest rendezvous, he watches in horror as she tells her lover she does not want to see him anymore. She is in love with James, she declares, the affair must end. Crushed, James immediately reverts to his old self—distant, reserved, passive. Soon they are fighting, just as they often did before the affair. One night there is a knock at the door. It is the other man, the lover, drunk and waving a gun. He threatens James, who says, Go ahead, shoot me, I don't care anymore. But the man cannot pull the trigger, and lays down the gun. Unexpectedly, the beautiful but enraged girlfriend picks up the gun, aims it at James, pulls the trigger. Now James lies in a coma, a bullet lodged deep in his brain, and he remembers everything—every detail—while praying to die...

Afterwards, you wait in the lobby for the first date couple to come out. They are silent, a good two feet between them. She is blank-faced, he stares at his shoes. You follow them outside, where it continues to drizzle. They pause at the corner, where you pretend to make a phone call at a public telephone.

                    HE
    I could use a stiff drink. You?

                    SHE
    (hems and haws)
    Well…

                    HE
    Just one.

                    SHE
    I better not. I have to get up early for work.

                    HE
    Aw, c'mon. One little drink. I won't bite ya.

                    SHE
    I don't think it's a good idea.

                    HE
    (a hardness in his voice)
    Oh. I see.

                    SHE
    I'm sorry.

                    HE
Hey, no big deal. Is it okay if I walk you home? I don't want you to be attacked or anything.

                    SHE
    All right. It's not far.

You watch as they walk off into the mist together.

Chapter Four: Our First Date

I called Caleb several days after the party and left a message on his machine. It took him a full day to work up the nerve to call me back, maybe because he knew I would say yes. We were opening a door, and neither of us knew what was on the other side.

We met at the Bloody Duck for a drink, with plans to see a movie and have dinner later. I wore my long pale blue dress, and when I walked into the bar I saw him watching the way my body pressed against the fabric. We sat at the bar drinking Guiness (him) and Bass (me). The jukebox got us talking about music again. We were both fans of Elvis Costello, and we sang the lyrics to "Beyond Belief" until people stared at us. That may have been it for me. I was hooked.

What's your most embarrassing moment? I asked between beers.

Oh God. Is this some kind of test?

It's a very simple question. I need to know. If we're going to become...closer.

If I tell you, you might not go out with me again.

That's not true. Unless you voted Republican or something.

No. Nothing *that* embarrassing. But let me see...

I waited. It's so interesting to discover what other people are ashamed of.

Well, he said, it would have to be the time I threw up at a friend's wedding reception.

Too much champagne?

Too much everything.

In the rest room or the reception hall?

Reception hall, he said. His face was burning.

In front of everybody?

Worse.

On somebody?

The bride's mother.

No!

Yes.

That's a good one.

Thank you, he said. I wondered if he knew I liked him. I wondered if he liked me too.

How about you? he asked. What about *your* most embarrassing moment?

That's easy, I said. The time my parents walked in on me and my boyfriend while I was giving him a blowjob.

Uh huh, he said. That would be awkward. Were you in the bedroom, or—?

In the kitchen.

The kitchen?

I find the kitchen very erotic. You know—all that stainless steel, the smell of food.

I know what you mean. Would you like another beer?

We tried to see *Shot in the Head* but it was sold out, so we went to the Retro 80 and saw *Wait Until Dark*, and then we went to Large Marge's, where he told me about the rat rumor.

It fell out of the ceiling, he said, pointing up at the cheap panels over our heads. It landed on an old lady's head.

Who told you that?

Miles. My roommate.

Well, I said. As long as they have good margaritas.

They do.

I didn't know you had a roommate, I said. What's he like?

Miles? He's...different.

He told me about Miles's PhD dissertation, on which he'd been toiling away for five years.

He's trying to determine the correlation between penis size and financial and social success.

That is different, I said. And how does he go about this?

He uses a ruler.

You mean he goes around measuring cocks? Himself?

I like saying *cock* in front of men. Their eyes get so wide!

He says he has to, Caleb said, his eyes wide. People lie about their size otherwise.

Has he measured *yours*?

I won't let him.

Why not?

It's not that I have anything against it. It's just, I don't know, it drives him crazy that he can't even get his own roommate to let him do the measurements. It's become an integral part of our relationship.

Maybe he'd let a third party measure yours, I said, and he blushed.

So... Why law school? he asked.

Why not?

It's that simple?

Pretty much. When I came to New York from California, my first job was as a secretary at this firm. They liked me, I liked them, one of the partners suggested I go to law school, they would help pay for it, and here I am.

And what'll you do when you graduate?

I'll work there for a while, see how it goes.

Entertainment law?

Yeah. It's fun, even though you have to deal with the slimeballs of the universe.

Really?

You can't imagine. Musicians, actors, writers. There's just too much damn money to be made in entertainment. The slimeballs are everywhere.

And you don't mind?

I can handle them.

I bet you can.

It was 10:30 by the time we got out of there. He asked if I wanted to stop and have a nightcap. I wanted to, and I almost did, but I had to get up early the next day and study. I was in my third year of a four year night program. The workload was outrageous. We talked for a long time while waiting for our trains. I was headed uptown, he was headed down.

So, he said. About that boyfriend.

Boyfriend?

You know. The one in the kitchen.

Oh. Right.

Is he still…

Long gone, I said.

When my train pulled in he leaned forward and kissed me softly on the lips. He lingered for an extra second, waiting for my tongue, but I kept it to myself. Not yet, I thought. Not quite. All the way home I couldn't concentrate on my law book. He'd looked handsome in black chinos and a white shirt. Simple but elegant. I thought about all the things we could do in his kitchen.

CHAPTER FIVE: CRISIS/OPPORTUNITY

Back at the Orenthal Hotel, couples are just returning from the concert down the street, where the stadium remains lit up like a space ship. They walk arm in arm, or arm around shoulder, talking reverently as they climb the iron stairs to their rooms.

Great show, huh? a woman says to you as you pass. She is tall, big-haired, with a warm, broad smile. Her man, looking a bit embarrassed, stares at your shoes.

You nod, rush up the steps, your key already in hand. What's *his* deal? you hear the woman grumble behind you. Inside Room 231, you check under the bed before relaxing. Disembodied voices float outside the window, doors creak open and slam shut, soft murmurs through the walls, music.

On the subway ride downtown he was torn between elation at having talked Sara into seeing a counselor—surely she'll see the error of her ways once we talk to someone!—and sadness at realizing just how puny this victory was. Sara was obviously indulging him.

His eye strayed to the beautiful woman sitting across the aisle. She was staring right at him with pale eyes that contrasted sharply with her jet black hair. He looked away, self-conscious, but kept tabs on her out of the corner of his eye. She continued to boldly stare at him, a mysterious grin on her face. What was she up to? He had always had fantasies about meeting women on the subway, someone strange and beautiful like her. When her stop came, she would nod slightly, rise, and he would discreetly follow her to a nearby apartment, a small, dark studio dominated by an unmade bed. Once inside, neither of them would utter a word as they kissed and groped and fell into bed. Why not? Sara was leaving him—why should he pass up such a golden opportunity? He looked directly at her now and she continued to stare back. She had full, pouty lips and a long neck. What would it be like to kiss her?

At 14th Street the woman abruptly stood up and removed from her purse a collapsible cane, white with a red tip, which she proceeded to unfold. The other passengers politely made room for her as she found the open door and stepped gingerly onto the platform.

Step in and stand clear, the conductor announced.

Feeling his face heat up, he covered his eyes with both hands as the subway doors clanged shut.

At the entrance to his apartment building he ran into Mia, their upstairs neighbor. Twenty-four, blonde, curvy, neurotic Mia. Occasionally she would come downstairs during the day and interrupt his work to discuss her latest life crisis, and because she had such a lovely face, and because he got such a bang out of her attention, he would indulge her. This had happened often enough that Sara started calling Mia his girlfriend, as in, Talk to your girlfriend lately? Sometimes, when he and Sara were having sex, he would think of Mia, of her bright green eyes, and it made it more exciting for him.

Hey, Mia said as he unlocked the door. What's up?

Not much, he said. What's up with you?

Oh, I'm back with Paul, she said.

Really? He was surprised. Paul was Mia's on again/off again boyfriend, a British graphic designer with a weakness for cocaine and gin. During their last heart to heart Mia had sworn off That Rat Bastard forever. Is this good or bad? he asked as he followed her up the stairs, her plump but shapely ass swaying before him.

Don't know yet. Ask me next week.

Well, good luck, he said, unlocking the apartment door. He wanted to get away from Mia. The more they talked, the more likely he was to blurt out something about Sara.

How's Sara? she asked.

63

A-okay, he said.

He stepped into the apartment. Mia remained in the hall, smiling warmly. She had freckles around her nose and under her eyes.

It's so hot, she said, wiping her face with the back of her hand.

Yeah.

Okay then, she said.

Back to work, he said.

Right. Say hi to Sara for me.

Will do.

Ta.

《《——》》

Ta, you think as you sit at the motel room desk, pen digging into your notebook like a butter knife.

Ta.

You climb into bed and shut out the light. The room is pitch black, the extra-thick window curtains blocking even the glow from the buzzing streetlamps in the parking lot. Music still tinkles from somewhere in the building. The sheets smell musty. Still thinking of Mia, you consider masturbating, but are too tired.

Breathe. Shut your eyes. Sleep.

You wake up in blackness. Where am I? It takes a moment to remember. There is a strange, sour smell in the room that you cannot identify. On your way to the bathroom you glance at your watch on the bureau. Ten o'clock in the morning. The room is so dark it may as well be midnight. Not a single dream all night long, just a death-like sleep.

You take a long shower during which you spend several minutes just standing there, immobile, as the hot water beats down on you. Yesterday was your birthday. You lean your head against the tile wall. Yesterday was my birthday.

You get dressed and mosey over to the hotel lobby to pick up some food from the continental breakfast tray. The room is full of couples dressed in running outfits. They're still talking about last night's concert. He has such dreamy hair, someone mentions. He sings like an angel. You grab two powdered donuts and quickly exit. The donuts, you find, are dry and stale.

Today, rather than drive, you take a bus downtown. You sit up front, watching through the windshield so that you don't miss your stop. The driver hums as he rolls through Saturday traffic. Other passengers chat with him when they climb aboard, commenting on the cloudy weather or wishing him a happy holiday.

Under the Burnside Bridge you discover the famous Saturday market. Arts and crafts and food and drink. Lots of bright t-shirts with rhinestones, cheap wallets, and ceramic animals. But the only booth that interests you is that of a Chinese calligrapher. Among the displayed samples of his work are the symbols for Crisis and Opportunity, written vertically on rice paper. You ask for a copy, and he dashes one off, the brush an extension of his small hand, then tells you to come back in ten minutes. Must to dry, he explains, holding up the rice paper for you to examine. When you return he has popped the paper into a simple wooden frame. You look closely at the symbols, making sure they conform to the ones on the back wall. Wouldn't it be amusing if the calligrapher had actually written something else, such as KICK ME, or I AM A SODOMITE? Who would know the difference?

At nearby Governor's Park there is a blues festival in progress. The park is a small, well-kept semi-circle of healthy green grass sloping down to the Willamette. At riverside is a large stage set up for live music. Several food vendors have parked their colorful vans around the perimeter, and the air smells of grilled sausage and french fries. Off to the side are two long rows of gleaming white port-o-potties, and in between, a row of portable sinks, complete with liquid soap dispensers. The next best thing to being home.

You find a spot on the grass about half way down the slope. Not many people have arrived yet, but the music is just starting and will continue until sundown. So far the audience consists mostly of Deadheads and bikers with their girlfriends, and a few other oddballs like you.

The sky appears unnaturally low today, a gray blanket propped up by the downtown skyscrapers and bridge towers. Still, it is warm and there is no smell of rain in the air. Boaters have begun dropping anchor just off shore to take in the tunes, currently being performed by a tight little trio called My Dog Blues. Their music is slow and simple, twelve bars of misery repeated over and over. Lately, any kind of music has made you physically ill, but somehow this stuff doesn't bother you. The vocals are mournful, guttural, practically indecipherable, the guitars heavy and chugging. Meanwhile, each thwack of the snare ricochets off the buildings behind you and rolls back down the park like an oak barrel into the river.

A few yards away stands a large man in full biker regalia—wind-beaten leather trousers and jacket, leaden black boots—along with a corpulent woman in unflattering tank top and jeans. They guzzle from cans of beer kept cold in foam holders and every so often the woman hoots and hollers along with the music, her belly and breasts jiggling like gelatin. On her left shoulder is a tattoo of a phoenix. As they kiss sloppily, you imagine them having sex. It is not a pretty picture.

As My Dog Blues drags out the ending of their final song, the biker couple twirls and laughs until they wind up in each others' beefy arms, their lips smashed together in a slobbery kiss that endures right up until the drummer's climactic cymbal crash, at which point the woman rests her greasy head on the biker's shoulder and sobs, I love you so much, Harold, I'm gonna *die*.

«««—»»»

The apartment was haunted for him now, a cold dark place populated by the ghosts of his marriage. One of these was Dilsey, who lay stretched out on the bed in a patch of yellow sunlight. He sat next to her and stroked her soft belly. She purred. He remembered going to the animal shelter with Sara, coming across this scrawny black creature with sad eyes looking out from her cage, lifting her into his arms. The purring cat had then placed her thin front legs on either side of his head, in effect giving him a hug. This is the one, he'd said. The shelter worker told them she'd been found on the street, half dead. But she endured, the worker said.

We'll call her Dilsey, Caleb said.

They became fast friends. Sometimes in the morning she

would lie across his chest and poke her whiskers into his face until he consented to patting her. Never again.

You want me to stay, don't you, Dilsey?

She lifted her green eyes to his and yawned dramatically. He lay down beside her for a while and stared out the window. He had lost all concept of time over the past three days. Except to make it to Martin's at his appointed hour he had not even consulted a clock. He'd slept, eaten, gone to the bathroom, sat around. He thought a lot about the future—not so much his own, which simply seemed barren, but about Sara's. She was with another man, laughing, making love, having beautiful children. A film loop that played over and over. Meanwhile, he glanced through the newspapers for an apartment to sublet, but he had not been able to make any calls yet. He never got beyond picking up the receiver. But he couldn't stay here much longer. It was just too painful to share the apartment with her. And he was glad he could not afford the rent on his own—let Sara stay here with all these ghosts, he thought. Maybe tomorrow he would look at a few places.

He climbed from bed and went into the living room. There on his desk lay the advance reading copy of *Rebound*, along with a sheaf of information provided by the Abacus publicity department. He stared down at the broken heart on the cover. Why couldn't they have assigned him something innocuous? Just last week he'd written releases for *Pork Bellies & Ostrich Ranches: Investments That Will Make You Rich*, and a tawdry legal thriller.

He forced himself to sit down and take out a note pad. He was going to write this if it killed him. From the fact sheet he got some information about the book's author, Philip Leakey, PhD. Apparently his previous book, *To Stay or Not to Stay: How to Escape an Unhealthy Relationship*, sold more than 100,000 trade paperback copies. He had appeared on *Oprah* and *Today*. The new book would be an Alternate Selection of the Book of the Month Club.

FOR IMMEDIATE RELEASE
In his previous bestseller, *To Stay or Not to Stay: How to Escape an Unhealthy Relationship*, respected therapist

Philip Leakey, PhD, provided readers with frank, common sense advice on how to untangle themselves from love relationships gone sour. Praised for its "honest and thoughtful examination of this age-old conundrum" (Arianna LaMotta, bestselling author of *Heartmending*), *To Stay or Not to Stay* sold more than 100,000 copies and has given thousands of love-torn men and women the courage to strike out on their own. Now, in his new book, **REBOUND: How to Survive Divorce in the 90s** (Abacus Hardcover/$23.95 FPT), Dr. Philip Leakey speaks to the millions of men and women still aching from the trauma of divorce, and offers practical guidance on how to kill your ex.

Okay, so he could make adjustments in the second draft, no big deal. So far, for the most part, it was going pretty well.

It has become a commonly known fact that more than 50% of all marriages end in divorce. Some are handled amicably, with both parties agreed on the terms of the split, but for too many, divorce is an emotionally wrenching, ego-shattering experience. As a long-time couples counselor, Dr. Philip Leakey has worked with thousands of husbands and wives who are in the midst of this traumatic process, and in **REBOUND** he shares his observations and conclusions about how to survive, thrive, and take bloody vengeance in the wake of a nasty divorce.

The telephone rang. He automatically reached to pick it up, but then stopped short. He did not want to speak to anyone. He would either have to pretend all was well or tell the whole story, and he was not prepared to do either.

He let the answering machine pick up. His own voice on the outgoing message sounded alien to him, like that of someone he knew a long time ago. There was a short series of beeps, then a man's voice.

Hello, this is Martin.

Martin was using his telephone voice, which was different from his office voice—more formal, as if he was afraid someone other than his patient might hear the message.

I have that name and number for you. He's an excellent counselor and I've spoken to him already. He's waiting for your call. His name is Phil Leakey and his number is…

Leakey. Leakey. Where have I heard that name before? Oh my God, Caleb said out loud. Philip Leakey! Philip Leakey, PH-fucking D!

Take care then, Martin concluded, and I'll see you next week.

On the back of the reading copy of *Rebound* was a murky photograph of the famous Dr. Leakey, who resembled Martin in many ways—meticulously trimmed gray beard, sensitive, probing eyes—except that his head was completely shaved. Bald men with beards, he thought—I've never understood them.

When the answering machine had beeped off he noticed that the little red light flashed twice, which meant that there was a previous message. He pressed PLAY and waited anxiously.

Hi, this is Andrea at Abacus? I was just wondering about the release for *Rebound*? You know—the divorce book I sent you last week? Are you gonna be able to get that back to me soon? Gimme a tinkle if there's a problem, okay? B'bye.

In the grand scheme of things—in a world where people were being bombed and raped, where children were starving, where old ladies had their toenails ripped out by soldiers—his predicament was minor, to say the least, and yet at that moment he felt as though the walls were sprouting poison-tipped spikes and closing in, and the air was being sucked from the room, and that God, or the gods, or the Spirits, or Fate—*whatever*—was conspiring against him and him alone.

Breathe, he said.

He picked up the book and tossed it against the wall, spooking poor Dilsey so badly that she leapt from her perch on the sofa and scrambled out of the room with a great clattering of claws on the floor.

«««—»»»

Having tired of the blues, you wander aimlessly around downtown, clutching Crisis/Opportunity to your chest and admiring the clean sidewalks. The farther you get from the river, the less you can make out the music, but the furious drum beat still bites at your heels.

You come upon a narrow park through which you walk toward the art museum. At first it seems as though you are the only one around but then you hear from behind you a man's voice calling out, Hey man! Hey! Yo! You try to ignore him but he continues to shout at you—Hey! Yo!—and as you approach the museum he has nearly closed the gap between you.

Hey guy, he's saying, Hold up there! and you are fairly certain he is not chasing you down to return a dollar bill that might have fallen from your pocket. By the time you reach the museum steps he is just a few paces behind you, and there's nothing left to do, is there, except to turn around and confront him.

Yo man, he says.

What?

Whoa, the man says, chuckling. He wears a sweat-stained t-shirt and polyester work pants, and his hair is ratty, with bare spots where you can see his sunburned scalp. I just thought you might like some smoke is all.

The truth is, you can do almost anything you want here. You can buy some dope, or you can ignore him and walk into the museum. You can take a swipe at him, or call the police. In this country, a guy like you can get away with almost anything.

Whaddaya say? the man asks. Smoke?

You are on the first step of the museum, about one foot above him.

Fuck off.

You are as surprised as he is to hear the words come out of your mouth, and you wonder if he can detect the slight, worried quiver in your voice. For a long time you two stand there, sculptures near the entrance of the Portland Museum of Art.

Okay, dude, the man says, showing bloody gums. He backs away, open-palmed, and as his bloodshot eyes lock onto yours he adds, See ya 'round, dude, then ambles back into the park. You wait a moment, watching him go, then enter the museum, where you loiter in the lobby for a bit, looking out the window until he's a few blocks away.

You purchase a ticket and enter the exhibition gallery, where you find you are shaking. What did he mean—See ya 'round? Will he be waiting for you outside?

You skip the Native American crafts—intricately beaded head dresses, deer skin drums, etc.—and head straight for 20th century painting. You prefer art that has zero practical value. As you browse the nearly empty gallery rooms, you start to get a little horny, for you a common reaction in museums. There is something chemical that happens to you around all this creativity. Soon you are sporting a semi-erection, which you attempt to camouflage by jamming a hand into your pocket.

Over near a typically amorphous Rothko is a middle-aged couple speaking in loud voices, as if they were in their own home.

Don't you see, Gerald—it's like music. You just have to let go of the intellect and allow it to *move* you.

Music? I like my music with lyrics. Cole Porter. Irving Berlin. The words make sense. I need *context*.

In the next gallery, standing before a grotesque Francis Bacon, is none other than ILSE. Though she is dressed in faded jeans, pink blouse and leather jacket—the spiritual antithesis to her synthetic airline uniform—you immediately recognize her. That hair. That skin.

She has not spotted you. She is consumed by the painting. And even if she does see you, there is little guarantee she would recognize you. You're just one of thousands of travelers to whom she has served beverages in the past week or so.

You pretend to admire the work of a local artist several panels down from the Bacon. With your expert, urban-trained peripheral vision you watch as ILSE moves on to the next painting. As she does so, she casts a quick glance your way, but shows no sign of recognition. Moving over to a garishly colored Pearlstein nude you notice the pounding of your heart. Can she hear it, too?

Quick! Slide your wedding band off and into your pocket!

When ILSE steps confidently into the next gallery you let out a deep sigh, then gather your meager reserves of courage. A plan has occurred to you.

ILSE is admiring a large canvas painted entirely in blue except for a blood-red streak down the left hand side. You stride purposefully to the adjacent painting and pretend to study its thick, painterly brush strokes. You are just close enough to catch a whiff of the familiar and perfumey aroma of soap on her skin. Your penis perks up a bit more. Hurry now, before she decides to leave.

You yawn, stretch your arms over your head, and bend over to touch your toes.

Hey, ILSE says. I *knew* I'd seen you somewhere before.

Excuse me? Oh, hello.

Caleb Caleb, she says, and her face erupts with that smile of hers. Brown eyes, soft, bowed lips, tiny, perfectly formed ears. Fancy meeting *you* here, she says.

Your day off?

Yeah, she replies, thrusting both hands into her back pockets, a maneuver that forces her breasts forward, which is to say *toward* you. Your heart skips a beat. How about *you*? she asks. Are you on holiday?

On holiday. She must have picked up this phrase overseas. She is utterly charming.

Uh huh, you manage to say. Has she noticed the bulge in your trousers? It feels as though the entire canvas of your life is precariously balanced on the throbbing tip of your penis.

I like to check out museums, you say. They can tell you a lot about a city.

And you never know who you'll run into, she says. Hey, is that the symbol for Crisis and Opportunity?

At this magical juncture, one might think the rest would be easy and inevitable: the flirty chat, the stroll around town, the brief pit stop at Bubba's for an amorous beer, the Big Etcetera. But reality—or your version of it—intrudes in the following form: you have a sudden, heart-stopping vision of the Orenthal Hotel maid searching through your carry-on bag. You can actually see it happening: a dark-skinned Guatemalan woman in a powder-blue uniform is vacuuming around the perimeter of the bed when she notices the carry-on and, curious as to why anyone would put the bag under there, she decides, out of curiosity to peek inside...

72

Madre de Dio!

What's the matter? ILSE asks.

Oh. I just remembered something. Something I forgot to do.

Is it something important? Can I help?

No!

ILSE jumps back. O-kay, she says, removing her hands from her pockets and crossing them in front of her chest.

I'm really sorry, you tell her as you back up toward the exit. But I gotta go now.

But—

And you are out of the room, taking the stairs two at a time to the lobby, where you push through the heavy front doors and out into the gray afternoon light. Jogging toward Burnside Street, where you can catch a bus back to the hotel, you make out the steady rhythm of a twelve bar blues from the riverfront.

Hey!

From behind you, a voice. Shit. It must be the drug pusher. He probably has a gun. Don't stop. Don't even hesitate. Burnside is just another block away.

The sound of footsteps on cement. He is running after you now. At Burnside you have to stop and wait for the traffic to slow before crossing to the westbound side of the street. C'mon, c'mon! The footsteps are getting closer. You picture his ashen face, his red eyes.

Hey!

You twirl on your heels and yell at the top of your lungs:

STAY THE FUCK AWAY FROM ME OR I'LL RIP YOUR FUCKING HEAD OFF!!

You are looking into a pair of shocked brown eyes.

ILSE?

She turns and runs—no, she *tears off*, as if you are holding a knife, and you are left with your heart pounding in your throat and the burning sting of fresh scabs on your arms.

Wait! you cry, but she's gone.

Back at the hotel you find that the room has indeed been cleaned, the bed neatly made, the thick smell of disinfectant in the air—but the carry-on remains undisturbed. You sit at the table and stare out the window.

The couple from next door passes by on their way to their room. Their door slams, you hear muffled voices through the wall.

«<«—»>»

This was his third night sleeping on the sofa. Sara was still out, probably with Corinne, no doubt living it up. He had watched television for hours, jumping from channel to channel, incapable of focusing on any one program for more than a few minutes, and he now lay in the dark, unable to sleep. Sara had volunteered to take the sofa but he wouldn't allow it—sleeping in their bed by himself, beneath the glowing stars on the ceiling, he would have been even more lonely.

He heard music playing upstairs, and the sound of dancing. Mia was having one of her spontaneous parties. She had called a while ago and he'd listened in real time to her invitation on the answering machine. He was tempted to go, to get drunk and flirt, but he would have to explain Sara's absence and he still wasn't up to telling either a lie or the truth.

So he lay there in his underwear, no blanket in this awful heat. The air from the window fan felt good but it did not stop him from sweating. On the news there had been talk of brown-outs and tension in the city's poor neighborhoods, extra cops were assigned to patrol the streets, fire hydrants opened all over town. He wiped a drop of perspiration from his eyebrow and shut his eyes.

Breathe.

(The night she lay across this very sofa as he inserted himself from behind. She held her breath and he kissed the soft, sweaty skin on the back of her neck. She took his hand as he moved deeper into her, the couch sliding, her hand squeezing tighter and tighter until his knuckles hurt...)

Breathe.

The sound of a key turning in the lock, the door swinging open, the hallway light spilling across the wall and floor.

Caleb?

He shut his eyes.

74

On her way to the bathroom she walked into the bookcase. Drunk. He could hear her pissing now, an endless stream that once struck him as happily domestic but now disgusted him. Probably drinking bourbon all night, her drink of choice when celebrating.

When Sara finally emerged, Dilsey was waiting for her. Hey, sweetie, she whispered, scooping the cat up. He could hear the purring all the way across the room.

Sara paused in the kitchen doorway and called out his name again, this time slightly louder. He breathed slow and steady, as if asleep, until she gave up and left the room, then he lay wide awake for another several hours, sweating, listening to the music and laughter from upstairs.

《《《—》》》

You wake up fully clothed, the room lit a pale green by the streetlight pouring in through the window. Where the hell am I? Headachy and confused, you slowly realize you've been awakened by a loud noise, and are suddenly jolted awake by the unmistakable sound of a woman moaning in rhythm to the squeaking of bed springs. The couple next door, just inches from your head. You immediately have an erection, but along with it comes a palpable sense of dread. This woman sounds an awful lot like Sara. Oh! Oh! *Oh!* she cries. Breathe. Breathe. Their bed is banging against the wall and you can make out the man's labored grunts. It's as though you're in the same room, the sounds are all around you. By the time they reach a raucous and simultaneous orgasm—*Mikey!* she shouts, *Mikey!*—you understand what it must be like to be buried alive, with no air, no light. In the silence that follows, you shut your eyes, swallow the bile at the back of your throat, and try to fight your way back to sleep.

CHAPTER SIX: THE FIRST TIME

It was a rainy spring Sunday. He was not expecting me, just lying around the apartment reading the newspaper, he said, daydreaming. C'est moi, I said over the intercom, and at first he didn't recognize my voice.

Who?

Sara, I said, sounding disappointed.

Sorry, he said when he opened the door. This intercom makes everyone sound like Betty Boop.

I told him I'd come to sew a button on his blue shirt, the one he had mentioned on the phone the day before, the one he said he was too lazy to fix. But before I told him anything I kissed him and passed a new button from my mouth to his, tongue to tongue, and he was so surprised he nearly swallowed it.

Where's your roommate? I asked.

He's at his boyfriend's.

Where's that blue shirt?

You'll fix it later.

We made love on his lumpy, second-hand sofa. The television was tuned to a golf tournament, and the hushed voices of the announcers lent an appropriately reverent tone to the proceedings.

He insisted I remove every article of my clothing. So I can see all of you, he said. I was shy. My entire body blushed. His skin was smooth and pale and tasted of salt. I allowed few preliminaries. I wanted him inside me as quickly as possible. For a long time, after he'd entered me, we lay perfectly still, watching each other's faces, and all I could think was what a perfect fit he was.

He was surprised, I could tell, by how much noise I made. As the rain tapped against the windows I moaned and sighed and growled, and toward the end, when our rhythm grew more frenzied, with my hands clasped behind his back, when I could no longer hold back the climactic jolt of pure energy that had accumulated inside me, I began to shout—not words, exactly, but lost syllables that ricocheted off the ceiling like balloons losing air—and for a few seconds I lost all control of myself, having been picked up by this wave and tossed and spun until I landed, exhausted, beneath him.

That was religious, I said.

We lay there for a while, breathing heavily, until we fell asleep. An hour later, Miles walked in and found us still naked on the sofa.

Who's winning the golf tournament? he asked.

CHAPTER SEVEN: HEAT RISES

You rise early and check out of the Orenthal, pausing only to grab two donuts—as stale as yesterday's—from the continental breakfast tray. On your way out you nearly collide with the couple from next door. They are holding hands and smiling warmly. You could hold the door for them but you do not.

Route 26 to Route 6 west, through gently rolling forests and farmland and towns so small they don't even bother to put up a stop sign. The sky is left over from yesterday—low gray clouds that seem illuminated from within. You are exhausted from a long night of sleeping and waking, sleeping and waking, but the wide open spaces and lush green trees relax you.

Near Tillamook you turn onto a dirt road that leads to an access trail to Munson Creek Falls—according to the guide book, the highest falls in the Coast Range. Noting that there are no other cars in the parking area, you are stricken by the urban dweller's irrational fear of nature. The trail—quite narrow, with dense, intensely green walls of vegetation and undergrowth—may be populated by strange creatures or militia people. You hesitate at the head of the trail. From off in the distance you can make out the rushing sound of the falls.

At various points along the trail you must traverse narrow gullies by inching across moss-covered logs, one step at a time, making sure the soles of your sneakers make firm contact with the slippery wood. So far, you have not encountered another soul.

(On the Appalachian Trail you came across a dozing porcupine. The path was narrow at that point and the prickly creature lay right smack in the middle. Neither of you had ever encountered such an animal and you were certain that if it was disturbed you would end up with poison quills embedded in your legs. C'mon, she said, very calmly stepping over the porcupine, which lay perfectly still and unaware. Come *on*, she repeated. He won't hurt you. But you couldn't move. You may as well have been on the edge of a mine field. We can't wait here all day, she said. She pretended to examine the porcupine from a few feet away. I think it's dead, she said. Really? you asked. He's not breathing, she said. You shut your eyes, raised one leg, hopped over. The porcupine did not budge, but a few minutes later, when you looked back, he had gone.)

Finally you reach what appears to be the end of the trail proper. From here you can see the falls, a shimmery sheet of water about one hundred paces farther on. It looks as though, by scrambling over a hodge podge of logs and steeply sloping rocks, you could make your way closer to a better view. You make a half-hearted attempt, but turn back after trying unsuccessfully to climb a moss-covered sheet of rock. You stand around for a while, a little bored, watching the far-off falls, then turn back.

Not much of a hike. Twenty, thirty minutes, tops. You walk quickly along the trail, ignoring the nearby flutter of birds and smell of blooming flowers. The sooner you reach the car, the sooner this feeling will go away.

About half way back you come across two hiking couples. They are about your age, more or less, the men large and mustached, the women plump and content-looking. Everyone carries bulging backpacks and is properly attired in khaki shorts and sturdy hiking boots. Howdy, the man in the lead says, but you do not reply. They grin pleasantly as they squeeze past you, headed toward the falls.

When you reach the lot you climb into the car and clutch the steering wheel. It is deathly quiet except for the drone of a fly that hovers over the back seat. You quickly turn and swat the insect with your palm, sending it sailing across the car and against the window. It lands, dazed, atop the carry-on bag.

You lean your head against the wheel and try to breathe. After a moment you hear the dull buzz of laughter somewhere behind you.

《《——》》

Ten days after Sara announced her decision to break up with him, he moved into a sublet apartment with a two-month lease. Maybe over the next couple months, he thought, Sara would come to her senses, and he could move back in with her.

It was a cramped two-bedroom apartment on the top floor of a six floor walk-up in the Village. The primary tenants were teachers headed up to New Hampshire with their twelve-year- old daughter to work at a summer school camp. They seemed relaxed and vaguely hippie-ish, with their simple, seemingly hand-sewn clothing and unkempt hair, and after just a few minutes of idle chatter with Caleb they'd decided he would suit them just fine as a sub-tenant.

You have good energy, Kate told him as he made out a check for the first month's rent. She and Earl had lived in the small, railroad apartment for seventeen years, she explained.

Really? he asked, wondering how two, and then *three*, people could live for so long in such a small space.

Oh, we've had to be ruthless, Earl told him. We don't save anything unless it's a matter of life and death.

They were leaving town the next day, they explained, taking only their clothes, so he would be left with all the furniture and appliances.

Want the full tour? Earl asked.

The furniture was spartan and practical, including a hideous, L-shaped sofa that left very little space to walk in the living room. The main bedroom consisted of a full-size futon, two gun- metal gray desks with matching filing cabinets, a dresser, and a tall bookcase crammed with pedagogically-themed books. The eat-in kitchen was equipped with all the necessary utensils and pots and pans, but he was warned that, in this summer heat wave, using the oven would make the room unbearable.

We're on the top floor, Earl reminded him. And you know how heat rises.

Which then brought them to Earl and Kate's prize possession: the air conditioner.

This little honey has saved our lives, Earl said, and then he demonstrated his ingenious method of conserving energy by draping a thick black curtain over the hall doorway.

That keeps the cool air in the living room, Kate explained. You may want to sleep in here on the real hot nights, she said. On the couch.

We'll do that ourselves tonight, no doubt, Earl said. Then it's off to cool New Hampshire tomorrow a.m.

Later, when Caleb got home there was a note from Sara saying that she was taking an evening flight to Los Angeles:

Back in a few days. Thanks for being so understanding. I love you,
—S.

The next morning he showed up, bleary eyed and exhausted from a sleepless night, at his new apartment. He carried two brown grocery bags full of underwear, socks, trousers and shirts, plus his laptop computer. Earl and Kate and their daughter were rushing around, packing last minute items, and periodically bringing their new tenant up to date on such matters as security.

When you go out, Earl told him, even if it's just for a few minutes, please leave a light on, and the radio too. Oh, and keep your eye on the super. He's a gypsy and his whole family's a bunch of thieves.

Earl, Kate said.

Well, it's true. Just be careful is all I'm saying.

He helped them carry their ridiculously heavy bags down to their Volkswagen, where he was handed the apartment key, and Kate gave him an unexpectedly moist kiss on the lips. Take care of the place, she whispered, as if telling him a secret.

Sure thing, he said, imagining what she looked like underneath that peasant skirt and blouse.

As they pulled away he waved goodbye, and with a friendly toot of the horn they were gone.

Breathe.

It was a long climb back to the apartment, six steep flights. Exhausted and sweaty, he lay on the sofa for a few moments, trying to digest the fact that, for the next couple months, this was his home.

First things first. Now that he had moved he needed to call his mother and finally tell her all that had happened. He was not looking forward to it. His parents had been married for forty-two years when his father died, and both his brother and sister were happily married also. Now he would be seen as the failure, the one who couldn't get it right.

In the midst of dialing he put the telephone down and began to pace back and forth in the narrow space between sofa and table. How was he going to put this to his mother?

Ma, Sara has left me... Ma, Sara and I have decided to split up... Ma, my life is in a shambles and I want you to make it better. He thought of Martin, who was always saying, Live in the moment, lead with your feelings, be spontaneous. He picked up the phone and dialed.

It rang several times, but just as he was about to hang up, relieved, she answered.

Hello?

Hey, ma.

Oh! I've been thinking about you. I haven't heard from you in a while.

I know. I'm sorry. I've been kinda busy.

On the wall, above the table, hung a painting of Kate, though he wasn't quite sure. The same eyes, but longer, wilder hair, and her skin was a fluorescent green. She was nude.

So what's new?

Well...

It would be so easy to avoid everything entirely, to make up a few vague comments about being busy with work, about the weather—all the stuff he usually talked about with his mother.

What is it? Is everything okay?

Yeah. I guess so.

What is it? Tell your mom.

Well...

He pictured her face: worried, sad, her big brown eyes full of concern for her baby boy.

Sara has left me.

He said it quickly, the way one might yank a bandage off a wound.

Excuse me?

Oh God—was he going to have to say it again?

Sara, he mumbled. She left...

Did she go to LA again?

Yes, he said. Business trip.

Why does she have to go out of town so often? his mother asked. I don't think that's right.

It's her job, ma.

Well, I don't like it.

Me either, but there you are. What can I do?

It's that city you live in, she said. How can you keep your priorities straight in that town, and being as ambitious as she is?

It's *fine*, ma.

Hmmph.

She didn't get it. He felt like a coward, but he couldn't tell her now.

Is it hot there? he asked.

Hot as Hades, she said.

They talked about the weather for a few minutes, then he told her he had to go.

All right then, she said. You take care of yourself now.

I will, ma. Goodbye.

Goodbye. Oh—honey?

Yeah?

Why'd you call in the middle of the day?

What?

You usually call in the evening. When the rates are cheaper.

Oh. I'm going out tonight, and I just wanted to check in. That's all.

Glad you did.

Me too.

Go out tonight and have fun.

I'll try.

A wife shouldn't leave like that.

I guess.

I'll light a candle for you.

Thanks. I need all the help I can get.

Sunlight poured in like boiling oil through the open window, but he did not turn on the beloved air conditioner. He was sitting on the sofa, staring at the portrait of Kate—her pubic hair was bright orange—when he became aware of a squeaking noise coming from outside. He went to the window. Six floors below was a restaurant courtyard with several tables set up for lunch, and beyond that was another apartment building. On its roof was a metal exhaust vent, the kind that spins in the wind, and it was in need of lubrication. Squeak squeak squeak with each revolution. He sat back down and tried to relax—breathe—but he could not get the sound out of his head. Squeak squeak squeak. A thick drop of perspiration rolled down his spine.

He was all alone here.

«« — »»

A few miles up Route 101 there is a billboard advertising the Air Museum—a former BLIMP hangar that is the LARGEST wooden structure in the WORLD! From the main road the hangar doesn't seem so huge but, as you approach, it looms like a mountain. You park in the building's huge shadow, pay two bucks at the door, and enter the vast interior.

A dozen or more vintage airplanes are parked in here but you are more interested in the space itself, the hugeness of it. A handout brags that seven football fields could be arranged side by side, with room left over. The sloped walls and ceilings are all constructed of wooden planks, with one end open—this is where the blimps would enter and exit—and you imagine the space filled with gigantic, silvery dirigibles.

Later, in the parking lot, you find a little boy peering into your car.

What's up, squirt? you ask. Your heart is pounding wildly in your ribcage.

The boy is surprised. He's maybe ten years old, tow-headed, big blue eyes, striped shirt.

Why don't you get the hell away from there, huh?

The kid does not move.

Go on, you say. Get outta here.

You take a step forward, and the boy runs off toward the far side of the parking lot, disappearing behind a row of minivans.

You look into the back window. The carry-on bag, still sealed tight, nothing to gawk at.

You head up 101 to the Three Capes Loop, a scenic drive along the ocean, hoping the sight of water will cheer you up. Soon, along the left side of the road, the trees begin to thin out, then disappear altogether as a ridge rises to hide the shore. You park in a small lot and when you shut off the engine you can hear the sound of waves crashing. You scrabble up a hill of fist-sized rocks to find yourself on the cusp of an expansive stretch of beach. The Pacific is a metallic gray that blends into the sky. Along the back edge of the beach lie hundreds of tortured tree limbs, like the salt-bleached corpses of aliens. You have read that these are the remains of trees washed from the banks of inland rivers that have since made their way to the ocean only to be tossed back by the waves. You walk among these gnarled monuments, touching their smooth skin, imagining their long journeys down flooded rivers into the Pacific. You climb into the outstretched limbs of one large specimen and watch the waves break. A man and a woman stroll down the beach hand in hand, using their free hands to stop their hats from blowing off in the harsh, salty wind. They say nothing, but their bodies move easily together.

Farther up the coast, at Cape Meara, you stop to see the famous Octopus Tree, a Sitka spruce sculpted by cruel weather into a tormented but strangely beautiful and natural piece of art. This tree, according to your all-knowing guidebook, is a source of great inspiration to all who visit, as it has learned to thrive under severe circumstances. You walk around it, admiring how the spruce's limbs thrust out and then upward, like the tentacles of its namesake.

You wait there until the only other tourists, a Spanish-speaking couple, move off down the trail toward the parking lot. From here you can see far enough down the path to know that no one else is on the way. You stand close to the tree, touch its rough bark. Then you quickly unzip your trousers and piss on the trunk.

Ahh.

On the wooded path back to the lot you come across the tow-headed boy again. This time he is with his mother, a distressed-looking woman dressed all in black. The boy is sobbing loudly. For some reason he seems much younger than before, maybe six or even five. He doesn't want to see a stupid tree, he yells. The determined mother pulls him along by one arm but by now he has managed to lower himself to the ground, and the mother does not have the strength to drag him. She lets him go and he collapses in a heap in the dirt.

Okay, the mother says sharply. But I will never take you anywhere again, not *ever*. Understand?

This just makes the boy cry all the harder. Exasperated, the mother leaves him lying there on the trail and heads back to the parking lot.

«« —»»

The first person he told was Miles.

Hello?

Hey Miles. It's me.

Who's this?

Stop kidding around. It's me.

Who?

Miles. Stop.

Ohhh. What's up, stranger? Why haven't you been returning my calls?

I know, I know. I'm sorry. It's just...

What? What's the matter?

I... I...

He couldn't speak. His voice box had slammed shut on him.

What's going on? Where are you?

It's Sara.

Sara? Is she okay?

She's fine. I mean, yeah, she's...

Goddammit, tell me.

She left me, Miles.

A long empty pause, then Miles said, Come over here.

Miles, I—

Come over here. Right now.

On the ride to Brooklyn he could barely breathe. The subway

86

was crowded and hot and full of angry, violent people. A man stepped on a woman's toe as he pushed himself in at Chambers Street and the woman cursed at him and the man told her he would kill her if she didn't shut her fucking mouth. At Grand Army Plaza he had to force himself through a wall of passengers, past glaring eyes and stiff elbows, to reach the door. Stupid fuck, somebody hissed as he squeezed by. Once on the platform, he turned around just as the doors closed and saw on the other side of the glass a short, stocky man dressed in a paint-spattered shirt. Their eyes locked and, as the train began to pull away, they both mouthed Fuck You at the same time.

Miles met him at the door to his apartment with two shot glasses full of whiskey. Drink this before you say anything, he said.

The whiskey coated his throat in a black heat. Miles poured another. All right then. Tell papa everything.

When the story was over he pushed the empty shot glass toward Miles and another was poured.

You know what, Miles said. I never told you this, and maybe I should have, but I never trusted her.

You didn't?

Nope. I can't explain it, exactly, but I just had a feeling from the very start that she was trouble.

Why?

Woman's intuition? I dunno. I mean, it was so obvious that you loved her, you know? It was all over your face, in your eyes, the way you spoke to her, the way you treated her, the way you talked about her when she wasn't around. It was obvious. But with her...

What? You don't think she loved me?

Aw, who cares what I think? I like Sara—don't get me wrong—she's a strong, intelligent woman. It's just... I gotta tell you, I'm not all that surprised by this. Another snort?

Definitely.

He couldn't taste the booze anymore, just the heat in his belly.

I feel like such a moron, he said. Why couldn't I see it coming?

Hey, cut yourself some slack. Who ever sees the bullet when it's coming at you?

It's just so *embarrassing*.

Embarrassing?

To make such a blunder. You know what it's gonna be like? Telling people that it's all over after having stood up in front of everyone and announcing, Hey, I love this woman and we're going to spend the rest of our lives together? I just want to crawl into a hole.

Jesus, it happens all the time. More than *half* the time, they say. Look at it this way—you're joining a great big club.

Yeah. The Loser Club.

That's bullshit. *She's* the loser. One day she'll wake up and realize this is one huge mistake. I guarantee it.

Hmph.

You tell your ma?

I tried, but not yet.

Here. Have another.

They drank all afternoon and into the evening. Every once in a while he would stare off into space and sigh as he remembered he'd soon be headed back to a strange apartment where he would sleep by himself and wake up by himself and...

Look, man, Miles said, you're better off without her. Just think: all those girls out there that you couldn't touch—now you can do whatever you want! You're *free*, man! There's millions of married guys who would give their left *nut* to be in your shoes.

Hell. I'm never gonna be with another woman.

Bite your tongue, mister.

It's true.

Okay, maybe it'll take a while to get back on the ol' horse, but like they say—*celibate* is just one letter away from *celebrate*.

Two letters.

Wha'?

Two letters away.

Two? There's the R—

The R, Plus *celibate* is with an I; *celebrate* is with an E. So—

A-E-I-O-U —- who gives a fuck? *You* know what I'm talkin' about.

I gotta go.

Yeah? You sure?

I'm sure.

Cuz you can crash here if you want.

Nah. I gotta get back. Gotta be by myself.

Hey—let's go to Smutty's and drink some more—

I'll see ya later. Thanks for the hooch.

Okay, man, but ya better call me. Alright?

Yeah. I'll call.

Ya better. Hey.

What?

Did you know the average erect penis is six and one quarter inches long?

I do now. Thanks.

He staggered down the stairs while Miles stood in the doorway watching him go. The news was out now. He shuddered in anticipation of all the humiliation to come—all the understanding looks on peoples' faces, the forced smiles, the awkward conversations. At the bottom of the stairs he heard Miles call out:

Take my word for it! You're better off without her!

CHAPTER EIGHT: THE PROPOSAL

Miles had invited us up to his parents' house in Westchester. It was summer, a warm Saturday, all worries and responsibilities seemed a million miles away. We'd spent the morning splashing around the backyard swimming pool. I wore a one piece blue swimsuit, Caleb wore loose, knee-length trunks with sharks on them. At noon Miles went inside to fix some sandwiches while Caleb and I raced from one end of the pool to the other. I let him beat me, then attacked him from beneath the water. He reached down, lifted me up, tossed me over his shoulder and into the water. I rushed at him and he swept me into his arms and held me there, floating in his arms like a baby. The sky was pale blue, a gentle breeze rustled the leaves in the trees, from somewhere far off came the reassuring sound of a lawnmower.

Hey, he said.

What?

Will you marry me?

I stared up at his wet, gleaming face. He was smiling.

What?

You heard me.

A sparrow landed with a flutter beside the pool and dipped its little beak in a puddle. We'd been dating for five months.

Y-yes. Okay. I'll marry you.

Really?

You heard me.

When Miles came out of the house we were kissing.

Hey, hey—none of that stuff in my parents' pool.

Shut up, Miles. We just got engaged.

Miles stood over us with a large tray piled high with cold cuts and bread.

You just got engaged?

That's right.

In the swimming pool?

Yup.

Well, I guess this calls for a drink.

That night we made love, and because he had drunk a lot he had a hard time coming, but he was determined, and he kept at it, pounding away to create the necessary friction, until I had to stop him, he was hurting me, and he fell gasping on top of me, sweat pouring off him, and promptly fell asleep.

Chapter Nine: Drift Logs

Farther up the coast the road rises and curves along the edge of the dramatic, rocky cliffs that overlook the ocean. You are sitting on a stone wall that runs along the rim of a sheer cliff at a pull-off area for sightseers. Far below you waves crash against the rocks, sending great spumes high into the air. Suddenly the sun emerges from behind the thick bed of cloud and turns the ocean a deep, plummy blue. You watch a gull soar on the air currents from here to an identical lookout about a mile down the road, then fly back again.

Nearby is a young couple eating home-made sandwiches, talking softly, laughing as they toss chunks of bread into the air for the gulls. Be careful! the girl shouts as her husband climbs the stone wall. What if he were to fall? you wonder. What if the girl looked away, or went searching for her camera, and turned back to find him absolutely gone? At first she thinks he's goofing around. Maybe he's hiding on a shelf of rock below the lip. But when she looks down, there is nothing, just a sheer drop to the roiling ocean. Did he fall? From here she can see nothing—no body on the rocks, nor in the waves. He has disappeared. Mister, she calls out to you—Did you see where he went? You have seen nothing. You were looking the other way. Her face is blank. She doesn't yet know how to feel. Terror? Grief? What *should* she feel? Anger? Another car pulls up and she runs over, asks if they have a cell phone. While she explains the situation, her tone now taking on the characteristics of pure panic, you walk to your car, climb inside, and pull away, thinking this is the beginning of an interesting story, or maybe even a film.

The ending comes to you several miles up the coast, at Gannon Beach, a huge expanse of flat, wet sand with rock formations like church spires jutting up from the surf. After grappling with the shock of her husband's disappearance for a year—his body was never found; the authorities surmise it was swept out to sea—the girl returns to the coast and visits a beach much like this one, deserted but for a few tourists and surfers dressed in black rubber wetsuits. She squats and writes with a stick in the wet sand: I LOVE DAVID. She ponders this for a moment, then adds a D to LOVE. Then she weeps, uncontrollably, for a full minute. The film version will show this in real time—long enough to make the audience uncomfortable. From here she revisits the cliff where her husband disappeared, and watches as a paper-white seagull circles above her. It is almost as though the gull wants to tell her something. She remembers one of the last things her husband said to her. Two gulls had been fluttering about, and he commented that they were probably about to mate. He made a joke of it, in honor of the morning they had just spent in a motel up the road. But maybe he was right. Maybe this seagull is the offspring of the original two. Maybe it holds the soul of her husband in its white breast. The gull circles in the air, squawks loudly, then flies off into the blue sky. A happy ending.

You now have the beginning and the end. The middle is always the hardest part.

The sun has long since disappeared behind low clouds that lie impaled atop a spire of rock. Drift logs clutter the beach and shallow surf. For some reason you have brought along your carry-on bag. Perhaps you had thought to toss it into the ocean—you worry it's slowing you down, making you remember things—but now you are not so sure. You walk a mile down the beach, switching the strap from shoulder to shoulder. The bag is growing heavier and heavier.

A sign is posted at the end of the beach: DRIFT LOGS CAN KILL. You can see the attraction of the smooth logs rolling on the water's surface. What dumb adventurous kid wouldn't want to ride them, like Thor Heyerdahl, across the sea to Tahiti?

On the way back you come upon a woman lying on a towel, reading a thick paperback. She wears a black bikini, has muscular limbs, and short brown hair wetted against her skull. As you pass by you try to make out the book's title, but her hand covers it. You want desperately for her to look up from the book, to lift her eyes to you, just for a second, but she's too deep into her reading. You whistle a tune, kick a stone. No response.

And what would you do if she *did* look up?

The question nags as you head back to the car, dragging the carry-on bag along the sand.

«« — »»

A week later, he and Sara went to a wedding. The bride was a former colleague of his at Abacus Press, and neither she nor the groom was aware of the separation.

I didn't want to tell them until after their honeymoon, he explained to Sara on the way uptown. I thought it might bring them bad luck or something.

He was surprised when Sara had agreed to attend the wedding. She hardly knew Patty and John, and she had never much cared for the people at Abacus. He could easily have explained her absence by saying she was away on business, but she had said okay, she would go with him, and while he was pleased at first—maybe she was having second thoughts about the separation—he now wished he was going stag. For one thing, she was wearing an absolutely ghastly outfit, a violet, chiffon-y dress, layered like the petals of a flower—though it reminded him more of one of those sculpted radishes used to garnish a meal—and cut well above the knee. He hated it and he hated her for wearing something she knew—she *must* have known—he would hate.

Then there was the tan. She had just returned from Los Angeles a few days ago and it was obvious she had spent most of her time at the beach. While he'd been holed up in his hot box of an apartment feeling sorry for himself she'd been playing volleyball and flopping around in the surf. It was all too much. When they met today at the uptown subway station he had wanted to run, to leave her there, but he couldn't. There was still a pull, a tidal tug of the heart that he was powerless to resist.

They got off the train at 79th Street and pushed themselves through the soggy air. A bank sign gave the temperature as ninety-nine. In this damn suit and tie he felt like a deep-sea diver making his way across the ocean floor.

On the front steps of the church were a few of the Abacus Press people, smoking and chatting.

Hey, he said with a forced smile. Good to see you. Greetings were exchanged, hands shaken.

Groovy dress, an Abacus office assistant told Sara.

The church was decorated with hundreds of flowers on the altar and at the end of each pew. How beautiful, Sara sighed. It was one of the oldest churches in the city and still had such quaint features as a raised stone pulpit and a small choir balcony. They sat on the bride's side of the aisle, sliding in next to Joe Peterson, the head of Publicity at Abacus, and his wife, Libby.

So she's finally going through with it, Joe whispered to him. I never thought I'd see the day.

Who?

Who?

Oh! Patty. Right.

Who else would I be talking about? Peterson asked.

Sorry. It's the heat.

He picked up a missal and pretended to read. Up in the balcony the organist played "Amazing Grace" while fresh-faced altar boys lit candles on the altar. Though the church had been modified with an air conditioning system, the humidity was so high that everyone was moving very slowly, fanning themselves with missals, blotting their brows.

Fifteen minutes after the ceremony was scheduled to begin, Peterson wondered aloud if perhaps Patty had decided not to go through with it after all.

She always *was* a smart girl, Caleb said, and Sara elbowed him in the ribs.

Then John and his best man entered through a side door and, along with the priest, took their places at the altar. The organist ceased her noodling, and everyone turned toward the back of the church.

There was a vast moment of silence. He held his breath. Why had he come here? Sara took his hand. He squeezed.

The organist launched into "Here Comes the Bride,"

everyone rose to their feet, and there came Patty, arm in arm with her beaming, gray-haired father, both of them taking dramatic, unnatural goose steps up the aisle. There were approving murmurs from the female guests as they took in Patty's traditional gown, long and satiny and blindingly white, and the gauzy veil over her face.

The procession seemed endless. Watching Patty's blurred smile beneath the veil, and John's terrified grin up at the altar, and with the rousing organ music shoving aside the dreadful moisture in the air, he felt only numbness. He dared not glance at Sara. He knew her eyes would be pooling with tears. She always cried at weddings.

The ceremony was a blur of ritual and music, except for the sermon, during which the priest—booming voice, bushy eyebrows, triple chin—requested that all those guests who were already married RENEW YOUR VOWS WITH JOHN AND PATTY—RENEW YOUR LOVE AND COMMITMENT TO A LIFETIME OF RESPECT, FRIENDSHIP AND HONESTY. The words were like heavy stones being placed one by one on his chest. He could not look at Sara, but he felt her presence beside him, like a ghost sucking all the oxygen out of the church.

Don't cry, he told himself. Don't.

When the newly wedded couple finally got around to kissing, Caleb stared down at his knuckles, squeezed to a pale bone white on the back of the next pew. This whole thing was a terrible mistake. He should not have come. He looked up to see Patty turn to the crowd, her veil tossed back to reveal blushing cheeks and a radiant smile. Applause, applause. As the chords to the wedding march filled the church, a thick drop of sweat dribbled down Caleb's vertebrae in perfect time to the bride and groom's movement down the aisle.

Well, they did it, Joe Peterson announced. A beautiful ceremony. Fabulous.

As the guests slowly filed out, row by row, Sara rested a hand on his arm. Are you all right? she asked, and for the first time since entering the church he looked at her face. There were streaks on her cheeks, a smudge of mascara under her eyes.

As well as can be expected, he said.

She squeezed his elbow and it was all he could do not to wrap himself around her.

As the crowd stepped out into the heat of the mid-afternoon, their merriment was replaced by grunts and groans as everyone quickly made their way to air-conditioned cars or taxis.

Share a cab? Peterson asked.

The reception was being held downtown at a fancy restaurant on the East River. He considered bowing out of the whole thing, but could not think of an excuse that would satisfy Peterson.

All right, he said, and Peterson stepped off the curb, whistled, and a cab immediately appeared. Peterson was that kind of fellow.

From West 79th Street to approximately east 57th Street Libby Peterson gushed over Patty's bridal gown, with Sara concurring. When Libby asked, What did you wear at *your* wedding, Sara? (the antique dress clinging to her body as she moved up the aisle, her hair pulled back into a complex bun, a few wispy strands hanging losoe to frame her face) Caleb detected a twinge in his lower bowel. After a mercifully brief description, Sara asked if the Petersons knew where John and Patty were going on their honeymoon.

Somewhere in the Caribbean, Peterson said. I can't remember which island.

One of the saints, Libby said.

St. Barth's? Sara asked.

Maybe, Libby said. Or St. Vincent. Like the hospital, she giggled.

《《《—》》》

Late in the afternoon, you end the day's drive in Astoria, Oregon, a bleak, desolate town at the mouth of the Columbia River. According to the guidebook, Astoria was the first American settlement on the west coast, but over the years it has lost one by one all the industries that kept it thriving—fishing, canneries, dairy farms, timber. Ramshackle turn of the century homes nestle into the steep hills that rise from the riverbank, but the downtown area at the river's edge is decrepit and empty. A ghost town.

The owners of the Jay Motel are Chinese immigrants, and the whole family pitches in, from the teenage daughter who takes your cash at the front desk to the boy helping his father sloppily paint the building's exterior. As you lug your bags to Room 10, father and son smile and bow, spilling gray paint onto the ground.

The door to Room 10 is located directly behind a Coke vending machine that perches crookedly on the edge of the cement walkway. The room is small, with fake wood siding, faded green carpeting, clashing curtains and a lumpy double bed. At the foot of the bed is an old television set—knobs, rabbit ears, no remote—on a wobbly metal stand. You slide the carry-on beneath the bed, then lie down to relax. Breathe. There is an artificial lemon smell in the damp air that competes with something else, a more natural but also more pungent smell. It makes you a little queasy, so you decide to take a walk.

The downtown streets are lined with stores closed for the holiday or else for good. The only places open for business are a small movie theater, an uninviting corner saloon, and a fast food sub shop. You see no other pedestrians except for a young man walking about a block behind you. He appears to be a drifter—disheveled, hunched, lugging a duffel bag on his shoulder. As you explore downtown, the Drifter seems to be following you. You turn left, he turns left, you turn right, he turns right, always remaining one block behind. You duck into the recessed entryway of a closed hardware store and pretend to window shop. Power tools, saws, wide leather belts with loops for hammers and screwdrivers. You wait a while but the Drifter does not pass. You peek out—no one in sight. Relieved, you walk on, but when you turn the corner there he is, one block ahead of you now, on the other side of the street. Though he is walking in the other direction you get the sense that he is watching you.

You climb a few blocks up a hill to get a view of the area. The early evening sun has just emerged, dipping below a cheap toupee of dark clouds and bathing the world in a syrupy glow. Washington state lies across the wide Columbia, connected by the imposing Astoria Bridge.

Ravenous, you stop into the sub shop for a sandwich. The place is empty except for the pimply teenager behind the counter. You order turkey with tomato and lettuce, and sit at a booth.

《《《——》》》

Walking into the restaurant where the reception was taking place was like walking into a meat locker. For about two minutes it was heavenly, with Oohs and Aahs echoing throughout the outrageously air-conditioned entryway, but then the perspiration that had dampened everyone's underclothes turned cold and people began to shiver. The only thing to do, as he saw it, was to drink, and drink heavily.

The reception was held in a large room with a polished wood floor and a wall of solid glass overlooking the river. Tables were carefully spaced around one half of the room, with the other half taken up by a dance floor and bandstand. A twelve piece orchestra was playing "Night and Day" as he and Sara made their way, swiftly, to the bar. He ordered a gin and tonic for himself, a bourbon on the rocks for Sara. The barkeep was generous with the booze. They took their drinks over by the window. The sky over Queens was thick with smog.

Well, he said, lifting his glass—here's to loving, cherishing and honoring until death do us part.

Sara ignored him. She watched the orchestra with what struck him as sad eyes. He hoped she was regretting her decision to attend the wedding; he hoped she was suffering.

That *was* mentioned at our wedding, wasn't it? he asked. The Till death do us part bit? What was the judge's name?

I don't remember.

Well, we could always look it up on the marriage certificate. If you haven't used it to line the litter box, that is.

Please.

Whatever his name was, I'm pretty sure he mentioned that. Till death do us part.

This is difficult enough, don't you think? Without that sort of talk.

Just speaking my mind is all. You always complain that I never share my thoughts and feelings, so—

Yeah, well, put a lid on your thoughts and feelings for now, all right?

The bride's sister was headed their way. He had met her a few

99

times at the office but could not remember her name. She was not as pretty as Patty, but was a little flashier, the life of the party type.

Hello! she gushed, gesturing toward Sara with an empty champagne glass. I just *adore* that dress! Where'd you get it?

The two women talked fashion for a moment, then the sister introduced herself as Penny. Penny and Patty, he thought. And there was a third sister, if he remembered correctly, named Pamela.

I've always wanted to meet you, Penny told Sara. Patty's told me all about you.

Really?

Yes. She says you're her fashion *idol*.

He rolled his eyes. He had no idea Patty felt that way about Sara. The two had met only a few times and there had never been any mention of this supposed idolatry. Maybe Patty was being facetious. Maybe Penny was taking the joke to the next level.

I need another drink, he announced, heading toward the bar.

After the cocktail hour, he and Sara found themselves seated at a table with three other couples, two of them married. There was Paul Guterman, from the Abacus marketing department, and his plump wife, Cynthia; Andrea Dubreau, from publicity, and her husband, Mark; and Stone Simmons, an up and coming editorial assistant, with his supernaturally beautiful girlfriend, Hank— short for Henrietta, as she immediately clarified. All three women remarked positively on Sara's dress.

So, how's freelance working for you? Guterman asked him.

Pretty well, mostly.

You able to make ends meet?

Just barely, but that'll change. I hope.

Helps to have a lawyer for a wife, eh?

Yup.

That reminds me, Andrea said. I'm still waiting on that release.

I know, he said, his face turning red. He had been avoiding Andrea throughout the cocktail hour for this very reason. I'm sorry. You'll get it this week.

It's not like you to be late.

I've had a rough couple weeks. Hectic.

I wish I could go freelance, Guterman said. I just like the sound of it. Free-lance.

Very King Arthur, Stone Simmons said.

Caleb loosened his tie and took a long sip of gin and tonic. The booze was kicking in. He could swear he was sweating quinine.

Throughout the meal—Cornish hen, crisp vegetables, sweet potatoes—he could not take his eyes off Hank. She sat to his right, offering a splendid profile. How would one describe her in a novel, he wondered. She must have been ten years younger than him but her brown eyes hinted at a serious, mature nature. Her short blonde hair was slicked back behind her ears, as if she had just emerged from a pool. Her skin was flawless, and as far as he could tell was completely free of cosmetics. A slight bump on the bridge of her nose lent her otherwise china-delicate features just the right element of strength and mystery.

So what do you do, Hank? he asked, having waited until the others were involved in conversation.

I dance, she replied with the perfect balance of pride and humility. I'm a member of the Hysterectical Dance Company.

No kidding? Is it modern dance? he asked, knowing nothing at all about dance, never mind modern dance.

You could say so, yes. Though we incorporate elements of ballet, tap, even ballroom dancing.

I'd love to see you dance sometime.

I'll make sure Stone lets you know when our next show comes up. But I'm just about to leave on tour. Four months in Asia and Australia.

Australia? he said, wondering how Stone could possible survive four months without this woman. I've always wanted to go there.

I'm very excited, she said.

Her eyes were the color of dirt—thick, fertile soil that things grow in.

Someone began tapping their knife against a champagne glass and soon everyone was joining in. Showing off for Hank, Caleb tapped out a Bo Diddley beat until the bride and groom were done kissing.

Hank clapped and said, They're lovely, don't you think?

Fabulous, he said. He could feel the booze sloshing around the sponge of his brain.

How long have you and Sara been married?

The question, posed in as friendly a manner as possible, and delivered through the world's most seductive and delectable lips, landed like a blow to the chin.

Five years, he told her.

My gosh.

Yes. And I am in desperate need of another cocktail. May I get you anything?

Sara caught his eye as he stood up, held up her empty tumbler. He could tell she was getting good and stinky. Stone said something and she absolutely yukked it up. Heeheehee.

After dinner, while the others danced to big band standards, he stood near the window and watched the river change colors. At the moment it was a dirty blue. Occasionally, however, he turned his attention to Hank on the dance floor. She and Stone Simmons jitterbugged and twirled and dipped like butterflies. When she spun, her knee-length skirt would rise umbrella-like to reveal smooth, powerful thighs that, he imagined, could crush watermelons.

Meanwhile, Sara remained at the table chatting with Guterman and a few others. He was pleased to see she was less jovial now, and he noticed her refusing several dance offers.

All of a sudden, before he could avoid it, he was accosted by a tuxedoed man with a video camera and an ungainly boom microphone.

Any messages for Patty and John? the man asked with artificial cheer.

Caleb stared at the dark eye of the camera, then up at the hovering boom. What on earth could he possibly say? Then he thought, what the hell, let's be honest here.

He raised his glass to the camera and said, I hope your marriage lasts longer than mine!

There was a pause, during which he finished off his drink. Gee thanks, the video man said, then he quickly moved on.

As the band strung out the final notes of an old Gershwin

number, he saw that the lanky, laughing Hank was fast approaching from the dance floor.

How about it? she asked, displaying the straightest, whitest teeth he had ever seen. Wanna dance?

Oh, I don't think that would be such a great idea, he said, feeling his face catch fire.

Well, maybe it's not such a *great* idea, she said, but it might be fun anyway. She was panting a bit from the previous dance. Her small but pert bosom heaved, her nostrils flared.

I dunno, he muttered as the band launched into "Love and Marriage."

Aw, c'mon, Hank said, grabbing his hand. Don't be such a chicken.

I'm kinda drunk, he said as she dragged him.

Fantastic! So am I.

Her hand was moist with sweat, and soft. Like a child being led by his mother, he followed her out to the dance floor.

《《——》》

The bell attached to the sub shop door tinkles. It is the Drifter. He walks to the booth next to yours, sets down his duffel bag, and sits, as if waiting to be served at his table. The pimply kid behind the counter just goes about his business, wiping down the counter, thinking about his girlfriend and how they're going to get high tonight. Meanwhile, the Drifter sits quietly, eyes cast down, a mysterious smile on his face. A wispy beard covers his unshaven chin, driblets of greasy black hair spill from under a wool cap. He glances over at you with eyes that are nearly transparent.

Would you like a sandwich? you ask.

You have no idea how old he is. His leathery face is lined and crusted with dust, but his eyes—they're so clear and youthful.

Another one of these, you tell the kid behind the counter, holding up what remains of your sub. The kid doesn't move at first, his eyes jumping from you to the Drifter and back again. It's okay, you tell him. I'm paying.

When the sandwich is finished you set the tray in front of the Drifter. Thanks, he says, taking the sub into his large, filthy hands.

He does not object when you sit down opposite him.

So, you say, I've seen you around town.

He nods. Seen you too.

Are you from around here, or just passing through?

He nods again, though in response to which option you are not sure. His eyes are nearly glowing.

You wanna hear a story? he asks.

You take a moment, and then, because you are more afraid of what might happen if you say no, you say yes.

The Drifter carefully wipes some mustard from his upper lip with a napkin. Okay then, he says in a voice both quiet and authoritative. One month ago I was living in Key West. I was renting a small apartment, one half of a one-story duplex not far from Old Town. I never had any problems there, no one ever bothered me and I bothered no one else. Then, one night, there's this commotion out on the front lawn. Shouting, cursing, some guy threatening some other guy. I look out the window just in time to see one man pull out a gun and shoot the other man in the face. It wasn't loud—it sounded like a cap pistol—but I knew it was for real when the man who got shot cried out, reached up to his face, and crumpled to the ground. The other guy ran off. When the police arrived they asked me questions but I was not able to help much. I hadn't gotten a good look at the shooter's face in the dark and I didn't know what the argument was about. My neighbor, an elderly widow, had slept through the whole thing, so she was useless to them. The police didn't seem to mind. They took a few pictures of the scene and an ambulance drove the dead man away.

The Drifter picks up his sandwich and takes a small bite. You're not sure if this is the end of his story or not. You notice he eats not like a starving man, in large sloppy bites, but more like a dainty old woman, nibbling, making sure not to spill anything.

The next day, he says, I went about my business—I was selling t-shirts to tourists down at Sunset Pier—and when I came home, about an hour after sunset, I noticed something lying on the front lawn. It was a shoe. A man's black wing tip. It must have belonged to the murdered man, though I hadn't noticed it the night before. I called the police and told them, but they said to toss it out. Obviously, the guy would not be needing it. And that's what I was going to do—throw it away—but first I thought...well, I wondered if I should try it on. I don't know why, exactly, except that the shoe appeared to be about my size, so I did. I tried it on.

Once again he pauses, but this time he does not eat. He stares at you with those strange eyes, a grin on his face. After a moment, he raises his right foot into the air. Sure enough, he's wearing a black wing tip.

Fits perfect, he says.

You glance beneath the table. On his other foot is a black high-top sneaker.

And that was the beginning of everything, he says. He commences eating his sandwich again, and only after a few minutes do you realize his story is over. Then, just as you are about to leave, he says, So—what's *your* story?

My story? you ask. No one has ever put this question to you.

Come on, he says. He glances down at the red scabs on your arms, then looks you square in the eye. Everyone has a story, he says.

You think for a moment. The kid behind the counter is hard at work cleaning the french fryer. The Drifter still stares, smiling. Is he hypnotizing you? You feel as though you are about to fall, and it feels all right. You take a deep breath.

Okay, you say, meeting his brilliant eyes. My story takes place on a small island in the Caribbean, where my wife and I spent our honeymoon. This island is famous for its dangerous airport. Pilots find it extremely difficult to judge the approach. The landing strip lies just on the other side of a natural V formed by two adjoining hills—it's like flying through someone's upraised and slightly parted knees to land on their belly. Only small planes are allowed to land there, and they are constantly plunging into the water at the end of the runway. My wife—and here you pause to think—*Sandra*, was terrified. For one thing, the airplane—which we'd boarded on a larger, nearby island—was tiny, about the size of a van. We could see right over the pilots' shoulders and through the front windshield. Plus, the plane wobbled terribly in the wind throughout the fifteen minute flight, and no matter how many times I pointed out the ridiculously beautiful water just a couple hundred feet below, Sandra remained mortified, her wide eyes glued to the front windshield. And as we began our descent, the plane did seem to be aimed directly at the hillside. We didn't know yet that the air strip was on the other side. Sandra squeezed my hand until it hurt. I let her squeeze, too, because I enjoyed it. At that moment she needed me, which was unusual in our relationship. She squeezed and squeezed as the plane barely skimmed over the pass and landed with a bounce on the tarmac, and she didn't let go until we braked just shy of a brilliant white sand beach. I remember the water was dazzling. This was just twenty-one hours after we'd been pronounced husband and wife.

You pause a moment. The Drifter watches you intently. Go on, he tells you. I'm listening.

Anyway, for our stay we rented a small, apartment-like villa just off the beach among several other identical villas near the airport. The bedroom was enclosed and air conditioned, the living room and kitchen were exposed, with a tiled roof overhead. Every daylight hour, on the hour, we heard the buzz of an airplane as it approached and landed with a screech a hundred yards away, and on the half hour we heard it take off again. It was not annoying. The regularity of it was comforting, actually.

To get to the point, after a few days of lying on beaches and dining out at snooty French restaurants, I found that the honeymoon was not turning out as I had hoped. Sandra seemed distant, detached—particularly, I have to say, when it came to sex. I need to interrupt my story here and say that my wife was beautiful. Not magazine beautiful, but real-life beautiful. There's a difference. Men stared at her, they called out to her on the street. I always enjoyed that, and I think she did also. This attractiveness of hers was heightened for me by the fact of our recent marriage, and I arrived on the island with the typical expectation one has about honeymoons, which is to say it was to be a veritable lovefest, non-stop sex from dawn to dawn, with breaks only for napping, eating and the occasional dip in the ocean to wash off the sweat. But, much to my dismay, in the first three days of our so-called honeymoon we had made love exactly once. *Once*! I tried

106

desperately to stroke Sandra's ego and compliment her, telling her how beautiful and sexy she looked in this or that bathing suit, or how much I loved her, how thankful I was that she'd married me, that she had saved my life. The irony is that I meant every word of it. Her response? I just don't feel like it right now, okay? I kept recalling a joke my old college roommate Mike Lieberman once told me:

Q. How do you cure a nymphomaniac?

A. Marry her.

It was very, very frustrating.

One night, we had dinner at a romantic little restaurant high up in the hills. We had rented a jeep-like car of the kind that everyone on the island seemed to drive, and on our daily visits to the various beaches I drove cautiously on the narrow, winding island roads. I found the roads treacherous, but I was constantly being passed and cursed at by the French. Just ignore them, Sandra said as we headed to the hilltop restaurant, and so I smiled and waved like an idiot until the belligerent French drivers were out of sight, all the time wishing I could run them off the road and into the sea.

Upon our arrival at the restaurant we discovered we were to be the only customers that evening. The place would not even have bothered opening its doors had not the woman at the villa rental office phoned to make a reservation for The American Couple. When we entered, we were greeted by the chef, who, doubling as waiter, sat us at a table overlooking the valley. In the distance, shimmering in a straight line above the trees and hills, we could see a thin blue ribbon of ocean. While we sipped wine and took in this view, we could hear the chef in the kitchen preparing our meal, a special seafood dish for lovers only, as he had described it to us in a delightful French accent. We were joined by a scrawny gray cat that rubbed up against our shins. Its mewing sounded like a baby crying.

Everything about this place was perfect, but I was in a foul mood. Earlier in the afternoon, after several hours of sunbathing at a nude beach, we had taken a nap. When I woke up I had wanted desperately to make love. I gently kissed Sandra's arm, her shoulder, her neck. But when I moved my lips to her face, she simply rolled over onto her stomach. Once again she explained that she did not feel like making love with me. When I pleaded, she said, Do you want me to do something I don't want to do? I was supposed to answer No, but I didn't, I answered Yes, *Yes*, that's part of being married! It went on like that for a while and we ended up in separate rooms, reading the books we'd brought with us. So, at the restaurant, high in the hills overlooking this paradise, and with the wine warming my face, I tingled with resentment. Deep down I realized I should talk it out, air my grievances calmly, rationally, be mature. But I knew she would win out, and I didn't want her to get the satisfaction. No. I held onto my anger, swallowed it along with dinner, and tried desperately not to imagine us doing this pathetic dance for the rest of our lives.

On the way home, we said nothing to each other. I drove faster than usual, almost recklessly, and when we arrived back at the villa, I noticed I had driven to and from the restaurant— perhaps a total of twelve miles—with the emergency brake on.

The Drifter laughs, but in his eyes, you are sure, there is understanding, not derision.

I'm sorry, he says. Go on.

Okay. On our last full day on the island, we hired a boat to go snorkeling. The crew consisted of two swarthy Frenchmen. I can't recall their names, but I'll call them Luc and Alain. We met them, as pre-arranged, at the dock, and immediately I felt inadequate. Luc and Alain smoked Gauloises and wore dirty skipper's caps and their arms and legs were tan and muscular. Sandra knew a little French and the two men delighted in chatting with her as they steered the small, uncovered speed boat out toward the reefs. Once, while Sandra stared down at the frothing emerald water, I saw Luc nodding toward her while he and Alain grinned conspiratorially. She was wearing a sheer white blouse over a two piece bathing suit. Apparently, they both liked what they saw.

As we cruised along with Alain at the wheel, Luc reached into an ice-filled cooler and brought out a gallon jug labeled JET FUEL in black magic marker. A special punch, he announced in heavily accented English, for our special guests. He filled four plastic cups and handed them around. *Salut!* Alain cried, and we downed the stuff. It was sweet but very powerful, and I felt the effect after just two cupfuls.

Soon I grew dizzy and addle-brained from the punch, and my stomach was heaving from the choppy seas. How long till we reach the reefs? I asked. Luc said it would not be long, perhaps ten minutes more. I felt my face turn cold and pale and sweaty. With every lurch and lunge of the boat my guts roiled. Luc spoke a few words in French; when Sandra replied they both laughed. I shut my eyes and tried to think of pleasant things but all I could see was the boat thrashing against the waves.

When we finally reached the reefs we had to endure a brief, painfully obvious demonstration of snorkeling techniques before we were allowed to leap into the sea. The surface here was smooth and relatively calm. With the heavy rubber flippers on my feet, I treaded water for several minutes, eventually relaxing enough to swim a bit.

Meanwhile, Sandra had swum several yards away, accompanied by Alain, and was gazing down beneath the water's surface while floating on her belly. I swam clumsily, nearly losing a flipper, over to where her bright yellow snorkel stuck into the air. She raised her head and exclaimed to Alain, This is *fantastic! Tres fantastique!* before returning her triumphant face to the water. I adjusted my mask and snorkel, plunged my face under the surface, and allowed the water to buoy my body. The water was like glass. About fifteen feet below lay the rough, knobby reef, and the fish were everywhere, entire schools of them, brightly colored in reds, blues, yellows, purples, with stripes and dots, their little faces surprisingly full of character. One fish in particular—I don't know what kind, I know nothing about fish— seemed as interested in me as I was in him. He was a deep, almost blood red, maybe six inches long, with yellow, cat-like eyes, one of which, I swear, winked at me. He appeared to be alone, floating just below me and staring up into my eyes. The more I watched him, the more his face took on almost human characteristics. His mouth opened and shut, opened and shut, as if he were talking to me. Hello, I muttered through the snorkel, and he shot away like a bullet.

After a while my mask began to leak. Treading water, I

readjusted the strap. Sandra was not in sight. I looked over at the boat. Luc was still on board, preparing lunch and talking to Alain, who now sat on the boat's edge smoking a cigarette. A little razor of panic ran across my chest. I swam at an angle to the boat to see if Sandra was on the other side. She wasn't.

Then I saw the yellow snorkel, impossibly far off, maybe a hundred yards or more. Why was she so far away from the boat? I wondered. I started to swim toward her. I went slowly, because the flippers were constantly on the verge of slipping off my feet. Luc had given me size nine and a half, you see, because, he claimed, they had no size nines. Meanwhile, Sandra seemed to be moving farther away. I couldn't understand it. She had never been much of a swimmer. I was worried she might go too far out and get tired, and then panic. With the mask jerked up onto my forehead and the snorkel flopping against my temple I started to swim a little faster. If I scissored my legs in a certain way and kept my feet at the proper angle, I found the flippers would remain secure.

When I was within fifty yards of Sandra, I felt a cramp in my abdomen. A small, sharp stab. I tried to ignore it. There was also the sour taste of jet fuel at the back of my throat. My strokes became sloppier. I had to pause to pull a loose flipper back on. The piercing stab in my gut intensified. And all this time Sandra remained far off, floating on her belly like a corpse.

The first big swallow of water came as a shock. It went down like something solid, took the wrong path, and ended up in my lungs. I coughed and flailed my arms to keep my face above water. It was then that I first heard Sandra calling out to me.

There was another sharp cramp and I went under for several seconds. Water shot up my nose. I cried out but my shout was muffled by the water. I felt a flipper fall away. My bare foot felt light and cool. I thought I heard splashing nearby but I could not tell if it was someone else or me. I looked down and opened my eyes, trying to catch sight of the lost flipper. I was thinking I must not lose it; it would be too embarrassing. I watched it float like a feather down to the ledge of the reef. I'll get it in a moment, I thought. I just need some air.

Alain reached me first, with Sandra right behind. Together they tugged me back to the boat. This was done against my objections. I'm okay! I kept shouting, Stop! I have to get the flipper!—all between violent coughing fits. Don't be stupid, Sandra said. You were practically drowning. She then said a few words in French, and Alain replied, simply, *Oui*.

And that, you tell the Drifter, was the beginning of everything.

The Drifter nods. Did the shoe fit? he asks.

Excuse me? Do you mean the flipper?

The shoe, he says.

What shoe?

You know.

You think a moment, unable to answer. The Drifter crumples the sandwich paper into a ball. Gotta go, he says.

Well, you say, somewhat disappointed, though you don't know why. Good luck to you.

The Drifter swings his duffel bag over his shoulder and walks out the door.

That guy, the kid behind the counter says. He comes in here almost every day.

Really?

For as long as I've worked here. Four months maybe.

But that's impossible, you say. He was in Florida—

The kid wipes the counter with a wet rag, smiling broadly— at you, or the idea of the Drifter in Florida, you're not sure which.

《《《—》》》

When the song was over, he staggered from the dance floor.

That wasn't so bad, Hank said. Was it?

He had danced miserably, stepping on her toes and just barely maintaining his balance, but it hardly mattered. He had been awash in her radiance. At one point he had put a hand on her waist and felt the strength and softness of her through the thin fabric of her skirt. At another point, when the music quieted to allow for a clarinet solo, her face had come to within inches of his own, and he could make out the intoxicating mix of sweat and champagne from her pores.

I need a drink, he said.

You were swell.

Then, after a lightning bolt smile and a gentle touch on his elbow, she walked away toward Stone Simmons and the others.

I'm ready when you are, Sara said, suddenly at his side. To go home, I mean.

He was torn. If he stayed, perhaps he could have another dance with Hank. But what was the use of that? He'd still leave here without her, and return to his stifling apartment alone. Sara hovered close by, waiting. How would he explain it if she left on her own? It was too much to think about. His head began to ache.

Okay, he said. Let's go.

Moments later, in a taxi caroming down FDR Drive, he placed his hand on hers and said, That was pretty awful.

Yup.

Listen. Can I stay over tonight? I just want to be with you. Just to sleep.

He had not planned to say any of this. If anything, he had wanted all day to lash out at her. It was as if the cumulative effect of all that rage was submission. He just wanted to be close to her now, like a child wants to be with the mother who has been away.

I don't think it's such a great idea.

Maybe it's not a *great* idea, he said, But it might be fun anyway.

I'm sorry, she said.

They both got out of the cab one block away from their—now *her*—apartment. They stood at the corner for a long moment, not knowing what to do or say. He resisted taking her into his arms, but just barely.

I guess I'll see you Wednesday, he said.

She looked confused.

At Dr. Leakey's, he added.

Oh. Right.

Don't forget.

I won't.

Then, without a kiss, without a hug or a handshake, she turned and walked away.

He walked briskly to his new apartment, and practically ran up the six flights, not caring if the sweat soaked through his clothing. Then he sat in the gathering darkness, panting, warding off tears. Breathe. It was as if all the heat from the bowels of the earth had risen and accumulated within this tiny space. But he did not turn on the air conditioner. Not even to drown out the incessant squeal from the spinning air vent across the way, or the sound of drunken laughter from the restaurant courtyard below.

He went to the window and gazed down at the illuminated dining patio. There was a party of twelve at a long table, six couples in their best Saturday night outfits. Someone said something and they all erupted into more laughter.

He went into the bathroom and unrolled a long strip of toilet paper. He balled up the paper and ran it under the tap. Sopping wet, the paper was heavy in his hand. He returned to the window. One of the women was leaning over to kiss her date. Her hand reached down into his lap.

He took aim.

The wet ball of toilet paper landed with a loud THWACK in the middle of the table. The kissing woman jumped back and yelped. Everyone quieted down before peering up at the windows of the apartment buildings that flanked the courtyard. He pulled his head inside to watch from the dark room. There was a quiet discussion among the diners, who then consulted with the waiter. The night was now quiet but for the squeaking air vent. A few moments later, the group settled their bill and left the restaurant.

《《——》》

As you are headed back to the Jay Motel you decide you cannot face lying on that lumpy bed watching television, so you stop by the local cinema. The film, *Bomb Scare*, has already started, but you've only missed the first five minutes or so. The theater is small and old, with pine slat floorboards that give a little as you make your way down the aisle, and Art Deco wall lamps shaped like pineapples. There are five other people in the place.

The movie is about a terrorist who has planted bombs at various New York City landmarks. As far as you can tell, he is planning to set them off, one by one, starting with the Flatiron building and moving on to the Chrysler building, City Hall, the

Plaza Hotel, et al. The city is, of course, in a state of panic. Meanwhile, the terrorist's kind-hearted brother—portrayed by Boyd Hart—who shares with his sibling a talent for chemistry, scrambles all over town looking for clues and defusing those bombs he can find in time. Buried under all this rubble of plot is a love story between the good brother and the bad brother's beautiful girlfriend, who teaches deaf children how to dance.

You nod off, dream of driving endless highways between cliffs of green trees, only to be awakened by an explosion. Apparently, the terrorist wired himself up with dynamite and threw himself from the observation deck of the Empire State Building. *Ka-Boom!* Boyd Hart and the beautiful dance teacher watch from above as the villain's remains are scattered to the four winds. Music swells. The end.

On the way back to the motel you can barely make out the Columbia River rolling silvery gray in the moonlight, carrying with it the occasional log destined for some beach down the coast. You take your time walking. The streets are dark and empty, the sky a cloudless bowl of stars.

Your room seems a little larger now that your head has cleared. The clean night air rolls in through the window, bringing with it the fresh aroma of pine. You think of ILSE, and the woman at the Museum of Advertising, the girl in the black bikini, Hank, and the beautiful dance teacher kissing Boyd Hart. You masturbate, then, overcome with emptiness, you crawl between the sheets. Breathe. The blanket is musty, the pillow thin. You hear a television from next door and the rumble of voices. From outside, the sound of crickets and leaves rustling. Just before you fall asleep you hear laughter and the steady drone of a fly.

CHAPTER TEN: THE MONARCHS

My parents live on the west coast, in the hills of Santa Barbara. Our first trip there together was at Christmas time, three months before our wedding. It was the coldest southern California December in sixty years.

There is no good way to introduce your fiancé to your parents. It's like lighting a firecracker. All you can do is say everyone's name and stand back.

What if they hate me? Caleb asked.

They won't hate you.

What if they think I'm not good enough for you?

They'll probably think you're *too* good for me.

You make more money than I do.

They don't know that.

What if they ask?

Lie.

I couldn't blame him for being anxious. My parents—my father, especially—can be intimidating. Born and raised in Texas, with faces like stone carved by hard winds off the plain, they come at life straight on, no tomfoolery, no pussyfooting, just hard work and taking care of family. My father works in the petroleum industry, clawed his way up from field jobs to management to V.P. over the course of thirty years. My mother teaches second grade. She doesn't need to—Daddy makes plenty of money—she *wants* to. Stern but generous, she's the kind of teacher that inspires both fear and love in her students. They often return to say hello and thank her long after they've moved on to high school and beyond.

When they picked us up at the little Santa Barbara airport, Daddy was wearing his usual outfit of faded jeans, spotless white cotton shirt and dusty cowboy boots. He is a tall, lean man, and he towered over Caleb as they shook hands. Mother is more diminutive but just as sturdy in her denim skirt and yellow blouse. One look in her eyes will tell you she has the world all figured out, or at least her little corner of it.

I held my breath the entire way home from the airport. I was waiting for them to say something stupid. I love my parents, but no matter how much money daddy makes, they are rednecks at heart.

They can't be all that bad, Caleb had said on the plane.

They're worse.

Everybody says that about their parents.

Why are you taking their side? I asked. You haven't even met them yet.

So do y'all plan to sleep in your old room? my mother asked in the car.

Mother, I said, testily, we're adults. Of course we're going to sleep in the same room.

Well, mother said, all I was asking was if you were going to sleep in your old room.

Where else would we sleep?

Sorry for asking.

See? I wanted to say to Caleb. See how ridiculous they are? But he was smiling. He was amused by all this, as if we were visiting some charmingly backwards tribe to examine their odd, archaic ways.

Within an hour of our arrival Daddy asked Caleb to accompany him on a walk around the yard. Looks were immediately exchanged—between Caleb and me, between Mother and Daddy, between me and Mother. This was more than a walk around the yard. This was the Man to Man.

For the next half hour or so Caleb was treated to an in-depth tour of Daddy's various home improvement projects, from the new tiles in the swimming pool to the improved fertilizer that would help grow the world's greatest tomatoes. I did my best to listen in, straining to hear at just about every window in the house.

Sara helped build this wall, Daddy told Caleb over by the stone wall that bordered the back yard. She and her sister and I

116

loaded these stones into my pick-up, then unloaded them and piled them one by one until the wall was completed. It took most of a summer.

Sara told me all about it, Caleb said, and I bit my tongue, regretting how I'd complained to him about building the wall, how I'd cursed my old man for ruining an entire summer with his slave driving ways.

She told you about the wall?

It's quite an accomplishment, was all Caleb said, and I could have kissed him.

They were looking down the hill at Santa Barbara's neat, orderly downtown, and, beyond that, the Pacific Ocean. It is my all-time favorite view. The sky was clear, the sun a perfect yellow ball sliding into the blue water.

Beautiful place you have here, Caleb said. I could see he was shivering. The temperature was in the low fifties, but when Daddy had gone out without a jacket, Caleb had to follow suit.

Worked hard for it, my father said. He examined the soil in the garden with the toe of his cowboy boot. Sara tells me you're in the book business.

Uh oh, I thought. Here comes something.

Yes, sir.

What is it you do, exactly?

I'm in publicity.

Publicity. Is that like PR?

More or less. Then Caleb gave him a brief description of his job, puffing it up a bit to make it sound a little more impressive.

I see, my father said. He kicked a clump of earth across the garden. Tell me—

And then my mother called from the kitchen for me to come help with supper. I had to wait until that night to ask what my father had asked about.

He asked me—and here Caleb did a pretty good imitation of Daddy—Do you think this work is important?

Oh no, I said. Did he really ask you that?

Yep. He was looking down on me from about a mile above and asked, Do you think the world is a better place because of what you do for a living?

Yeah, he asks that because, you know, the world is so much better off with petroleum. What did you say?

I was stymied. I mean, the answer was No, but I couldn't say that, so I had to come up with a lie, and quick. I said, I think the w-world is a better place w-with books in it. And if I can get s-some of those books read, then, y-yes, I think it makes a difference.

Excellent answer!

Then your dad put his big ol' hands in his jeans pockets and said, You know I put everything I had into raising my two girls. Her mother and I both did. There's nothing like having a family. I hope you'll do the same with my Sara.

Oh my God.

I-I-I'll do my best, sir, I told him.

What did Daddy say next? I asked.

He said, All right then. Let's go inside. It's colder than a nun's twat out here.

He never!

Honest to God.

«« — »»

My sister Susan showed up on Christmas Eve.

What the fuck's up with the weather? were her first words upon arriving at the airport.

Charming, I said, giving her a hug. Slightly behind her, as usual, was Henry, her husband.

Then Susan turned to Caleb and said, And I suppose you're the fool who's gonna marry my sister.

That would be me, he said, extending a hand, which she ignored in favor of a bear hug.

It's your funeral, she said. This here is my own patsy—Henry.

Caleb shook Henry's moist little hand.

Welcome to the Wacko family, Henry said.

Back at the house my mom made a fuss over Susan, but it seemed forced, as if to make up for my father's cool reception. Daddy was not enthusiastic about Susan's lifestyle. She was at the time a waitress at a restaurant in Taos, and to make matters worse Henry was a poet. Contrast that with my being in law school and working full time as a paralegal at a big time New York law firm and you'll get the idea.

But at least the whole tribe was together now, and the Christmas tree blinked in the sunken den, and the stereo was tuned to an all-Christmas-carol station, and mom had made her world famous salsa.

Let's open up some wine, I said.

Later that night, in accordance with family tradition, we opened our Christmas gifts. Everyone was cheerful, even Daddy, whose face was a deep pink from the wine.

From his future parents-in-law, Caleb received a very nice black leather wallet and matching belt.

Picked them up down in Meh-hee-co, my father announced. Like a lot of people, he was so much more likable when pickled. He made jokes, occasionally pinched my mother's behind, and his Texas accent thickened until it twanged like a taut guitar string.

My gift from them also originated south of the border—a colorful peasant skirt. Just like the seen-yor-itas wear, Daddy announced.

From Susan and Henry, Caleb received a book of poems by Pablo Neruda.

One of the world's greatest, Henry declared.

Practically murdered by Pinochet, Susan added.

Pinko poet, Daddy said with an impish grin.

Our faces turned red, green, yellow in the blinking lights from the Christmas tree. I felt relaxed for the first time since we'd arrived. Caleb smiled, as if he knew what I was thinking: nothing terrible was going to happen.

I opened his gift last: a silver ankle bracelet with his name engraved on it. I immediately put it on and didn't take it off until we arrived home three days later.

My gift to him was a hat, a pork pie, the same type he had once pointed out to me in the window of a hat shop on Broadway. He was touched that I remembered. He put on the hat, which fit perfectly, leaned over, and kissed me full on the lips.

That night I had to stifle my moans with a pillow so my parents wouldn't hear us fucking in my old room.

On Christmas morning my father cooked up some fluffy Texas-sized pancakes and announced over breakfast that we would all go see the monarchs.

The monarchs? Caleb said.

You'll see, I said, doing my best to smile mysteriously.

We piled into two cars and drove across town to a housing development near the coast.

What's all this about, anyway? Caleb asked.

I told you, you'll *see*.

It's a family tradition, Henry said.

We parked on a residential street that dead-ended at a cluster of trees. The air was crisp and cool, the sky a deep blue. From beyond the trees came the sound of waves crashing. We entered the woods, two at a time, Caleb and I last.

I love this, I said, taking his hand. It's my favorite part of Christmas.

We walked a short way before coming to a bowl-shaped clearing. Look, I said.

He followed my gaze. It took a moment to see. The trees were alive somehow. The trunks, the branches—they undulated and shivered.

What the—?

Then he heard the fluttering, like leaves in a breeze, but more subtle.

Aren't they gorgeous? I asked.

That's when he saw them—the butterflies.

My God, he said.

The trees were covered with them, thousands and thousands of butterflies, their delicate wings twitching and flapping. Some of them were in flight, zigzagging through the air like tiny kites in a storm.

Wow.

They're migrating south, Daddy explained. They stop here every year at this time.

We walked into the middle of the clearing, directly beneath the black and yellow flashing of the monarchs. Caleb put his arm around my waist and squeezed.

Looky here, Daddy called. This one's tagged.

We gathered around a butterfly that had alighted on a log. Attached to its gentle wing was a numbered tag.

That way they can track the migration pattern, Daddy said.

I wonder if that tag makes it harder to fly, Caleb said.

Nah. This little guy gets along all right.

And as if on cue, the little guy lifted into the air and fluttered away.

They must be cold, I said.

That's why so few of them are flying, Henry said. They're conserving their energy.

We stood for a long time underneath the butterflies, Caleb's arm draped around my waist, both of us smiling like idiots.

Do they make you happy? I asked.

Yeah, he said, bending to kiss me. I shut my eyes and heard the far off crash of breaking waves, and the close beating of a million wings.

CHAPTER ELEVEN:
CAPE DISAPPOINTMENT

The name pulls you: Cape Disappointment. The southern tip of the Long Beach Peninsula, the southwest corner of Washington state.

You remain jittery from this morning's exchange with the motel owner during check-out. He informed you in poor English that someone in Room 9 had complained of a bad smell.

Bad smell?

Yes. Bad smell from Room 10.

Really?

You smell too?

I didn't notice.

No bad smell you too?

No.

Yes. Okay. Thanks very much.

You had to force yourself to eat a bowl of oatmeal and a side of bacon at Big Boy. But now you are across the river, in a completely different state. No one can touch you.

The trail to the Cape Disappointment Lighthouse leads from a small parking lot past a small beach cove that resembles a set for a south seas movie. Lush green vegetation overhanging the water, nearly blocking the cove's narrow mouth to the ocean. Something catches your eye. A child's striped shirt hangs from the branch of a gnarled, long-dead tree that has washed up on shore. Someone is running an ice cube up your spine.

Heading on toward the lighthouse you round a bend in the trail and stumble upon a large doe munching fitfully on the well-manicured lawn. Between you, but much closer to the animal, a woman lies on her back on the grass, perfectly still. For a moment you wonder if she is asleep, or dead, but then you see her eyes move. She is simply observing the deer. As you approach, the doe looks up, its narrow jaws chomping, then nonchalantly returns to grazing. You pause several yards short and admire her light brown hide, her reflective chestnut eyes. The woman on the grass turns and smiles at you. Sun-bleached hair, leathery skin, muscular calves between khaki shorts and hiking boots. Her eyes are friendly, but there is the unmistakable message: say nothing. She has been here who knows how long, inching herself closer to the animal, gaining its trust. One word and the doe may bolt. You tiptoe past the scene only to discover that the lighthouse is closed to the public, then backtrack past the woman and deer, neither of whom has budged, neither of whom take any notice of you. When you are around the bend, you find a rock, heavy and perfectly fitted to your palm. You toss it into the brush, creating a racket of breaking branches.

You take Route 101—a thin gray line on the map—up the coast, with occasional stops to take in the view. At one point you drive on the beach, the sand as hard and flat as pavement, mile after mile, the air so thick with mist and salt you can barely make out the ocean.

In Aberdeen you stop for lunch at a fast food pizza restaurant. Grimy windows, tables scarred and peppered with scraps of food. The pudgy young waiter seems put out when you ask him to wipe your table clean. His bright orange polyester uniform is one size too small; it looks as though he's tied a thick tube of pepperoni around his waist. You order a cheese and sausage pizza and watch him waddle off to the kitchen. No doubt the cooks make fun of him behind his back; they've nicknamed him Extra Cheese.

The restaurant is nearly full with the lunch crowd, mostly groups of three or four escaped from their dingy offices, their ties loosened, fat purses swaying from chair backs, debating good-naturedly about whether to order a pitcher of beer.

Relax. Breathe.

《《——》》

He was pacing out on the sidewalk when Sara arrived. She was five minutes late for their 4:00 appointment.

Couldn't you at least get here on time?

Take a pill, she replied nonchalantly. She wore, as if to taunt him, a tight-fitting dress through which he could make out the tips of her nipples.

Sure, he said. No big deal. It's just our marriage we're dealing with here.

Dr. Philip Leakey's office was in an old townhouse on Perry Street. Next to the bright red door was a gold plaque: PHILIP LEAKEY, PH.D., COUPLES COUNSELING. Sara went straight up the stone steps and pressed the buzzer.

The door swung open almost immediately. Remembering the author photo, he was surprised to see such a large man, over six feet tall and at least 250 pounds. But this was definitely Philip Leakey—shaven head, gray beard, intense eyes. He greeted them in the deep, grave voice of an undertaker, then ushered them into his ground floor office.

They sat on a long leather sofa against the wall, with Dr. Leakey facing them in an armchair beside his cluttered desk.

Let me make one thing clear right off the bat, Leakey said. I am not a marriage counselor. That is to say, I am not here to save your marriage. I often find that couples should not, in fact, remain together in an intimate relationship. Whether that's applicable to your case, I don't know yet. But I want you to know that what I will do is help you discuss your feelings toward one another, and, if you like, to help you deal with whatever decision you make. Understood?

Caleb nodded glumly. Already he felt like this was a losing proposition. Meanwhile, Sara sat at her end of the sofa, a half mile away, attentive and perky. Her nipples were even more evident in the chilly air conditioned room.

So—how can I help you two?

Caleb looked over at Sara, she looked back. He began to formulate an opening statement, but she beat him to the punch.

Basically, she said, I've left him, and I want to live on my own.

On the wall, behind Leakey's desk, hung an elegantly framed print of *Christina's World*.

So you've separated?

Yes.

And do you see yourself on your own for a short time? A long time? Forever?

Next to the Wyeth print was Dr. Leakey's diploma. Caleb tried to make out the name of the university, but it was difficult from this angle.

I don't know exactly, Sara said. I just know that, for now, our marriage just isn't working—for me—and I'm not sure it can be saved.

Why's that?

Sara thought about it. She was probably trying to come up with a way to say it that would not wound Caleb too terribly. He stared down at his shoes.

Over the last year or so, I've lost any attraction I once had toward him (oh God—the way she refers to me, as if I'm not in the room). The marriage has become stagnant and safe and, for me, unsatisfying (did she rehearse this?). It's gotten to the point... (spit it out! say it!)...I'm not only not attracted to him, I'm sort of repulsed (!!!). I'm sorry, she said, looking over at Caleb. I know that's hard to hear. And I do love you, but it's just...it's just not working for me.

Dr. Leakey turned to him, watching. Waiting. So—how do you feel about what Sara just said?

(I would like to kill her.)

I guess I'm not surprised. (Is that my voice? Flat. Dead.) I mean, I'm not exactly satisfied either. I know things have been lousy lately. I know we haven't been happy. But this—breaking up—it just seems so drastic. To be honest, it seems like the easy way out.

This is *not* easy, Sara said.

I'm not saying it's *easy*. What I mean is that it's *easier* than staying together and trying to work things out.

Is that what you want to do? Dr. Leakey asked.

Yes.

Look, Sara said, I'm doing this for *me*, all right? I *need* this. For once in my life I'm going to do what I want to do. Not what *you* want—what *I* want.

This was delivered with such an air of finality that it was followed by a lengthy pause. Dr. Leakey folded his hands—they were like slabs of ham—across his ample belly and watched them silently. On the desk was a photograph of a little girl in a sun dress, but there was no picture of her mother. Was he divorced?

How do you imagine your relationship, Leakey finally asked, if you decide to split up for good? Sara?

We've been here, Caleb thought, all of fifteen minutes—the clock hung by the door, ticking like a clock in an Ingmar Bergman film—and here is our couples counselor leaping to the conclusion that we're splitting up for good!

I hope we can be friends, Sara replied. I genuinely like you, she said to Caleb, and respect you, and would love to remain close.

You bitch, he thought. How could you say such a hateful thing?

Dr. Leakey turned his big face toward him. This guy's not on my side at all, Caleb thought. He's already decided this marriage is dead in the water. How did he do that? What did he see?

And you? Leakey asked.

Dunno.

You don't have any idea—any fantasy—of what your relationship would be like if you split up for good?

Can't imagine it.

What pops into your head?

(I'd like to toss her out that window there.)

Maybe we'd be friends, maybe not.

Leakey looked from one to the other of them. He wore a puzzled yet somehow pleased expression. What's unusual here, he began, is the lack of anger between you two. Not that you aren't angry—I imagine you're both furious. It's just that neither of you seems willing to express it directly.

I'm not angry, Sara said.

That's difficult to believe, Dr. Leakey said. You've been driven to the point of leaving your husband—an extraordinarily difficult decision, one that will drastically change your life. And you're not *angry*?

Sara looked down at her very expensive shoes.

Caleb saw his chance. I'd just like to point out here, he said, that this extraordinarily difficult decision was made *unilaterally*, without any prior discussion with me—her *husband*—the other person whom it would so drastically affect.

Leakey smiled. Are *you* angry?

Of course I'm angry. My wife is dumping me.

And have you told her how angry you are?

Well… I think she knows how angry I am.

Yes, I'm sure she's picked up on it, but have you told her outright? Have you said, point blank, I AM ANGRY AT YOU?

No.

Why not?

I guess I'm afraid it'll make things worse. Ruin my chances.

Leakey nodded, as if he knew that would be the answer, then turned to Sara and asked, Why don't you tell *him* that *you're* angry?

But I'm *not* angry.

This was ridiculous. Caleb couldn't take it anymore. Oh come on, he said, feeling a surge of power course through him. Every time you say something nice to me—You're a good person, I like you, I want to be friends with you—it's laced with strychnine. You're *furious*.

Sara's face was blank, and he realized for the first time that she was just as confused as he was, that she was just as terrified and unsure of herself. For the first time, he got the feeling that this mess may not be entirely his own fault.

I get the impression, Dr. Leakey said to Sara, that you're also afraid of the effect your anger might have.

Sara's eyes twitched, then the rest of her face seemed to soften and contort into a tortured expression. I don't want to hurt you, she said.

What *hurts* me, Caleb said, is when you tell me how great everything's going to be, how much better off I'll be without you, all that rosy future crap. *That* hurts.

Her cheeks turned pink, then crimson. She was either about to cry or take a swing at him. Then the tears started rolling, great shiny dollops of water cascading down her cheeks. All she could say, in a hoarse, cracked voice, was, I'm so sorry. I'm so sorry.

《《—》》

When your pizza arrives you eat it too quickly and burn the roof of your mouth. It's so difficult to eat slowly when there's no one to talk to. The sausage tastes like cardboard. You stare out the window at the low-hanging, steel-gray sky. A dead fly lies on the sill, its wings spread in defeat. You signal Extra Cheese for the check.

On Route 101 tall pine trees line the road like undulating skyscrapers, blocking out all but a narrow strip of sky. Occasionally you burst through to an area that has been cleared of timber, entire hillsides as desolate as some napalmed stretch of Vietnam, with stumps stretching off into the distance like the gravestones of long dead soldiers.

Dead dead dead, a thin, whispery voice says from behind you. You turn on the radio to drown it out.

In Port Angeles, a small, quaint town overlooking the Strait of Juan de la Fuca, you stop at the Visitors Bureau, where a pleasant, retired lady volunteer advises you about local motels. You settle on the Cochran, which she assures you is clean and convenient to downtown.

And don't forget! she shouts as you reach the exit. There's fireworks on the waterfront tonight! Ten o'clock sharp!

You'd nearly forgotten—it's the Fourth of July.

The Cochran Motel is indeed a tidy establishment, and you get the cleanest, largest room you've had so far. You wash your face, change your shirt, lie on the bed for a moment to collect yourself. With your eyes shut you can still feel the movement of the car in your body. You leap up, rush for the door.

It's a short walk to the pier, where you find a tavern, the kind of touristy place you would not normally patronize, but you're tired and thirsty and don't feel like searching. It's called Landlubbers or Windjammers or something like that, and is populated with more ferns than people. The young barkeep is griping to a regular about the big crowd they're expecting later tonight.

Lots of tips, though, the regular says.

It ain't worth it.

Hey. Money is money.

Still ain't worth it.

128

You order a beer and drink as fast as you can. Through a large plate glass window you see a paper mill up the strait, its tall smoke stacks like a row of birthday candles. Across the water and lining the horizon is Canada. The clouds seem to be breaking up now, exposing raggedy patches of deep blue.

«««—»»»

Tell me, Dr. Philip Leakey said to Sara, How do you picture Caleb in a year or two, assuming you split up for good?

Oh Christ, Caleb thought. Here Leakey goes again with these scenarios based on the *assumption* that there's no chance of reconciliation.

I see him happy, Sara said. With a girlfriend who's in love with him, who can give him what he really needs.

Caleb looked toward the door. This was like a prostate exam.

I see him thriving, she continued. You see, I think I've held him back, in a way.

How so?

I don't know, exactly. But I think with me out of the picture he'll be freer to do the things he really wants to do. He won't worry about whether it's all right with me.

(I'm right here. I'm right in this room. Stop talking like I'm somewhere else. In the past.)

So it's *you* who holds him back?

Well, maybe indirectly. I mean, he holds *himself* back, of course, but I often get the feeling it's because of me.

I see, Dr. Leakey said, rubbing his beard. He turned to Caleb. And what do *you* make of this?

I'm sure Sara's correct, he said, his eyes focused on his left shoe, third eyelet from the top, where the lace was twisted. I'm sure I'll find a girlfriend lickety-split, someone who's just crazy about me, who wants to have sex with me all day and all night, and I'll go on to achieve all my wildest dreams, curing brain cancer and winning Academy Awards and all those other things that Sara has prevented me from doing all these years.

A smile broke out on Leakey's face. Are you angry about what Sara said?

I'm an open book, doc.

Yet you don't tell her, not directly. Instead it comes out as sarcasm.

What can I tell you? You're on the money.

Why don't you tell her that you're angry?

He looked at Sara and was surprised to find her receptive—chin raised, eyes wide and unblinking, the hint of a friendly smile. It was unnerving.

All right, then. These little fantasies about my happy future—they're just ways to soothe your guilt. But you know what? They make me feel terrible. Just terrible. Because I don't see myself as happy without you. I see myself happy *with* you. Not now, maybe. Not in the last year. But I see us working through all this. Your little snapshots of me are very convenient for you because you don't have to do any real work. You walk away and it's nice and clean. I can't *stand* that. It pisses me off. Why can't you give it another chance? Huh? Till death do us part—remember? You won't even *try*, for Christ's sake. You're a fucking quitter, and—yeah—it pisses me off.

That did it. That got her angry. Her face was beet red.

You think this is easy for me? You think I haven't asked myself a million times whether I'm doing the right thing here? I *hate* having to do this. It hurts like hell, but you have to understand—I have no choice.

Bullshit! You do have a choice. You can try to work it out with me. You owe me that, Sara. You owe *us* that.

No! She started bawling. I can't take another minute of it. I'm too unhappy.

Caleb was at a loss. He knew things were bad, but he didn't know they were *this* bad. Jesus. It was as though their marriage was physically painful for her.

Why didn't you come to me before? he asked her. We could have come here then and worked it out.

Dr. Leakey offered her a tissue. Caleb wanted to slug the guy. Sara wiped at her face. Her eyes puddled up again immediately, reflecting light from the far window.

I was afraid, she said. I was afraid.

«‹‹—››»

Landlubbers is starting to fill up with the pre-fireworks crowd. You pay up and leave, time for some dinner. On a little side street you find a Mexican restaurant recommended by the guidebook, but it's closed. A sign on the door: CONGRATS TO SHARON & JORDAN!!! with a little caricature of a bride and groom wearing sombreros.

Next door is a Chinese restaurant, the Lotus, where you are seated in a large booth of red vinyl. It is so red and so shiny you feel as though you're sitting in a huge, wet mouth. You also feel conspicuously alone and are tempted to dash, but then you see your waitress approaching. A sultry brunette with a welcome air of New York haughtiness. Even in the humiliating uniform— black trousers, white long-sleeved blouse, red suspenders—she carries herself admirably. There is barely enough time to yank off your wedding band and stuff it in your pocket.

When she asks if you want a drink—a beer, you tell her—you swear you can detect some sort of identification she has with you: she feels alone in her life, and you, alone in this big red booth, remind her of that. Maybe she's from somewhere else, maybe she's earning some quick money so she can continue her travels, maybe she lives in a decrepit rooming house where she has to share the bathroom with salesmen and junkies. In any case, there is a look in her eye that belies the business-like attitude. You imagine she is a voracious lover.

«‹‹—››»

So, Dr. Philip Leakey said, How do *you* see yourself in a year's time?

More grim divorce scenarios, Caleb thought. This is like some twisted parlor game.

«‹‹—››»

You picture Room 28 at the Cochran Motel, the waitress emerging naked from the bathroom.

I can see myself alone and miserable, he told Leakey, watching Sara out of the corner of his eye. She was staring down at her shoes again.

Why is that? Leakey asked.

I won't be able to trust anyone, for one thing.

And how do you see Sara? In a year?

«« —»»

You lie on the bed waiting, your cock as hard as a log. She crawls onto the bed and kneels astride you, her face above yours, and grinds herself into you, soft little bird sounds fluttering from her throat.

«« —»»

Oh, Sara won't have any problem finding someone. She's never gone more than a few hours without a boyfriend.

Leakey turned to Sara and asked, How do *you* see yourself in a year?

She thought a moment, then said, Lost.

How so?

Well, despite what he says about my never lacking a boyfriend, I never manage to make it last, do I? I'm beginning to wonder if I'm capable of being happy. I mean, if I can't be happy with someone as good and decent as *him*, then how can I be happy with *anyone*?

Oh *please*, Caleb groaned.

«« —»»

Your beer arrives. The waitress insists on pouring it into a frosted glass. It takes forever. You try to think of something to say, but come up with the usual nothing. She smiles for the first time and scurries away to another table. It was a sad little smile, as if she knew what you were thinking.

Isn't it natural, Caleb asked Dr. Leakey, even *inevitable*, that a marriage goes through this sort of crisis? Where one, or both, parties will see the other as unattractive, where they're miserable and hopeless? Isn't it *normal*? Why aren't we exploring how things might be if we were to stay together instead of talking about what'll happen if we *don't*?

Sara was shaking her head, like a child refusing to eat her cauliflower.

Go on, shake your head, Caleb said, but let me tell you something: *real* marriages go through some serious ups and downs, okay? And grown-up people find a way to keep it going, or at least they try. They find new, more realistic terms of love. That's the hard way, sure, and I don't even know if I'm up for it, but I'd sure like to try.

How many times, Sara said, in how many ways do you want me to say it? *It's over*, okay? Maybe I'm immature, maybe I'm a quitter, I'm a stone cold bitch—whatever. Blame it all on me. But it's over. It's over.

A thin, clear, but impenetrable membrane slammed down like a garage door between them.

Well, Dr. Philip Leakey said, shifting his large bulk in his chair. We've about run out of time. Perhaps we should discuss what you'd like to do next.

Neither of them said anything.

Would you like to come back for another session?

Nothing.

It may help to air some more of your feelings.

Caleb nodded. I would. Come back.

Sara?

She seemed calm, even serene. I guess so, she said. But I can't commit to anything beyond that. It's like he's just trying to talk me back into getting together, and that's not helpful.

Fine, Leakey said. I think it's a good idea, frankly, because all these problems you have with talking about your anger are not going to go away, and will affect your separation as much as it did your marriage. Most importantly, neither of you will find any satisfaction until you deal with this anger in a productive way. And this is the place to do that. We can meet next week, if that's good for you.

Caleb and Sara nodded.

So, Leakey said, wrapping his paws around the chair arms—all that remains to discuss is my fee.

«‹‹—››»

Chicken and broccoli in garlic sauce, the waitress says as she sets the plate in front of you. Can I get you anything else?

The contrast between her blue eyes and jet black hair creates an almost unbearable tension. You look away.

Not right now, thanks.

There is a fine wiggle to her walk as she moves on to another table.

«‹‹—››»

They left Dr. Leakey's office together. It was a shock to step out from the air conditioned townhouse into the heat.

Can I come over? he asked. I'd like to see Dilsey.

She hesitated, then said, It's not such a good idea. I have things I need to do and... Oh, I don't know. After all that, I'm just not up to it. Sorry.

They walked on, and he felt coiled up inside, knowing that, as of a few weeks ago, putting his arm around her would have been perfectly acceptable. And now...

At the corner: Why don't you stop by and see Dilsey tomorrow, while I'm at work? You still have a key, right?

Looking away: Okay. I guess I'll talk to you later.

Rush hour traffic flowed around them. Sara had an expression of—what? pity?—on her face, as if she were looking at a crying child. Then she pulled him to her for a quick but potent hug before walking away.

He stopped at a bookstore on the way home. He couldn't bear the thought of the hot, humid apartment. But he couldn't stay long in the store—after ten minutes in a bookstore he always had to move his bowels. It was an allergic reaction. Something about the paper and spores and dust. Sara always ridiculed him about it, and they would often get in arguments.

On a large table near the entrance was a stack of blank-paged notebooks and scrapbooks on sale. On his way out he impulsively selected and purchased a small notebook in which to collect his thoughts. Maybe that would help with his anxiety.

Sure enough, it was blazing hot back in the apartment, with not even a trace of a breeze from the open windows. He paced the rooms, swearing under his breath, trying his best to ward off the panic. He could barely breathe. The only way around it, he was convinced, was to see Sara. It made no sense—he knew it would probably make things worse, in the long run—but he couldn't budge the idea from his mind.

He grabbed the phone and dialed. The answering machine picked up. Her voice on the outgoing message was like a razor cut. It used to be *his* voice on the machine. She was now officially living without him.

He slammed the telephone down, grabbed the copy of *Rebound* lying on the floor, and ran downstairs. The sidewalks were still jammed with people returning home after work, along with tourists and dog walkers. At the entrance to Washington Square Park, he was accosted by the usual faces. Smoke...Smoke... If one of them gets in the way, he thought, I'll knock the fucker down.

The park was cacophonous. Barking dogs splashing in the fountain, clusters of students and slackers singing along with guitar players, screaming children. He wandered among them, disconnected, a silent satellite escaped from its usual black, empty orbit into a space crowded with caroming asteroids.

He sat on a bench on one of the tree-lined paths, making sure to find a spot not too close to anyone else. On the next bench over sat an elderly couple quietly licking red popsicles. Across the way a young man read a newspaper.

Breathe. Calm down.

After a moment of decompression, he opened the book.

Introduction

The first thing I tell my clients when they come to see me is that I am not a *marriage counselor*. I call myself, instead, a *couples counselor*, because, after more than twenty years experience, I have come to understand that not all marriages are for the best.

He slammed the book shut. His stomach ached. He hadn't eaten any lunch—he'd been too nervous about seeing Dr. Leakey—and he had no appetite now either. The thought of food made his stomach ache even more.

Hello.

A large woman, with fleshy arms and a puffy face, stood before him.

May I sit and talk with you?

Caleb looked around. Was this a joke? Some kind of scam?

May I?

She was young, maybe twenty or so, with the smile of an innocent.

I guess so, he said.

She sat quite close to him and introduced herself as Angela. Are you single like me? she asked.

Her face was remarkably open. He got the feeling she would tell him anything about herself. This made him anxious.

He showed her his wedding band and told her he was married.

Oh! she exclaimed. I thought you might be single because you were alone.

I'm just alone at the moment, he said. He couldn't stop looking at her face. Her eyes were so dilated they looked like black holes.

It's a lovely day! Angela said, gazing up through the trees.

Too hot, he replied, though at the moment there was a slight breeze cooling his face.

I *like* the heat, she said. It comes from the sun, millions of miles away.

Yes.

The light takes eight minutes to get here, she said. Did you know that?

She sat perfectly still, hand in her lap, big black eyes level with his.

I've been living here a whole month, she said, and I don't know where the good restaurants are. Do you know any good restaurants?

Well, what kind of food do you like?

I like everything!

He told her about DeMeo's, and she pulled a pencil from her purse and made him write the name and address on a scrap of paper.

Thanks! she said. I'm going to walk around now. Have a nice day!

She stood up and walked away, a joyous bounce to her step. All of a sudden he was famished.

«««—»»»

The waitress sets the bill on the table, along with a fortune cookie and two slices of orange. You smile, she smiles back—friendly?—and heads off to the kitchen.

You open the cookie. ALAS! THE ONION YOU ARE EATING IS SOMEONE ELSE'S WATERLILY. Whatever that means.

You lay your money on the table, including a twenty-five percent gratuity. Before you leave, you write a note on the back of the fortune and set it on top of the cash. YOU ARE VERY BEAUTIFUL. You move quickly to the door, and just as you see she has reached the table, you exit and hightail it up the street.

There are thousands of people crowded on and around the pier. You push yourself through the throng, patting at your trouser pocket to make sure your wedding ring is still in there. (There was that time in Florida when it slipped off in the water. Luckily the tide was low and you were able to spot it on the sandy ocean floor. But what an awful feeling to discover it missing, like a premonition of disaster.) You sit on a concrete step leading to a grassy area beside the pier. You are surrounded by moms, dads, kids, grandparents, friends, everyone laughing and talking loudly. There is a chill off the water but the sky is clear and salted with stars.

All of a sudden a noise from out on the water—SHWOOP!—and a streak of sparks straight up into the sky. The crowd gasps, holds its collective breath, then cheers as the rocket explodes into red, white and blue streamers.

The fireworks go on for a long time, great fiery flowers erupting one after another until clouds of sulfur-smoke drift off the water like fog. A little girl nearby oohs and ahhs every time a rocket bursts. Somewhere a baby is bawling.

During the show's long, drawn-out climax, you stand and walk toward the street, turning away from the strobe-like flashes. Face after upturned face, no one can see you. The noise is deafening.

Hey, she says, suddenly right in front of you. Remember me?

There is the trace of a smile, and her face seems softer, more open. In the light from the fireworks it turns red and blue and white.

Of course I remember you.

Enjoying the show?

Huh? It's hard to hear her over the noise.

Enjoying the show? The *fireworks*?

Sure. What's not to enjoy?

I missed most of them.

A particularly spectacular rocket bursts into mile-long golden sparkles. The crowd sighs.

Wow, she says.

You watch together as the fireworks play out. After what seems to be the final explosion you turn to her and say, My name's Caleb. I'm from out of town.

Sheryl, she says, shaking your hand. I'm from right here.

Listen, can I buy you a drink or something? I'm traveling alone and could sure use the company.

She looks deep into your eyes to gauge your character. You look slightly away.

All right.

Landlubber's is jammed. The barkeep zips from beer tap to ice box to cash register with a stricken look on his face. You squeeze through to the far corner of the bar and order two beers.

She asks the predictable questions—where are you from and

why are you here? New York, you tell her, and because you felt the need to get away.

New York City, eh? That's cool. She tells you she grew up in Port Angeles but is saving money to leave. I want to move to Des Moines.

Des Moines? Why on earth there?

Because I want to be landlocked.

You're kidding.

No! I really do. You see, this place, it's on the very edge—of the sea, of the country—and I always feel like I might just slide right off. Know what I mean?

You nod vigorously. Yes, yes. I do know what you mean.

Two more beers. When she asks what you do for a living you exaggerate only slightly, telling her you work for several publishing houses. You know from previous experience that people generally assume you write books rather than brief, hyperbolic press releases that no one ever reads. She is impressed.

Is that why you carry that notebook around?

This? Yeah. Just to jot down ideas.

A real New York writer, she says. Very cool.

She rests a hand on your forearm and takes a long swig of beer. You are both pressed up against the bar by the throbbing crowd.

Why did you need to get away? she asks.

Hm?

From New York. Why'd you need to get away?

You look across the room, at nothing in particular.

Do you ever feel like you can't breathe? you ask. Like everything around you—the people, the buildings, the sky—is leaning on you, squeezing the breath out of you?

I feel like that *here*, she says.

Good—you understand.

Where are you staying? she asks, looking you boldly in the eye.

Uh...the Cochran Motel.

Is it nice?

Yes. It's fine.

It's nearby?

Uh huh.

Will you show me? She gives your arm a squeeze.

Be glad to.

When you get outside she slips her arm through yours. You feel like a fake, an impostor, in a strange town with this beautiful stranger at your side.

I have to be honest, she says. I was hoping I'd find you at the fireworks.

You don't say anything. Your face is burning up.

I found your note, she says. It was so sweet. It made my day.

I wondered, you say, looking up at the sky. You've never seen so many stars. The neon sign for the Cochran Motel glows bright red down the block.

I've never done this before, she says.

What?

Gone out with a customer. I get asked now and then but I never go. But then no one ever left me a note like that.

Outside Room 28, just as you're about to insert the key, she pulls you close and kisses you. Her lips are soft and moist.

THIS IS THE FIRST WOMAN OTHER THAN YOUR WIFE THAT YOU HAVE KISSED IN MORE THAN SIX YEARS!!

She runs the tip of her tongue across your lips, then pulls back. Let's go inside, she whispers.

You open the door, motion for her to enter. She pauses on the threshold, stiffens.

Oh God, she groans. What's that *smell*?

What smell? you ask, though you can smell it too.

Oh come on! Don't tell me you can't smell that. Jesus. It's like someone *died* in here. She covers her nose and steps outside. I'm sorry, but I can't go in there.

But—

No, really. You should say something to the management. Oh God, she says, turning away. What the hell *is* that?

It's not that bad, Sara, you say, moving into the middle of the room. See? I don't mind it.

She looks at you in a new way, as if her eyes had just adjusted to some change in light. My name's Sheryl, she says.

140

I know that.

You called me Sara.

I did?

Listen, she says, backing away, I should head home.

No!

Yes. I'm sorry, but this… it's just not going to work out.

Let me walk you home then.

No! That's okay. I'll be fine. Honest.

But Sheryl—

It was nice talking to you, Caleb. If that's your real name. Goodbye.

And then she's gone.

You slam the door. Fuck you! you shout, pacing the room. *Fuck you*! You check under the bed. Goddamn thing stinks to high heaven.

You're all charged up now. You pace the room. You turn on the television. Baseball, cartoons, talk shows, old sitcoms. You stumble onto some softcore porn on channel 69. A bruised blonde with two tattooed guys in a hot tub. You try to masturbate, but it's no use.

Maybe you should leave the carry-on in the car next time.

CHAPTER TWELVE: NO PAIN, NO GAIN

You are awakened from a deep dark sleep by a group of rowdies out in the motel parking lot. They laugh and holler like a gaggle of drunks stumbling home from the bar in the middle of the night, but when you part the thick curtain you find it is actually a dazzling, bright morning, and the rowdies are in fact a group of senior citizens organizing themselves for the next leg of the their vacation adventure. There are four couples, all dressed in the latest AARP casual wear—pastel pullover shirts, khaki trousers, cotton skirts, virginal white walking sneakers—and loading up two large American-made sedans with Samsonite luggage and ice coolers.

C'mon, Moe! What's keepin' ya, buddy?

There in a flash! Forgot my tooth brush!

He'd forget his colostomy bag if it wasn't attached to him!

Let's get a move on! I can smell those eggs a-fryin'!

I'm starved!

Where's that bottle of Beam?

How'd *you* sleep, Martha?

Like a corpse! Musta been the hooch!

Frank snored all night long! Like sleeping next to a garbage truck!

Anyone seen that bottle of Beam?

I think we drained it, Moe! C'mon! Let's get goin'!

And so on, for a good half hour, until they finally climb into their luxury cars and drive away. The clock reads 7:03. Wide awake now, you climb from bed. Through the small window above the toilet you see nothing but clear, inky blue sky, and you decide on the spot to drive up to Hurricane Ridge.

After a quick breakfast of donuts and juice you load up the car, this time making sure to put the carry-on in the trunk. Ignoring the muffled objections, you roll down the windows to air out the interior. It is a stunning morning, not a cloud in the sky.

There is just one road up to Hurricane Ridge in the Cascades—uphill for twenty miles on a winding two-laner—and all the way up you do not see another human soul. Even the park entry booths, normally manned by rangers, are deserted at this early hour.

Up up up you drive, the rental car straining at the steeper grades, whole families of deer standing beside the road, barely pausing to watch you pass by. At times the road skirts the edge of the mountain and you catch glimpses of dramatic, bowl-like valleys until, coming round a bend, you are presented with the sight of Mount Olympus and her sister peaks, massive, snow-capped, spookily silent and still, as if resting between cataclysms.

The road ends at a visitors' center, which is closed until nine A.M. and completely deserted. You park in the lot and emerge into cold, crystal clear air that tingles in your lungs. There are patches of snow up here, and it's chilly enough that you need to pull on another shirt. You make a snowball, in July, and toss it at a tree.

A short hiking trail winds through some pines and along the rim of the mountain. Miles away, across the valley, stands Hurricane Ridge, its pure white snowcaps broken up by patches of blue-green pine.

Straight up above, a jet slices through the blue sky, leaving a thin white chalk line in its wake. People are up there, sleeping, eating, reading books, talking to one another. Perhaps one of them is looking down.

Breathe in the clean air. Breathe.

Soon another vehicle pulls into the lot. A man climbs out, eyes you for a moment, nods, then walks to the visitors' center and unlocks the front door. You walk back to your car, admiring the crunch of your shoes on the snow. Before climbing inside you take one last look at the ridge.

It was here millions of years ago, you think, and will remain long after you are gone.

You start the car and drive down the mountain.

«《—》»

The To Your Health Club was located in the two-level basement of a large co-op building down the street from Caleb's apartment. On his first visit as a member, Caleb found the weight machine room nearly empty. He consulted a list of the various machines and the recommended weight levels for someone of his size and experience. The list had been provided by a muscle-bound trainer named Bruce who had sized him up as a novice.

Just go right down the list, Bruce had advised. Three sets of twelve on each machine. And make sure to stretch and drink lots of water.

The day before, on impulse, he had taken a tour of the facility. He was shown the weight room, the dance/aerobic studio, the stair machines and treadmills, the small lap pool. He appreciated the order of the place, and the dank smell of perspiration that hung in the cool, air conditioned atmosphere. And he liked the woman who gave him the tour. Dana? Dina? She had a raspy voice that was dangerously sexy even as she outlined the costs of membership. Annual fee, $800, plus a one-time joining fee of $200.

So what do you say? Dina asked, batting her long eyelashes.

He'd read somewhere that it's always possible to dicker with these health club people, that they often knocked off a few dollars if you pressed them.

Where do I sign? he asked.

There were ten machines on Bruce's list. They had strange, exotic names: Bicep Curl, Deltoid Extension, Shoulder Press. Most of the machines—their tall, shiny metal frames made him think of guillotines—were lined up with their padded seats facing the mirrored walls, so you could watch yourself sweat and strain. In the middle of the room were racks of free weights and exercise bikes, and over in the far corner stood the imposing Gravitus Maximus, a sort of space-age chin-up machine.

Bland, soft rock music oozed from ceiling speakers throughout the club.

There were only two others in the room, a middle aged man with a barrel chest that threatened to burst through his STATEN ISLAND—THE REST OF NY CAN GO TO HELL t-shirt, and a young woman in a black, two piece spandex outfit. The man stood near one of the mirrors, grunting and grimacing as he hoisted a massive dumb bell with his gloved right hand. Meanwhile, the woman was seated at the Leg Curl machine, her eyes glazed as she paused between sets.

With trepidation, he approached the Seated Pectoral. Each machine bore an illustration demonstrating its proper use. The man in the Seated Pectoral illustration was wide-shouldered, with bushy hair and a noticeable bulge in his tight-fitting workout shorts. There were two lever-like handles that, apparently, he was to push away from himself. First he adjusted the seat height and weight level. The trainer had suggested he begin at fifty pounds. The previous user of this machine had lifted two hundred pounds.

He sat facing the mirror. From here he had a perfect reflected view of the woman at the Leg Curl. He watched as she lifted a padded bar with her shins. Her exposed, sweat-filmed belly was as tight as a snare drum. Her bare arms looked sculpted from marble. With each exertion she let out a little grunt. (Sara in her sexy, skin-tight aerobics tights, stretching, stepping, gyrating along to a workout video as you watch from your desk, unable to concentrate with all those women on the television sweating and grunting away and this real-life version within easy reach. No sooner is the tape over than you leap to your feet and grab her from behind.

Ugh. Cut that out. I'm all sweaty and gross.

Sweaty is sexy.

Not for me it isn't. I'm taking a shower, now leave me alone.

Can I scrub your back?

No.

Wash your hair?

No.

But when she is done she might allow you to brush her wet hair as she sits on the bed, Dilsey stretched across her lap, and then with an air of annoyance she might allow you to open her terrycloth robe enough to expose a bright pink nipple, which she might, if you're lucky, permit you to squeeze and fondle until she either will or will not set the cat aside.)

He tried to concentrate on his own contorted face in the

mirror as he pushed the handles forward, lifting, by a clever series of pulleys, the five brick-like weights. The first few heaves were relatively easy—he even wondered if he ought to adjust the level to sixty pounds—but by the fifth lift the weights seemed to become heavier, as if gravity had all of a sudden become more pronounced. By the eleventh repetition his face was a bright pink, his mouth pulled back into a grimace. Remember to breathe, he told himself, puffing. After twelve lifts he lowered the weights with a loud clank and sucked at the dank air. Three sets of twelve, Bruce had told him, on ten different machines.

While he rested, the spandex woman moved to a different, slightly more complicated exercise machine. She knelt on all fours and lifted, by kicking back one leg at a time, a weighted foot pedal. From this angle he could make out the perspiration that glistened on her neck. With each kick she lowered her head, her light brown hair falling over her flushed face, and let out a throaty groan.

Caleb frantically shoved the machine levers forward, being careful to exhale with each thrust. One…two… As if timed to coincide with his own expulsions of air, the woman's rhythmic groans increased in volume as she strained to complete her own set of twelve. Five…six… Her legs were long, shapely, kicking back endlessly. Ten…eleven … At twelve he made sure to set down the weights quietly, then shut his eyes and breathed. The burning sensation in his chest was not unpleasant.

After a moment he repeated the sequence once more. One (breathe in)…two (breathe in)…By ten he was sure he could not continue. His arms might pop out of his shoulders at any second. Four (breathe in)…five (breathe in!)…

He opened his eyes. His face in the mirror was crimson and shiny with sweat. Six …seven… His chest was on fire, his arms throbbed. He considered leaving the building before he injured himself. Eight… Meanwhile, the spandex woman had moved on to the Inner Thigh machine. Nine… Seated at a slight upward angle, as if in a dentist's chair, she spread her legs onto padded panels that she then forced together. Ten…eleven… he was forgetting to breathe.

Twelve.

On the way to the Seattle ferry on Bainbridge Island you encounter a massive traffic jam. A sea of cars crawls, stops, crawls, stops. Every so often a herd of vehicles speeds past in the opposite direction, which can only mean that there is one lane open somewhere up ahead.

No one is moving now. People are turning off their engines. Some get out of their cars and walk up the shoulder of the road to check out the trouble, or just stretch and relax. There is an entire family sitting on the grass, eating sandwiches and drinking sodas. You remain in the car, engine off, window down. From someone else's car you can hear the eerie falsetto of Roy Orbison.

In your rear view mirror you spot a woman walking up the middle of the road. She pauses beside your car, stands on tip toe, hands over eyes, gazing off into the distance.

What the hell? she says.

She is young, early twenties, in a short summer dress, white with red polka dots, dark hair hanging loose to the middle of her back, long smooth legs and bare feet, bright red toenails. You worry she will cut herself. You feel old.

Do you know what's going on? she asks you.

Must be down to one lane up ahead.

What a drag.

Yeah. Where you headed?

Vancouver.

Nice.

Yeah. Well. See ya.

As she turns to go, you realize she not once looked at you.

«‹‹—››»

He set the weight level of the Seated Butterfly at a sad forty pounds. The machine was a sort of upper body version of the Inner Thigh, with weighted forearm panels that were to be forced together in front of the face. Across the room sat the spandex woman resting between sets, her face flushed and glowing from exertion.

He returned to his own reflection in the mirror and yanked the panels together. One (a vein bulging in your forehead, a bluish worm under rice paper)...two (the barrel-chested man sets down the dumb bell and sits at the Bicep Curl, right next to you, and sets the weight at the highest level)...three (an older woman enters, thin except for a slight roundness in the belly, dressed in black dance tights, and steps up to the Gravitus Maximus)...four (the older woman, wearing an obvious wig and large dangling ear rings, sets down her handbag and adjusts the weight level) ...five (the vein in your forehead is pulsing)...six (the spandex woman grunts as she forces her thighs together—eight, nine, ten—the numbers like the names of lovers)...seven (the barrel-chested man commandingly hoists the two hundred-plus pounds, his biceps like mangoes beneath his sweatshirt)...eight (the older woman reaches up and grabs the handles, and with a swift, confident motion, lifts herself in a perfect chin-up)...nine (your chest sizzles like a steak on a grill)...ten (you cannot possibly do this series two more times, your arms are going to snap like breadsticks)...eleven (just one more now, do it for her across the room, for the spandex woman, as she wipes the sweat from her face with a soft white towel)... twelve.

He carefully brought the weights to rest. His head throbbed, and there was a vague stabbing sensation in his rectum, but he had done it. He imagined himself at Jones Beach, his shoulders wide, his pecs like inverted ice cream bowls, and next to him the spandex woman lying face down on a bright yellow towel, her bikini top unlaced. Meanwhile, the older lady at the Gravitus Maximus lifted herself—one, two, three...—without breaking a sweat.

«««—»»»

At the ferry landing cars are being directed up the ramp and into the bowels of the ship, all with commendable efficiency. Amazing, really, how much weight this ferry can carry. You recall a recent news story about a similar vessel capsizing in some frigid channel somewhere, death toll in the hundreds. What must it have been like to feel the massive ship flip like a toy in a bathtub, spilling everything and everyone into the cold, salty water? Breathe. You lock the door and climb the stairs to the passenger deck.

Out on the foredeck the air blows crisp and cold off the sound, but the sky remains a sheer blue. Seattle lies across the water, its downtown skyscrapers clustered like a glass and steel Stonehenge. To the north rises the Space Needle, to the south the Kingdome. You are relieved to be headed toward a veritable city after these past two days of wide open space and forests.

As the ferry pulls away you notice a man standing nearby: about your age, wearing baggy Army-Navy store olive trousers, a grimy long-sleeve sweatshirt and an old faded Orioles baseball cap. At his black-booted feet lies a bulky backpack as well-traveled as its owner. For a split second you make eye contact, which you immediately regret—he has picked up his backpack and is fast approaching.

Hey, he says, setting down the pack. His face is unshaven, his eyes droopy from either a lack of sleep or medication.

Hello, you say.

This is my first time in Seattle, he says. He does not look at you when he speaks, but instead gazes off toward the skyline.

Me too, you say.

You can now make out huge red boat cranes south of downtown Seattle. They look like monstrous insects.

Do you know of a cheap place to stay the night? the man asks. I'm gonna ring up a friend of mine but I'm not sure he's in town.

You get the impression he is speaking in some sort of secret code, that he is a CIA operative who has mistaken you for a contact.

I think the Y is cheap, you tell him, remembering something about it in the guidebook. You were even considering staying there yourself—until now.

The Y, he says.

You nod, thinking, You could sure use a shower, pal.

Thanks, he says, then he drags his backpack across the deck to the railing.

During the remainder of the crossing you keep glancing over at him. He suddenly looks familiar. Not anyone you know personally but someone whose photograph you've seen. You wonder if he's an escaped killer, maybe you've seen him on the news. You look hard as he gazes off toward the shore, but it does not come to you.

«««—»»»

After waking up and finally realizing where he was, Caleb lay in bed another half hour, afraid to set his day in motion. Just moments earlier he had rolled over fully expecting to find Sara lying beside him, sleeping so soundly he could drape a leg over her without disturbing her. For a few seconds he was panicked, and jolted up in bed to see a portrait of Earl and Kate's daughter, with a white rabbit on her lap, staring down at him from the wall.

Oh, right, he thought. *This* place.

He was hungry, but getting to the kitchen to prepare a bowl of cereal seemed a task fraught with danger. Last night he'd seen a cockroach scuttling up the wall above the sink. He hated bugs. Lying in bed he imagined the kitchen swarming with them. He looked up at the portrait. The rabbit's eyes were a strange, candy red. He would take it down, he decided, and the one of Kate also.

Breathe.

His thoughts turned to Martin. At their session yesterday the therapist had been impatient, pushing him to talk more, encouraging him to go further.

What would you like to do to Sara?

I dunno.

Oh, come on. What do you *feel* toward her?

Hurt.

Toward her!

Anger?

Exactly. But you have no thoughts or ideas on how to *act* on this anger? No fantasies?

Well...

Yes?

I want to yell at her.

All right. What would you say?

Uh...I'd say, I'm angry at you, you...

150

Yes?

You *bitch.*

Great! What else?

I can't believe you fucking dumped me, you *bitch.*

Marvelous. Anything else?

I want to hurt you, you *cunt.*

How?

Physically.

Okay. Keeping in mind that this is a fantasy, what exactly do you want to do to her?

I want to strangle her.

Okay. And how would you go about it?

I guess I'd grab her by the throat.

Uh huh.

And I'd squeeze real tight.

Yes.

And she'd fight back a little, maybe scratch me and stuff, my arms, but not too much.

You would overpower her.

Yeah. And then her face turns blue.

Mm hmm.

And she goes limp.

And do you go all the way with this? Do you actually kill her in this fantasy?

I don't know.

How does it feel to talk about it?

It feels pretty darn good, actually.

You realize that fantasies are normal, don't you? That thinking about it and talking about it under these circumstances are acceptable? Of course, *acting* on them is another matter entirely.

Of course.

Do you think you could tell Sara how you feel about her?

What? That I want to strangle her?

Not that. I'm thinking more about your *feelings.* Your *anger.*

That's what Dr. Leakey said. We both have trouble talking about our anger.

That's right.

And so on. Now he lay in bed running it through his mind, and he imagined what would happen if Sara refused to accept his anger, if she refused to take him back into her life, and he saw himself snap and grab her by the throat, her white throat that he used to kiss so tenderly, and he squeezes as hard as he can, compressing her windpipe as if it were a rubber hose until no air can possibly get through, she cannot breathe—How does it feel, you *bitch*? Not to be able to breathe?—and her eyes plead with him to let her go, which he does, finally, and as she gasps for air he holds her tightly, and against all the odds and laws of emotion she holds onto him, she holds him and weeps uncontrollably on his shoulder, I'm sorry, she cries, I am so so sorry..

《《—》》

Now you remember who he is. A writer you recently saw interviewed on television, a cult figure, author of novels about transients and whores, a known depressive with several suicide attempts behind him. He remains at the rail, watching Seattle become less a vague scattering of landmarks than a distinct collection of individual structures and neighborhoods. You consider approaching him, asking if he is who you think he is, but you are hesitant, you haven't read any of his books, and even if you had, what would you say to him? So, when the announcement is made for drivers to return to their vehicles below deck, you head toward the stairs.

Waiting behind the wheel as the ferry slowly glides into the dock it seems as though the car is moving rather than the ship, a discrepancy in perception that makes you a bit seasick. Thinking it might help, you examine a map of downtown Seattle, pinpointing the exact location of a nearby bed and breakfast, the Brentwood, on First Street.

You roll off the ramp onto a street that rises sharply to a plateau and the city's grid. Left onto First Street and into late afternoon traffic, pedestrians clogging the crossways, endless red lights. You keep thinking of the Writer. If only you had recognized him earlier, when he was speaking to you, you might have connected with him somehow.

The Brentwood is around here somewhere, it should be on this block, but all you can see is a movie theater, the Eros, with an obtrusive marquee displaying today's double bill—XXX! *Two in the Bush* and *Cock-o-Mamie*! Pulling up in front you notice an entrance next to the box office, marked with a small plaque: Brentwood Bed & Breakfast UPSTAIRS.

Once inside, having parked the car in a lot across the street, you are given a tour by an attractive blonde named Ada or Addie. She walks with shoulders thrust back, like an athlete, and speaks in an assertive, confident manner. She tells you she is a graduate student at the University of Washington—business administration. This place would be a financial mess if not for her help with the books. Her jeans are cut raggedly above the knees.

There are six rooms, only one of which is available for the next two nights. It has no windows, though it does have a skylight and gets plenty of sun—When the sun is actually shining, Ada adds with a laugh. There is an antique double bed, an easy chair, a bureau, and several tasteful etchings on the off-white walls.

It's a little cheaper, Addie tells you. Which is good, right? Her smile clinches the deal.

After paying in cash and signing the register—Samuel Shepard—you return to your room, shut the door, and lie on the bed. The skylight is like a window to a deep blue ocean. A ceiling fan chops at the air, swish swish. There are voices in the hall, laughter. Will you be able to breathe in this place?

Outside you find a short line has formed at the Eros box office, two couples and a few loners. You are tempted, but then cross the street to a corner saloon named Jugsie's, where several bohemian types are reading newspapers and quietly talking. You sit at the bar with a stack of post cards, but the barkeep—a tough-looking woman with several silver rings adorning her ears—does not seem to notice your arrival. She is busy washing dirty beer mugs, lowering them one by one over a soapy, spinning scrubber then dipping them into a sinkful of hot water. You would call out to her but then it is her job to tend bar, which should include keeping track of new arrivals.

Dear Sherman & Shelley,
Greetings from Seattle. As you may have read in the funny
papers I am on a solo tour of the Pacific NW, trying to
find myself & with luck put some of the pieces back
together.

The barkeep still has not approached, though you could swear
she looked up and right at you, saw you sitting there, beerless,
parched, and nevertheless continued washing dirty mugs. You
remain silent. A line has been drawn in the sawdust.

Highlights thus far: Hurricane Ridge (big mts.), Ruby
Bch. (big ocean), & the many locally brewed beers (big
hangover).

Won't Sherman and Shelley, for whom you still have a lot of
affection, be heartened to know their soon-to-be former son-in-
law still has a sense of humor?

Still searching for MYSELF, however. Perhaps I'll find
something among the rubble of Mt. St. Helens.

There. She looked right at you, and yet she continues washing
glasses. If there is anything you cannot tolerate it's rude, inept
service. You'll give her the time it takes to finish this post card.

I think of you often & miss you in advance. Hope all's
well in SB. With much love,

You sign the card, then take your time filling out the address.
Still no service from the bartendress. With a dramatic sigh and
loud slap of hand on bar, you make for the exit. En route, you
glance back to see her still at her unending task, eyes down,
oblivious to your very existence. Looking around the place—does
anyone notice this? Does anyone care that this barkeep has
completely ignored you?—you notice that everyone here is
female, even that one over there in the suit and tie. Oops. You
swallow hard and push through the door.

You wander for a while among the vendors down at the pier, then make your way to a small park overlooking the sound. There are a few couples and groups lounging on the grass, but there are also several like you, alone, eating or drinking, reading books. South of here stands the truly hideous Kingdome, its roof green with mold, and beyond that, like an apparition, or a huge cheap painting, the snow-capped Mount Rainier.

Turning now to gaze over the sound, where a ferry is just departing for Bainbridge Island, you notice a familiar figure across the park: the Writer sits on a bench beside his backpack, a notebook on his lap, staring off into the distance. After a moment of stillness, he jots down a few words.

You are only a few yards away, on the grass directly behind him. It would be simple to approach him, ask him a question or two. Are you so-and-so? Are you working on a novel? Would you like to get a beer? You stand, walk toward him, pause. He seems so deep in thought, as if searching for just the right word to describe the sound. You could practically reach out and tap his shoulder. Then he gasps, and you nearly jump out of your shoes. He bends over toward his notebook and starts scribbling. And scribbling.

You decide to check on the car. The lot across from the Brentwood is nearly empty now, many of the downtown workers having left for home. You open the trunk, making sure the carry-on is still there. Maybe you should have left it at Hurricane Ridge, buried in a snow drift. The heat and close quarters have intensified the odor somewhat, but you don't think it can be detected with the trunk shut. You slam it closed, and try to ignore the stench as you walk away.

The sun is at half-mast now, sending shadows across the macadam. Downtown is eerily empty, but things pick up as you near Pioneer Square. This must be where people gravitate toward in the evenings—there are bars and clubs and restaurants. The buildings are old and quaint, none more than three stories tall.

You stop in a bookstore for a moment, just to kill time, and sure enough, within moments, you feel the urge to defecate. It happens every time.

Excuse me, you say to the woman at the information desk. Is there a public rest room?

Over there, she replies, pointing her bony finger. She wears a pinched expression beneath a firm helmet of suspiciously blonde hair. It's just past Self-help, she adds.

That's very appropriate, you tell her, and you detect a little twitch at the corner of her prim little mouth. No doubt she uses no other bathroom but her very own.

There is just one rest room and the door, alas, is locked. You remain in the aisle, the sweat breaking out on your forehead as you concentrate on clenching your sphincter muscles.

After a moment you turn the knob again—the universal signal of lavatory urgency. The person inside clears his throat—it sounds like a man—to let you know the room is indeed occupied. This charade goes on interminably. You whistle a tune, he whistles back. You hum, he hums. In the meantime, you peruse the self-help books, attempting, unsuccessfully, to distract yourself from your straining-to-burst colon. Breathe.

One title leaps out at you: *To Stay or Not to Stay: How to Escape an Unhealthy Relationship*, by Philip Leakey, Ph.D. No no no—leave it there. You pull out the book next to it instead, *Heal Thyself: Mind Over Body*, and, flipping through the index, your eye settles on the word Gastrointestinal.

You turn the knob, this time more frantically.

Just a *moment*, the occupant calls out. Now he's angry at you. The guy's in there reading an entire issue of *Time* magazine and he's pissed at *you*! Now he's going to take his sweet time, he's going to be extra thorough with his hygiene, he'll wipe himself a hundred times, then make sure to use lots of soap and water on his hands and dry them completely.

Finally, there is the sweet music of a flushing commode, followed by the jangling of a belt buckle. Then, silence. Where's the water from the tap? Why isn't he washing his hands? Just when you are beginning to think, with mounting fear, that this guy is a two-flusher—you had a friend in college who claimed to have one bowel movement per week; he would be in the john for a full hour, then exclaim upon his return, It was as long as a freakin' *python*!— the door convulses, there is the scratch and slide of a small bolt lock, and the man emerges at long last. He pauses, gives you a stern look, and you nearly mow him down on your way inside, slam the door, slide the bolt, throw down your trousers.

Bliss.

While sitting there, you pull out your pen and write on the wall. FOR A GOOD TIME CALL SARA, complete with telephone number.

Later, feeling that delightfully light-footed, post-evacuation sensation, you stumble upon a saloon promisingly named The Bulbous Nose. Above the glass-paneled door swings a wooden caricature of a man's head, complete with a swollen, potato-like nose. Inside, honky tonk growls from the jukebox as several customers lean wearily against a long bar scarred with carved initials and misshapen hearts. The barkeep, a round fellow with handle-bar mustaches, greets you pleasantly as you pull up a stool, and when you order a pint of stout he nods in a way that displays genuine appreciation of your decision.

While waiting for the frothy stout to settle you take a good look around the dimly lit room. Pressed tin ceiling, dusty bar-length mirror, high-backed booths along the opposite wall, most of them unoccupied, an ancient but still operational puck-bowling machine, the aforementioned juke box—45s, no CDs. Aside from small bags of peanuts—50 cents a pop—there is no solid food sold here. This is a bar, pure and simple.

When the stout has settled, you hoist your glass, toast your grimy reflection, and drink.

«« —»»»

Yoga classes at the To Your Health Club were held two evenings a week in the aerobics/dance studio, a large room with a shiny hard wood floor and mirrors along one entire wall. Caleb arrived ten minutes early, and, following the lead of those already there, took an exercise mat from the closet and staked out a place for himself. He removed his shoes and socks, lay on the mat, and shut his eyes. With his shoulders aching from his so-called workout yesterday he hoped this yoga session would be relaxing.

Breathe.

It had been a long day. He had attempted once again to read Dr. Leakey's book, but he could not get beyond the first several pages ("This book is designed especially for those who have been left rudderless after the unexpected crash of separation and/or divorce… Finding your way again is a long, painful, but very necessary process, and one that very often requires help from experts"). He jotted down a few pertinent ideas but gave up early in Chapter One—or, Stage One: State of Shock, as it was called. The book made his hands feel cold and numb. He slammed it shut wondering if *Sara* felt rudderless too. No—she probably felt free, liberated. At last! She would no longer have to tolerate his conservative sense of fashion, his moodiness, his insatiable need for sex. So he'd put the book aside and fell asleep on the sofa for an hour and a half.

Hello everyone, the instructor announced, having entered the room without fanfare. Is anyone here for the first time?

Timidly raising his hand, Caleb glanced around the room. A sizable crowd had shown up, but he was the only first-timer.

Welcome, the instructor said with a warm smile. My name's Sara—

Oh God. What were the odds? She was tall, with light brown hair tied back in a ponytail. She wore a sleeveless, skin tight exercise outfit that showed off her well-toned shoulders and arms. She yanked off her sneakers and socks as she spoke.

—and if you have any questions, please feel free to ask me after class. Okay?

He nodded blankly. Sara's toenails were painted fire engine red.

They began class by sitting in a cross-legged position and chanting Om—the universal sign of peace, Sara explained. Her pitch was steady and strong.

Next came the sun salutations: mountain pose, forward bend, runner's pose, plank pose, upward dog, downward dog, runner's pose, forward bend, back up to mountain pose. This was repeated several times at an increasingly faster pace, until he felt warm and slightly sweaty.

At one point, during the downward dog, Sara came over and rested her hand on his back.

Okay, you want your back nice and straight, she said softly. It was as if they were the only two people in the room. Breathe, she said. His eyes strayed to her long, narrow feet—and those red toenails. Keep your eyes on your belly button, she told him. Is she a mind reader? That's it, she said, and her hand felt so warm and soft that when she moved away he found he missed it.

Breathe.

Miles had called earlier today while Caleb was forcing himself to eat lunch. He was losing weight—his trousers were slightly big on him—and sometimes he felt weak and dizzy, but he never actually felt hungry, and when he did eat he hardly tasted anything. Salad, rice and beans, peanut butter and jelly—it all had the taste and texture of a communion wafer.

What's up? he'd asked Miles.

That's what I called to ask *you*, Miles said.

I'm eating lunch.

What're you having?

Left-over pizza.

My favorite.

Except I didn't bother to heat it up.

Just stick it in the window.

No shit.

What is it—ninety five in the shade?

At least.

What the hell is that noise?

What noise?

That squeaking noise.

Oh, that. I don't even hear it anymore. It's from across the way. One of those spinning roof vents.

God almighty, that would drive me insane. Doesn't your air conditioner drown it out?

I never use it.

You're a mad man.

Tell me about it.

Look, what've you been doing with yourself, besides the usual masochism?

Going to the gym.

You joined a gym?

I know—it's hard to believe.

Any good looking girls there?

Nothing but.

You remember my old friend Stu?

The newspaper writer?

When he and his wife split up, man, he went *crazy*. Fucked everything in sight. The guy was on *fire*.

Yeah, well. I'm still working on an opening line.

Let's hear it.

My wife just dumped me and I'm going to kill myself if you don't go out with me.

That's very catchy. They'll be crawling all over you when they hear that.

Ha ha.

You and me, we're going to go out one of these nights, okay?

Where to?

Someplace where even *you* can find some action. Soon as I finish this chapter of my piece-of-shit dissertation.

I'll be waiting by the phone.

Hey, did you know that less than one thousand penises in the world are more than twelve inches long?

I do now.

Hey. Some advice.

Yes?

Forget about that bitch.

What bitch?

That's my boy. Smell ya later.

Right. Bye.

Sara ran the class through a difficult series of standing poses that left his legs shaky and tingling. During these poses he tried to concentrate on his breathing, directing his breath to his strained quadriceps, or his calves, or his groin muscles, and to keep his gaze fixed on his own pink face in the mirrored wall. But he kept losing track of his breath, and he kept glancing at the reflections of those around him, comparing his poses to theirs, or at Sara, who darted from person to person with advice and that comforting touch. He couldn't believe how much he wanted her to return to him, to stand behind him with her hand on his back or his neck or his legs, gently prodding him to bend that tiny bit farther. It wasn't sexual, though he found her wildly attractive; it was more of a spiritual thing. During a balancing pose—torso bent forward, one foot on the floor, the other thrust straight back, arms pointing ahead to form a horizontal line with the back leg—she stood in front of him and told him to reach farther with his hands. Touch my palms, she said, holding them just beyond his fingertips. Just another inch, she said, and when he did it, when he touched her palms, she said, simply, Great, and he felt like the king of the world.

While taking a walk this afternoon he had stopped at a magazine store. On display were the usual titles—*Time*, *Newsweek*, *People*—as well as a large assortment of pornography. He picked up a *Rolling Stone* and absently thumbed through it, but his eyes kept straying over to the porn. He was always amazed at the variety. There were magazines devoted to large breasts, small breasts, big asses, foot fetishes, blondes, Asians—you name it. The covers were mostly hidden by the magazine slots, but he could make out the titles—*Swank, Chic, Oui*—and the faces of women in various poses, some of them actually engaged in what appeared to be the act of sex, their eyes squeezed shut and their ruby-lipped mouths opened wide in ecstasy. A man nearby was shamelessly flipping through a copy of *Pink*. With his expert peripheral vision, Caleb could make out shot after shot of exposed female genitalia.

Emboldened by this man's nonchalance, he pulled from its slot a copy of a magazine that struck him, from its relatively tasteful cover, as less gynecologically obsessed: *Lithe*. The cover photo was of a blonde, lithe indeed, and naked as a newborn, her golden skin aglow with some sort of oil.

After a quick glance around the store to make sure no one he knew was there, he rifled through the magazine, catching glimpses of reasonably attractive models posed on beds, chairs, deserted beaches—mostly nude but some sporting panties or an open silk robe.

Before he could change his mind he plopped the magazine down on the counter along with a five dollar bill. Ten eternal minutes later he was back in the apartment, his heart beating rapidly—and not just from running up the six flights—his lower bowel gripped by the fist of catholic shame, his penis already engorged. He sat on the sofa and slowly paged through the magazine. On page thirteen was a woman who vaguely resembled Sara. She was kneeling against a bed, her torso flat across the covers, her smiling face turned toward the camera. As he looked through the rest of the magazine he periodically returned to this page, imagining himself kneeling behind this woman, as he'd done so many times with his wife, touching the smooth skin of her ass.

This scene played over and over in his mind now as he lay on the mat in the Corpse pose. Sara had turned down the overhead lights, the room was deathly still. She had told them to empty their minds of all distractions, but his, as usual, was overflowing. There were the two Saras, plus the Sara on page thirteen. There was the magazine, hidden beneath the futon. There was *Rebound*. There was his mother, and the spandex woman, and Miles. All this, and still he felt like the only person on the planet. Sara quietly told the group to wiggle their toes and fingers, then to stretch their arms and legs, to roll onto their sides (the first time they'd slept together she told you she never slept on her left side; when you sleep on your left side, she explained, the weight of your other organs presses on your heart) and come up into a comfortable seated position for the final chant. This time his voice was stronger, more resonant. Sara then touched her palms together and quickly bowed to each individual in the room, one at a time. When she got to him, he bowed back, and she smiled. Then, without making a sound, he put on his shoes and socks, stood up, and walked home.

«««—»»»

The barkeep—how does he keep those mustaches so perfectly coifed, their tips coiled like the tails of two warring scorpions?—asks if you would enjoy another pint of stout and you answer affirmatively. How could you not?

Sitting at the bar are three young women recently arrived. They entered the place in a whirlwind, and agitated, as far as you could tell from the conversation, by their inability to get into a nearby club. They are now regrouping, armed with a copy of the local alternative weekly and sipping cheap beers bought to appease the barkeep.

They are quite a threesome. One, clearly the leader, is loud and cruel. Her response to all queries from her friends is, Don't be such a dumb bitch, though she somehow manages to make it sound like an endearment. She would be attractive if she laid off the rouge.

Number two is the intellectual of the bunch. Wire-rimmed glasses, loose-fitting jeans and blouse, dry delivery of wisecracks that go sailing high above the others' heads. She too would be attractive if only she knew it.

Number three is the follower, the least bright, the main recipient of the leader's insults. She is also the prettiest. Long, soft brown hair, full lips, and eyes like those of the does you keep running into out here. Your guess is that the other two keep her around to attract men.

You tap your trouser pocket, feel the small, hard lump of your wedding band.

LEADER: Hey, we aren't bugging you, are we, mister?

YOU: Not at all.

(All three stare at you now.)

LEADER: Whatcha writing there?

YOU: I'm writing down everything you say.

LEADER: Well, aren't you sneaky.

YOU: Very.

INTELLECTUAL: Are you from around here?

YOU: I'm from New York.

ALL THREE WOMEN: Wow!

PRETTY: New York! I've always wanted to go there!

(They proceed to ask all the usual questions. Do you feel safe there? Have you ever been mugged? Is it expensive? Have you seen *Phantom of the Opera*?)

INTELLECTUAL: What're you doing way out here?

YOU: Just wandering.

LEADER: (incredulous) Why?

YOU: It's beautiful here. The mountains, the forests, the water. I need that every so often or I go crazy.

LEADER: Well, I'm going crazy being *here*. (the others concur with murmurs) It's so frigging *boring*.

(You ask them questions about themselves. It turns out they are not from Seattle. They live in Tacoma. They drive up here

163

every weekend to escape. The Leader is a hairdresser, the Brainy One is a mail carrier, and the Pretty One—you can hardly believe this—is a mom.)

PRETTY: I have a one year old boy. (smiles) Dylan. I'm raising him on my own.

YOU: Where's his father?

INTELLECTUAL: Good for nothing.

LEADER: Rat bastard.

PRETTY: Yeah. He shows up every once in a while to see Dylan, but what he really wants is money.

(Looking into her eyes you find it easier to believe now. There is a weariness there, from lack of sleep, from worry and responsibility. They all went to high school together, you learn. About a million years ago, the Leader says, though it's actually closer to five. Those high school years, you bet, were the brightest of their lives.)

LEADER: All right, you bitches—let's make a game plan.

(You can tell she is angry that you've upset the balance of power, you've stolen her limelight. You would be happy to return it to her. But the Pretty One, who sits closest to you, continues your conversation while the other two convene.)

PRETTY: Isn't it scary traveling around on your own?

YOU: Sometimes. Not as scary as raising a kid on your own, I bet.

PRETTY: That's a good point. But usually I'm too busy to notice how scared I am.

YOU: Where's your little boy tonight?

PRETTY: With my mom. She's my number one babysitter.

YOU: Are you girls planning to stay out all night?

PRETTY: That depends. We can crash at Lottie's (nods toward Leader) brother's place over near U. Dub., but we're not sure yet. Where're *you* staying?

YOU: A B&B on First Street.

PRETTY: B&B?

YOU: Bed and Breakfast.

PRETTY: Oh.

YOU: It's above a porno theatre.

PRETTY: Really? Dylan's father is into that. I hate it.

LOTTIE: Hate what?

PRETTY: Pornos.

LOTTIE: Oh, yeah. (gives you the hairy eyeball) What? Are you into that?

YOU: No! I was just telling, uh –

PRETTY: Didi.

YOU: I was telling Didi that I'm staying at a bed and breakfast above a porno theatre.

LOTTIE: Uh huh.

DIDI: They're just so… (thinks about it, then decides against discussing it at all) I guess I've sworn off men.

YOU: Because of Dylan's dad?

DIDI: And a million others.

(You imagine her in the arms of some dunderheaded football star, too drunk and tired to ward the brute off, receiving his thrusts with bored patience, prying herself away at dawn. How would she respond to someone gentle?)

LOTTIE: Hey! What happened to your arms there?

YOU: Oh. Uh…brambles.

LOTTIE: Brambles?

YOU: Yeah. I was hiking down in Oregon, near this big waterfall, and there were these brambles –

LOTTIE: Bummer.

DIDI: Looks like it hurt.

YOU: It did. (beat) Didi is a nice name.

DIDI: Thanks. Oh, and this is Lottie (points beer bottle at Leader).

LOTTIE: And this bitchlatoid (wraps an arm around the Brainy One) is Marnie.

YOU: Pleasure to meet you ladies.

LOTTIE: Ladies? Aren't *you* polite?

DIDI: What's *your* name?

YOU: Sam. As in Shepard.

DIDI: Nice to meet you, Sam Shepard.

YOU: No. I mean –

DIDI: What?

YOU: Nothing.

MARNIE: Wasn't he the one who killed his wife?

YOU: No. I mean, that was a *different* Sam —
LOTTIE: Well, you cunts, we're off to the Flame. Drink up!
(They drain their beers and collect their handbags.)
LOTTIE: We'd invite you along, mister, but it's chicks night
out, you know?
YOU: I understand.
LOTTIE: So long, then.
MARNIE: Be good.
(Didi lingers a moment)
DIDI: I really admire you. I hope you find what you're
looking for.
YOU: I admire you too, Didi.
(Hold a moment)
YOU: The Brentwood.
DIDI: Huh?
YOU: On First. Above the Eros theatre. Room six.
DIDI: Oh. (disappointed) Right. Well. See ya.
(Didi exits.)

«««—»»»

Late that night he left the steamy apartment and walked over
to Sara's place, and stood across the street staring up at the
window. It was four o'clock. There were no lights on in the entire
building, the street was quiet, a bone-colored moon hung above
the rooftop. Twice he crossed the street and hovered in the
doorway near the buzzers, tempted to press number two, the one
still marked with both their names, but both times he retreated to
the other side, where he paced in a fit of anxiety. She was up
there, right now, sleeping in their bed, where he used to sleep,
warm and soft and smelling of cotton and sweat. For a while he
was sure he could see Dilsey sitting in the window, her favorite
spot, but after a while he figured it was just a shadow. When a
police cruiser passed by he casually walked away, glancing one
last time over his shoulder, wanting and not wanting to catch a
glimpse of her, but the window remained dark.

Maybe it's because you're a little drunk, but the walk back to the Brentwood seems twice as long as before. The air is crisp and slightly chilly, the sky so clear you can glimpse stars through the haze of city lights. The downtown streets are empty but about half way home you hear footsteps behind you. You turn to see a figure two blocks away—a man, walking, like you, at a brisk pace. There is nothing particularly threatening about him—no strut or drug-addled stagger—but you make sure to keep moving, gauging the distance between by the volume of his footsteps. He is gaining on you. When he is within one block, you cross the street. If he follows suit, you will run like hell. You glance back and see he's carrying a backpack. You cannot make out his face, but you recognize now the lope of the walk. He takes no notice of you as he passes on the other side of the street, and it is not long before he is out of sight.

When you reach the Brentwood there is a line outside the Eros for the late show. You take the stairs two at a time and nod at the night desk clerk, a large, bespectacled young man reading a comic book. Inside your room, you turn on the lamp and sit on the bed. Your feet are throbbing. There are muffled voices from next door. The timbre of the voices is strangely tinny, artificial. You remove your clothes, climb into bed. The sheets smell fresh. After a while there is the sound of moaning. Shit. Not again. Then music, a thumping disco beat that no one in their right mind would listen to. Do they have a boom box in there? The bed starts to vibrate with the bass.

As the groaning grows louder and more hysterical, you imagine an alternate scenario: you and Didi, thrashing about in a hot tub while Lottie and Marnie look on.

You consider masturbating, but you're you so drunk and exhausted that you fall asleep amidst the droning music and howls of pleasure still seeping through the walls.

Chapter Thirteen: Michigan

I slept most of the way on the plane, my head resting on his shoulder, dreaming short, machine-gun flashes of images and events, mostly work or school related, but some untraceable, short vignettes of walking down stairs or tripping on rugs. Meanwhile, Caleb remained wide awake, terrified.

It'll be fine, I told him after we'd landed. It turned out fine with *my* folks.

Your folks are reasonable people, he said.

No one's ever said *that* before.

We rented a car at the airport and headed east on I-94. It was a spectacularly grim winter day, the sky a battleship gray above skeletal trees, sooty clumps of snow on the median. I had to laugh when we passed the giant auto tire beside the interstate. That is just so *midwestern*, I said. This was my first trip to this part of the country. I'd lived far west and far east and skipped everything in between. Back home he'd had to break out a map to show me where we were going. All those big states in the middle, I'd said, half joking, I can't keep them straight.

Almost there, he said as we pulled off the expressway. His knuckles were turning white on the steering wheel as we got closer. I patted his knee, told him it would be all right, but he ignored me.

His mother—I'll call her Claire—lived in a fairly new subdivision in the suburbs. Caleb had never lived there himself—Claire had moved shortly after his father died, leaving behind the house he grew up in. He did not consider the new house home.

Welcome to middle America, he said as we pulled into the subdivision. The houses were nearly identical, with minor variations in color and detail, the lots all the same size, with well-groomed yards that bore the extra burden of distinguishing one home from the next. How do you know which is which? I asked.

He admitted that he had to count the houses from the corner of Lindy Lane—one, two, three, *four*—to know which was his mother's. He pulled into the driveway and turned off the engine. Here we are, he announced. Ready?

More ready than *you*.

The only sound was of a jet flying somewhere above the clouds. The yard was tidy, with stubborn little patches of snow in the corner against the house. The front door was locked. Caleb pressed the doorbell, waited.

Don't you have a key? I asked.

Yeah. I'm just surprised that…

He unlocked the door. Hello? he called, stepping inside. The house still smelled new, a combination of fresh pine wood and wallpaper paste. Hello? Ma?

Maybe she's not home.

But she knew we were coming, he said.

While he searched the house I examined a wall of photographs in the front room. Caleb as a small boy in a milk-white bathtub, his strangely large head poking up from the rim. Caleb with his siblings, the middle child looking lost and sad.

You were right, he said, returning from his search. Her car's gone.

You were so cute, I told him, pointing to a photo of him standing stiffly in a back yard—a little boy with a mischievous glint in his eye, as if he had just buried the family pet up to its neck and no one knew about it yet. You look like a little devil, I said.

Still am, he said, pinching my ass.

Hey. None of that.

His mother showed up an hour later. She'd been to the hairdresser's, she explained as she walked in the side door. A short but ample woman in an attractive wool skirt and long sleeve blouse, her hair done up into snow-white cotton candy. After hugging her son she stopped in the middle of the kitchen, put her hands on her wide hips.

So you're Sara.

Hi, I said, extending a hand. She took it in a firm grip, squeezed.

Sit down, you two. What do you want to eat? They probably fed you nothing on the airplane. Am I right?

Well—

Peanuts, maybe. Right?

Uh—

That's all I got coming all the way back from Florida last month. One measly bag of dry, stale goobers!

For the next few hours, we sat trapped at the kitchen table while Claire prepared snacks and then a full supper.

I don't need any help, she said firmly when I offered to make a salad. I know where everything is, she added. I turned to Caleb, whose face was hard, unreadable. I nudged him, encouraging him to help his mother, but he shook me off.

How are you doing, ma? he asked when his mother took a breather to gulp at her second glass of red wine.

Me?

She seemed genuinely taken aback.

Well, she said, I guess I'm fine. Now—have you two settled on a date?

We discussed wedding plans over supper. She had effortlessly prepared chicken Kiev, utilizing the least number of dishes and trays and utensils as is humanly possible. I smiled, recalling the time Caleb had called his mother a bit brusque, and I thought he'd said *brisk*.

The thing is, she said while cutting her chicken into precise, bite-sized squares, I'll be back in Florida next month.

Oh, Caleb said.

When I saw he was not going to say anything more, I piped up:

There're tons of flights out of Florida to New York in March. I bet it's easier to get to New York from *there* than it is from *here*.

Yes, she replied, still chewing on a morsel. Would you like some more chicken, dear?

We weren't allowed to sleep in the same room at Claire's house. It was never actually said—it was a given. Nevertheless, after she had gone to bed, and we'd cleaned the kitchen to within an inch of its life—My mother, Caleb said, can spot a crumb ten miles away—

and we'd brushed our teeth and unpacked in our separate rooms, Caleb sneaked into the guest room and into my bed.

Your mom's not so bad, I said. I was lying, of course, but I thought it might make him relax. I rubbed my hand across his chest.

She seems perfectly nice, I added, moving my hand down to his belly.

He made no move.

I slid my hand beneath the elastic band of his underwear and said, I kind of like her.

Still he did not touch me or say a word.

What's wrong?

Nothing.

Tell me.

It's nothing, really.

Tell me.

Well. I don't think she likes you.

What?

I shouldn't have brought you here.

How can she not like me? What'd I do?

Nothing. I can just tell.

How?

She's not herself.

How?

I can't explain. I can just tell. Maybe we should leave tomorrow.

No way. I want to know what you're talking about. She seemed perfectly fine to me. We seemed to get along.

She wasn't herself. Trust me.

Well, what should I do?

There's nothing you can do. It's the way she is.

This is so weird. Did she say something to you?

Not really.

What's that mean?

Well, when you were in the bathroom, right after dinner, she said…

I remembered returning from the bathroom to find the two of them stone silent, identically blank expressions on their faces.

What? What did she say?

She said you were a real career woman.

A what?

A real career woman.

What's *that* mean?

I don't know, but it isn't good.

But I *am* a real career woman.

I know. But it sounded so...*bad*.

What is this—1970? *Career woman* is a bad word?

I know.

So, she doesn't like me because I have a career? Because I'm in law school and have a decent job and a future? These are *bad* things?

I know.

Stop saying that.

We lay there for a while, not touching. Through the wall we heard his mother cough. Caleb sighed, climbed from bed, and went back to his own room.

CHAPTER FOURTEEN: GREEN

When you wake up the next morning, light is flooding through the skylight, igniting the white walls and seeping through your shut eyelids. You feel well-rested, if a little hung over and dry-mouthed. You lie there for a moment, taking in the room. You recall last night: Didi, the writer, the couple next door. Where is Didi at this moment, you wonder. And Sheryl. And ILSE. And...

The smell of coffee and toast comes wafting under the door. You climb from bed, throw on some clothes, and make your way to the large community area where breakfast is served. Ada— Addie?—meets you there.

Good morning, she says. Will you be having breakfast?

Please.

We have eggs, cereal, toast, fruit—

Cereal is fine for me. And fruit.

Coffee?

Juice, please.

Coming right up.

You run to the bathroom for a quick piss. When you return to the large country style table you find another customer there, a round little man with a ring of brown hair around his otherwise bald head.

Morning! he says.

He introduces himself as Dennis or David from somewhere in Iowa or Idaho. His grip is vise-like, his speaking voice unnecessarily loud, as if he lives at home with his hard-of-hearing mother and can't shake the habit of yelling.

First time in Seattle?!

Yeah.

Dennis then goes on about his many trips to the area, and how much he adores the Brentwood—this compliment offered while Addie presents you with a large bowl of corn flakes and a plate of sliced melon, apples and strawberries—and the myriad opportunities for bicycling both in the city and in the outlying regions. You nod and make approving noises throughout.

Say! he says with a mischievous glint in his eye, You didn't by any chance notice the NOISE LEAKAGE problem last night, did you?!

Noise leakage? Is this the guy you heard through the walls? It's hard to believe Dennis capable of driving a woman to such a frenzy that she would shout, repeatedly, *Give it to me, baby! Give it to me up the ass!*

Apparently, Dennis says, there was some sort of problem with the sound system at the Eros! You know—the DIRTY MOVIE HOUSE downstairs!

Oh, you say, as if you hadn't noticed there was a DIRTY MOVIE HOUSE downstairs.

Some of the other customers complained! Dennis says. You'll get ten per cent off your bill if you mention it!

Ten per cent, eh?

At first I thought it might be the newlyweds in Room One! David says, But it was the music that tipped me off! That, and the fact that the bride—have you seen her?! No?! Well, she doesn't seem the type! You know—to make all that racket!

You nod and take up a spoonful of corn flakes while Dennis tells you about how the theater manager was here earlier, along with the landlord, to apologize to Marge and Ted, the owners of the Brentwood.

It was a bit awkward, as you can imagine! But they promised the problem would be taken care of! But we'll see—or HEAR, rather—tonight!

David chuckles as Ada re-enters with a plate of eggs for him. Thanks, sweetheart! he hollers. When she's gone he asks you what brings you here to Seattle.

Nothing in particular, you say. Just the urge to travel. And you leave it at that. You are eating quickly now, feeling a bowel movement headed your way.

How can you take living in New York?! Dennis asks. Don't get me wrong—I love to visit! New York's a blast!—but to live there?! No way, Jose!

Well, sure, you say, it can get to you, but—

I don't know, Sam! I think I'd lose my marbles!

Just then Ada returns to refill David's coffee.

Sam here's a little shy! Dennis yells. But he ALSO had a little trouble sleeping through last night's, uh, DISTURBANCE!

You look from his face—part conspiratorial, part fraternal—to Addie's. She is embarrassed.

I'm so sorry, she says.

Oh, no bother—

Marge will take ten per cent off your bill. They promised it won't happen again. Just mention it when you check out.

Thanks, you say.

See?! Dennis says when Ada has left. No problemo! The squeaky wheel and all that! Well! he says after a long slurp of coffee, What're you up to today, Sam?!

Not sure, you say, then immediately regret it. That's all you need—this guy haunting you all day long.

Beautiful day! Dennis says. Me, I think I'll drive up north aways! There's a glassmaking outfit up there makes the most delicate little baubles! Ever seen glass made, Sam?!

Can't say that I have.

Pretty wild! It's sand, you know! Silicon! That's why old windows, like these here, they distort after a while! Gravity! They get thicker toward the bottom! See?!

You have finally reached the bottom of the endless bowl of cereal, and make a great show of wiping your lips with a napkin.

Well, I'm off, you say.

You wouldn't be interested in joining me, would you?! Glassmaking tour?!

Oh, you say, frozen in mid-stand, I don't think so. That sounds horrendously dull, actually. Thanks, anyway. And you walk quickly away without looking back.

From inside the communal bathroom you can hear Dennis and Addie chatting, though you can't make out the words.

When you return to your room, you stretch your arms up,

bend over to touch your toes. Your back is stiff, probably thanks to the soft mattresses you've been sleeping on. Your palms brush the carpet, your nose comes to within a couple inches of your knees. Breathe.

Something smells rotten. You run the fabric of your trousers under your nose. That's not it. Then the smell is gone. Perhaps Ada went past the door with the kitchen trash. You stand up, raise your hands toward the skylight, feel your spine elongate. Breathe.

Out on the street the air is cool and smells of the sea. As you pass the parking lot you see your car remains safe and sound. You do not get too close. Still, the attendant eyes you as you pass by, as if you are a car thief on the prowl.

«««—»»»

He was ten minutes early for their next appointment with Dr. Leakey. It was the hottest day of the summer so far, with temperatures hovering at one hundred and humidity to match. He stood beneath a scraggly tree on the sidewalk, trying to get some relief in its sparse shade. There was hardly anyone else on the streets—everyone was in their air conditioned apartments or offices or movie theaters. Air conditioner units droned in windows up and down the block.

He looked at his watch. Five minutes till, and still no Sara. He hadn't spoken to her in a few days, not since she called to say hello and ask how he was doing. He'd told her he was well, that he was working on a press release. In truth, he'd been thumbing through *Lithe*, his pants unbuckled, one hand thrust down his jockey shorts. The woman on page thirteen looked more like Sara with every passing day.

Sara had sounded a bit depressed on the phone, and when he asked her about it she confessed that she was feeling lonely in the apartment.

I could always come back, he told her, but she ignored the offer, going on to say that Dilsey must miss him too because she'd also been acting sad lately. Of course she's sad, he told Sara. There's no one there to rub her belly all day long.

She talked about her work for a few minutes but he did not

176

listen—he was scrambling for the right thing to say, something that would get her to invite him over, but he never found it and when she said goodbye she added, I love you, which made his mind race even faster.

Four o'clock and still no sign of her. He watched the east end of the street, expecting to see her round the corner in a hurry, her face plastered with that familiar combination of remorse and defiance. Maybe the trains are running slow, he thought, or she may have taken a cab and got stuck in traffic.

Four-oh-five. He was getting angry now. Obviously she did not take this process as seriously as he did, or was it that she did not want to have her actions and motives held up for examination?

At four-ten he began to worry. Perhaps there had been an accident. The subway train had caught fire, the cab had hit a telephone pole. This is not like her, he said to himself, even if she is reluctant to come.

He walked to a public telephone on the corner and called Sara's office. Virginia, Sara's assistant, answered on the second ring.

Hi, Virginia. It's me. Is she there?

Hey. Hold on a sec.

So she *was* still there. He felt his anger return now. What excuse would she come up with?

Hi, she said, a little breathless.

Hi. He waited for her to address the situation, but she said nothing.

Where are you calling from? she asked.

Oh, a phone booth down the street from Dr. Leakey's.

Dr. Leakey? *Oh my God!* I completely forgot! Oh shit. I'm sorry, honey. I can't believe I forgot!

He let her go on for a minute.

What should we do? she asked. Should I come down there? But by the time I get there—

Don't bother. I just called to see if I was right. I'll talk to him and get back to you.

Listen—you have to believe me. I'm really sorry. I've had a crazy day and it just slipped my mind.

Sure. Fine. I'll call you later.

He hung up before she could apologize any more, then walked back to Dr. Leakey's door and pressed the buzzer. Sweat rolled down his spine and pooled at the elastic band of his underwear. He wanted to scream.

The door swung open, releasing a wave of frosty air. Dr. Leakey stood looking down at him as if from a cloud.

I've been waiting.

The skin around his left eye was badly bruised and swollen, with the color and texture of an over-ripe plum.

Sara isn't coming, Caleb said. He felt like a child informing his parents that their other child, Sara, was indeed as bad as he'd claimed all along. I just called her office, he said. She says she forgot about the appointment.

I see. Well... Leakey rubbed his beard.

The cold air felt good. It was like peering into a refrigerator.

Do you want to come inside? We can do some individual work. Or we can reschedule. Up to you.

Caleb wasn't sure what he wanted, other than to strangle Sara. When it became clear he was stymied, Leakey said, Why don't you call me later. We'll make another appointment.

All right. I'll call you later.

Leakey nodded and shut the door. In that moment all the heat of the afternoon wrapped itself around him and squeezed. He knew he would not call Leakey again.

«《—》»

You take a city bus out to the university area. The campus is huge, with one of those massive, open-ended football stadiums and a meticulously planned campus hub complete with a view of Mount Rainier. Hundreds of summer term students walk about with their books and cigarettes and frisbees and their dogs with red bandannas around their necks. The students strike you as terribly young, and the women are beautiful as only twenty-year olds can be—fresh-faced, with excellent posture, their pert bodies barely clothed on such a warm summer day. Somewhere on this campus, you think, one of them is being made love to by her boyfriend.

You sit on the edge of the large round fountain at the campus's most central point. Several ducks have gathered near a woman tossing bread scraps into the water. They quack madly and fight each other for every crumb. One especially large duck, more eager than the others, has climbed up onto the edge to boldly face the woman. She laughs and drops a long sliver of crust at his bright orange feet.

Must be a male, she says.

You're not sure if she's talking to you or to herself. You are the closest person to her, but not so close that a casual conversation would feel natural.

He's so aggressive, the woman adds, and when you look at her she appears to be smiling at you. She has light brown hair that falls straight and thin to her shoulders, and a plain but pleasantly open face.

I keep wondering, you tell her, if that duck's going to leap into your lap.

It wouldn't surprise me, she says. She is squinting—the sun is very bright—which gives an edge to her smile. Her teeth are very white and a tad crooked. She seems a little old to be an undergraduate.

You thrust your left hand into your trouser pocket. Why do you even bother to wear your wedding band anymore?

Are you a student? you ask, scootching a little closer.

Used to be, she replies. She continues to toss bread. She has a large bag with two or three loaves. Graduated last year, she says. I just haven't left yet.

It's hard to leave sometimes.

Yeah.

She seems sad now, her eyes cast down toward the water. The duck on the edge squawks impatiently until she provides him with another hunk of bread.

Are you in grad school or something? she asks.

No. I'm just passing through.

By yourself?

Yep.

As you explain where you're from, you try frantically to remove your wedding band from your finger inside your pocket.

It's difficult to do without the other hand, and the warm weather has swelled your finger so that the ring is tighter than usual.

New York, huh? That's cool. What're you writing in that book there?

As she asks this, she glances quickly at your lap. Has she noticed your one-handed grapple with the ring? You stop the effort for a moment.

Oh, it's just a sort of journal. Things that have happened to me lately.

She turns back to the ducks.

Like what? she asks.

You take this opportunity to resume your attempt to de-ring, using your left thumb to try to shove the band down your finger. It won't budge.

Well, like this morning, on the way out here, I didn't have the correct change for the bus. And the smallest bill I had was a ten. But the driver, he let me ride for free.

What're you doing? the woman asks.

Hm?

Are you playing with yourself or something?

What? You feel your face flame up, the heat spreading to your shoulders and down your spine.

What's going on in that pocket?

Nothing! you cry, but you keep your hand in there anyway, as if you still had some kind of chance with this woman.

I could call the campus police, you know. My boyfriend works there. I could have you arrested.

No! I mean—I haven't done anything! Look! you shout, revealing your hand. I was just playing with my ring. It's a nervous habit is all. I was nervous!

By now you are standing, backing away, wanting to run. She is smiling, at what you're not sure.

I was just playing with my ring! you say again, and just before you take off, the aggressive duck takes a step toward the woman, and she nudges him into the fountain pool, where he splashes about and squawks like the others.

《《——》》

180

He walked the streets of the Village like a zombie, every step a struggle in the heat, each breath a minor victory. Soon his entire body was drenched in sweat, so much so that it almost ceased to be a bother. He wanted a drink, an ice cold beer, and was headed to the Bloody Duck when he passed a small travel agency. He paused to gaze at the posters in the window. Luminous white edifices and purple seas on a faraway Greek island, the rolling green hills and stone fences of Ireland, mountainous ice floes off the coast of Alaska.

Inside the cramped office, two gun-metal desks sat side by side, one of them occupied by a middle aged woman reading *People* magazine, the other empty not only of a travel agent but also of any papers, writing utensils, pamphlets, or anything else for that matter—just an empty desk without even a chair. The air conditioner, an old model fitted above the doorway, wheezed and spewed lukewarm air that smelled of soot.

Can I help you? the woman asked, barely lifting her eyes from the magazine.

He told her he wanted to take a trip, that he would go almost anywhere, just so long as it was soon and wouldn't break the bank.

He sat on the edge of a molded plastic seat while the agent— she did not volunteer her name, nor was there a name plate on her cluttered desk—checked for air fares specials on her dusty computer.

Most of the specials this time of year, she explained, are for flights headed south. Florida, the Caribbean. Warmer climates. I don't think you had that in mind, did you?

He said no, he would prefer someplace cooler, and she continued searching, her thick eyeglasses reflecting the green figures on the computer screen.

Here's something interesting, she said. Round trip to Portland, Oregon. Oh my—this is an excellent deal, she added, quoting the price.

How soon can I leave?

Well, this is an unusual situation in that you can leave as soon as…let me see here…you can leave as soon as this coming Friday.

Friday? He considered for a moment. Friday was his birthday. Why not? he said. I'll do it.

He walked out ten minutes later with a ticket in his pocket, round trip to Portland, Oregon. He hardly noticed the heat as he made his way to the Bloody Duck, where he drank a pint of ale, imagining the lush green forests of the Pacific Northwest.

«««—»»»

At Lake Union, in Seattle, there is a kayak rental office nearly hidden among the boat showrooms and restaurants that line the southwestern shore. You park the car in the lot and sit for a moment, collecting yourself. You are still a little shaken up by the encounter with the woman at the fountain. You pull at your wedding band, twisting and turning it on your finger until it finally comes off. You feel like tossing it in the garbage, but you put it in your pocket instead, where it feels like a small piece of lead.

The staff at the kayak rental office is young and energetic. There is an air of summer camp with the fresh faces and the sound of water lapping against the wooden docks. You are assigned a single-seater, fire engine red, and are outfitted with a sleeveless canvas over-shirt that attaches, by a series of metal snaps, to the opening in the kayak.

A young man wearing a bandanna and scraggly goatee instructs you to climb aboard. You sit on the dock and place your feet in the wobbly kayak's small opening. There ya go, the young man says as you plop your ass into the boat. You immediately experience a lovely sense of floating. You seal yourself in with the metal snaps, and the young man hands you a double-sided paddle.

Okey dokey, he says, then he shoves the kayak away from the dock. Have fun, man.

It takes a few minutes to acquaint yourself with the feeling of floating so low in the water. Every movement you make affects the boat's balance. At first you're sure that the slightest misjudgment will tip you over, but after a bit of jostling you realize it would take serious effort to capsize. You aim the kayak's nose toward the open expanse of water beyond the docks and begin to paddle.

Earlier, when you picked up the car, the attendant—he was in

182

his early twenties with a scraggly beard and a pony tail, the name Eddie embroidered on his beige uniform shirt—had given you the skunk-eye.

Is there a problem? you asked when paying up.

Not a thing, Eddie said, looking at your face as if memorizing it for later.

But you don't want to think about that now. The water is calm, with the occasional chop from a speedboat or jet ski. As you skim across the surface like a snake, a sense of tranquility comes over you. You run a hand through the water. It is refreshingly cold. Home seems like another planet away, with all its horrors and degradations and blood-smeared streets.

The lake is small enough to row across quite easily, but there is a bowl-like effect toward the middle that lends it a certain majesty. To the southwest stand the downtown skyscrapers against a blue sky. To the north is a small park with neatly mowed grass, and, nearby, what appears to be an abandoned factory. Straight east is a marina jammed with small craft, including a bright red tugboat.

Just as you pass the middle of the lake a small pontoon plane appears to the north. It seems to be descending, its insect-like buzz growing steadily louder. In fact, it seems to be headed to the exact spot where you now float. When you realize the pilot has no intention of altering his course, you begin to paddle in the direction of the marina. For some reason, however, no matter how furiously you paddle, you're getting nowhere. Is there some weird current keeping you in the middle of the lake? The plane is now less than a hundred yards off, its wings bobbing in the breeze a mere fifty feet above the water's surface. You paddle harder, but it's no use, you're making no progress. What a ridiculous way to die, you think, just as the airplane passes overhead—perhaps twenty feet high, no more—you can feel the tug of air, like when a truck whizzes by on the freeway—and lands smoothly atop the glittering water. You watch, out of breath, as the plane glides toward a long dock. You feel as though you've been warned.

«««—»»»

Back at the apartment he devoured a slice of greasy pizza. The beer had gone straight to his head, fueling his excitement about the impending trip. The tickets lay on the kitchen table in front of him. LaGuardia - Portland - LaGuardia.

The heat in the apartment was overwhelming. He told himself that, later, when he went to bed, he would turn on the air conditioner. But not yet. For now he would endure.

The kitchen window looked out onto an interior airshaft, and not five feet across was the window to a similar kitchen in another wing of the building. This, he had surmised, was the kitchen of the superintendent and his wife—the Gypsies Kate and Earl had warned him about. Like him, the Gypsies rarely used their air conditioner, and often had their window wide open. Tonight, the wife was fixing dinner. If Caleb stood or sat in a particular, rather impractical, spot, he could see her at the counter—or *some* of her, depending on the angle. This evening he had a view of her from knees to chin. She wore a very American outfit of cut-off jeans and sleeveless t-shirt.

Over the past week he had occasionally seen the super's wife out on the front stoop where she passed the time with her friends, talking in an unidentifiable eastern European language with the occasional English phrase tossed in. She was always quick to smile and nod in a friendly way as he entered or exited the building. She was not beautiful, but her blue-black hair and equally dark eyes seemed exotic to him, and struck him as an unmistakable sign of sexual energy. While the view through the window tonight denied him these particular physical attributes, he was able to feast on the sight of her plump arms and strong thighs, and to imagine her dark-hued limbs wrapped around him.

At the moment, she was preparing a salad, slicing large chunks of lettuce into a bowl, dropping in plum tomatoes, adding a few olives. She worked slowly in the heat, pausing every few moments to wipe perspiration from her face. At one point she reached up beneath her shirt and scratched between her small, firm breasts. He recalled the stretch of smooth skin between Sara's breasts, the scent of sweat and musk that settled there on a day like today.

The phone rang. At first he couldn't tell if it was his or the super's, but when the woman across the way did not move, he

184

knew it must be his. Still, he remained in the kitchen, allowing the answering machine to pick up. Earl had insisted on leaving his own outgoing message—an annoyingly cheerful greeting followed by a wordy explanation of where he and Kate and their daughter could be found—and when it was finally over Caleb heard Sara's voice, like that of a ghost, wafting through the apartment toward the kitchen.

Hey. It's me. Are you there? I'm really, *really* sorry about this afternoon. I honestly forgot—it was a horrendous day at work, and well, it just slipped through my sieve of a mind. I hope you forgive me. Call me about making another appointment. It won't happen again, I promise. Okay? Call me. *Okay?*

The click rang out like a pistol shot. Throughout the message he had debated about whether to pick up or not. He'd felt a sense of panic, a vertiginous sense of losing an important opportunity, yet he had not budged from his seat in the kitchen.

The phone rang again. This time he lunged for it. Maybe Sara had forgotten something. Maybe she wanted to get together.

Hello?

Dude.

Miles. Hey.

Sounds like you were expecting someone else.

No. Not at all. What's up?

You and me. Tonight.

Yeah?

Yes, indeedy. There's a new club in SoHo. Sally told me about it, said it's happening.

Miles, you know I hate clubs—

Uh-uh, my friend. We're gonna go out, we're gonna have a few drinkies, we're gonna dance with some beautiful people.

I don't know.

It's called Green.

Green?

As in money. Or envy.

Or nausea.

Nice. That's a very good attitude you have there. I'll come by at nine-thirty, we'll hang out, maybe stop for a beer somewhere on the way. Okay?

Sure.

And dude?

What?

Turn on the frickin' a/c before I get there, okay?

By the time he returned to the kitchen the super's wife was gone. He heard the sound of a television, voices and canned laughter spilling into the air shaft. His pizza was cold.

«««—»»»

You've been sitting in the car in the parking lot for a half hour. Your arms are still wobbly from paddling so hard, your body compass still registers the motion of water. And you can still feel the yank of air pressure when that pontoon plane skimmed over you.

That was quick, the young kayak attendant had said when you returned. Yeah, well, you told him, I forgot something I have to do.

Your stomach growls, reminding you that you haven't eaten since breakfast.

You drive through hectic rush hour traffic, looking for a place to eat. Over a bridge to Scheck Street, an Italian flag fluttering outside a pleasant-looking restaurant, Bundi's Trattoria.

The place is crowded despite the early hour. An indifferent hostess refuses to look you in the eye when you tell her you have no reservation. She disappears around a corner, and you examine the framed photographs on the wall—sports stars, film stars—*To Sal Bundi, with warm regards, Boyd Hart*—and a few faces you don't recognize.

The hostess returns and wordlessly beckons for you to follow her out onto a covered patio dining area, past picnic-style tables occupied by large, very loud families. You are seated at a table for two next to the kitchen door. Perfect, you tell the hostess, and she wrinkles her nose as she walks away. Before you know it, a waitress appears—young, pretty, with green eyes and red hair—and you order a glass of wine.

The kitchen is noisy, with pots clanging and the chef shouting and dirty plates being hosed down, but you are amused by the activity, the waiters and waitresses coming and going, their faces hard and determined as they struggle with huge trays laden with bowls of steaming pasta. The waitress returns with your wine. You order linguini with pesto—a fine choice, she tells you before plunging into the kitchen.

《《———》》

By the time Miles arrived the sky had turned a sickly greenish-gray as storm clouds rolled in from the west.

It's gonna break, Miles said. Relief is near.

When they reached the club it was still early enough so that no line had formed outside. The bouncer—six feet four inches, muscles barely contained within a shiny sharkskin suit and salmon-colored shirt—examined them with eyes that said, Hey, if it was one hour later you guys would be shit outta luck, then he unfastened the velvet rope and let them through.

Just inside the door was a curtained foyer and another well-dressed muscle man. Twenty bucks, he said. Each. From behind the curtain came throbbing dance music, computer generated bass and percussion that vibrated the bones in Caleb's feet. He still couldn't listen to *real* music—music with melodies and lyrics—but this stuff struck the right impersonal note. He and Miles paid up and the man swept open the curtain.

The club consisted of one large, high-ceilinged room. At its center was a sunken dance floor lit by racks of swiveling lights and the ubiquitous mirrored ball. No one was dancing. Around the perimeter of the floor were small tables and metal chairs, about half of which were occupied.

Let's get a drinkypoo, Miles said.

Along the far wall ran a long black onyx bar with no stools. As he followed Miles across the room Caleb felt self-conscious. In a pair of old black chinos and a plain white shirt he was no doubt being disdainfully inspected by the few customers, the men in their silk shirts and Armani suits, the women in their tight mini-dresses and dangling earrings.

The barkeep was an astonishingly beautiful woman wearing a fishnet dress with only a thong underneath. Miles ordered two gin

187

and tonics, and Caleb tried his best to keep his eyes off the woman's small, pointed breasts. She moved efficiently among the bottles, and quickly returned with two thin cocktail glasses and two words: Eighteen dollars.

First round's on me, Miles said, handing over a twenty.

At these prices, Caleb said, we better drink slowly.

I bet you'd like to drink *her* slowly.

Her? She'd eat me for breakfast.

You wish.

They leaned back against the bar and surveyed the room. The music was loud, the lights dizzying. Every so often a strobe flashed, making Caleb slightly woozy. One couple finally moved out onto the dance floor where they gyrated several feet apart, seemingly oblivious of each other. Most everyone else remained near the bar, and nearly all of them were men. Ten of them, Caleb counted, posed a few feet apart along the entire length of the bar, like whores in a cathouse waiting to be chosen. A few of them looked like they could be models, with perfect hair and the latest trendy clothes, while the others were clearly Wall Street types flashing Rolexes and red suspenders.

Well, he shouted to Miles, at least I stand out in this crowd.

To your credit, his friend said.

The drinks were weak, and he finished his quickly. For a moment he considered leaving, cutting his losses, but he knew Miles would not allow it. He ordered two more gin and tonics, this time shamelessly eyeing the barkeep's pale breasts as she prepared the cocktails. Her nipples were small and rosy-pink. He wondered how many men she had to reject every night. The number must have been staggering.

As he waited for his change he heard Miles mutter, Uh oh.

A small group had just arrived. Among them was Corinne. She was with some of her Eurotrash friends, music business clients clipped from the pages of slick magazines. He quickly scanned the group for Sara, but she was not among them. They settled at a table beside the dance floor.

You're not leaving, Miles shouted into his ear. Not yet.

Come here, Caleb said, pulling Miles to the dark corner of the bar. I don't want Corinne to see me.

Why not?

I don't want Sara to know I was here.

What's the big deal?

I can't explain. I just don't want her to know.

You're afraid Corinne will tell Sara, and then Sara will know you're not at home pining away and feeling awful. Right?

Caleb didn't answer.

Miles laughed. What you should do is get some foxy girl to dance. *That's* what you should do.

Corinne and a few others moved on to the dance floor. She looked sexy in a tight red dress, her black hair falling to the middle of her back. She moved slinkily, her arms gliding out in front of her like snakes. He had always thought she was attractive. He wondered now what she thought of him.

How about *her*? Miles asked, pointing to a woman standing at the other end of the bar. Tall, wafer thin, with a pale, angular face. She was tapping her foot to the music.

I can't.

Porque no?

I can't dance to this shit.

It's easy. You just move your hips and arms. Like this.

No.

It'll make Sara's blood boil when she hears about it.

No.

All right, all right. I'm just trying to help out.

Why don't *you* go dance with her?

Maybe I will, Miles said. Though I'd much prefer that gentleman over there—the one with the shaved head.

Go for it.

Miles shoved off from the bar. He spoke a few words to the man with the shaved head, and they headed toward the dance floor. Meanwhile, the tall woman was fending off two men in matching pin-striped suits.

This was his chance to run. Corinne had returned to her table, where a vampirish young man was biting her neck.

He headed toward the door, keeping to the shadows as much as possible. The exit was behind yet another set of thick, black curtains, just beyond the entrance. He stood at the threshold and took one last look. Corinne was laughing with Dracula, while Miles flailed away on the dance floor, his bald partner making small, rabbity moves in his wake. Feeling like a complete failure, Caleb parted the curtain and left.

The door, when it slammed shut, swallowed all club noise. The wind had picked up, sending bits of paper and plastic swirling around the street. There was the smell of rain in the air.

As he started walking uptown he glanced back toward the club, where a line had now formed behind the velvet rope. Just entering was a woman who, from a block and a half away, looked an awful lot like Sara. He saw her only from behind, but he was pretty sure it was her. Thank God I got out of there, he said out loud, picturing Sara on the dance floor with those night creatures, their long bony fingers running over her, their pointed teeth flashing in the darkness.

He walked quickly up Hudson Street as the first of the night's raindrops fell heavily upon him.

«««—»»»

After the waitress has brought you your pasta, after she has smiled warmly at you and told you to enjoy your meal, after you have impulsively patted your trousers pocket to check on the status of your wedding band—you discover it is not there.

From your pocket you remove a tissue, a stick of gum, some lint. No ring. You check your other pocket. Car keys, keys to the B&B, another tissue. You check the floor under the chair, under the table. Nothing.

It must be in the car. Without thinking you stand and head for the exit.

Is there something wrong? the hostess asks.

I left something in the car, you tell her. I'll be right back.

You're outside before she can respond. Half-way there you realize that she might think you're skipping out without paying the bill. You almost turn around to explain the situation, but cannot. You must find the ring.

You search the seat and floor. You run your fingers between the seat and the back cushion. A dime and two pennies. The back seat and floor. A gum wrapper. But no ring. Wine-tinged acid rises in the back of your throat.

The kayak!

You are half way there before you realize that now you really *are* running out without paying the bill, but you cannot stop yourself. You feel like a man with his trousers on fire headed for a barrel of water.

At the kayak rental desk you explain the situation—leaving out the part about your wife deserting you—to a woman who looks as though she graduated from middle school just last week. The woman is mortified for you and asks if you remember which kayak you rented.

It was red! you shout, looking beyond her to the docks. There are dozens of kayaks piled up against the wall, and a third of them are red.

Do you remember the number?

What number?

She explains that each kayak has a number on its side. You tell her you don't remember any number, and she groans.

She announces your predicament to the others and soon there are five of you unstacking the kayaks and examining their interiors. Because the boats are hollow, you have to lift one end, then the other, to see if the ring rolls from the farthest point. It takes fifteen minutes to check every kayak—no luck.

Are there any red kayaks being used right now? you ask.

There are six kayaks out on the lake, you're told, and at least two or three of them are red.

I'll wait, you say.

Soon two red kayaks are returned at the same time, but a quick search comes up with nothing.

Two blue kayaks and one yellow show up, leaving one kayak left on the lake.

We don't know for sure it's a red one, the young staffer says. But we close in half an hour, so we'll find out soon enough.

At ten minutes till, the last kayak appears. It's red. Everyone on the dock cheers.

Did you find a ring in your kayak? you ask the woman in the boat as she reaches the dock.

A ring?

You help her out then yank the kayak onto the dock to examine its interior.

Nothing.

Water builds up behind your eyes.

Sorry, mister, someone says.

Doesn't matter, really, you say, half choking. I'm not married anymore, anyway.

They look at you as though you've just announced this was all a prank, that you didn't really lose your ring at all, that you just wanted to watch them jump through hoops.

Well, one of them says, good luck, anyway.

Back in the car, you lean your head against the steering wheel as one huge tear rolls down your cheek. You feel it reach your chin, where it pauses and dangles for the longest time before falling and landing with a thud on your lap.

«‹‹—››»

Rain drops rattled the apartment windows, lightning flashed, illuminating the bedroom for a split second—Kate and Earl's daughter, the white rabbit—followed by a sharp crack of thunder. He lay in bed praying this storm would break the heat wave.

The phone rang. He did not move. From the next room he heard Earl's outgoing message, then a loud beep.

Where'd you go, man? he heard Miles say over a wash of music. I guess you saw Sara, huh? I think I (music) that bitch Corinne. Oh well. Bound to step on a few toes on the dance floor. (music) That guy I was (music)? Mr. Clean? He (music). Well... (someone yelling) tomorrow. (click)

A bolt of lightning touched down nearby, followed instantly by a bone-rattling peal of thunder. He lay there waiting for the next bolt to strike.

«‹‹—››»

Back at the First Street parking lot you lock up the car, pay in advance this time for the overnight space.

You again, Eddie says.

You try not to look in his eyes as you hand over the money.

See you later, he says.

You want to get away—away from the car, from the carry-on. You don't know where you're going, all you know is that you also cannot face your tiny, windowless room at the Brentwood, not yet. The sun has dropped below the horizon, the night air is warm and dry. Downtown is deserted, just like last night, though there are merry sounds coming from the restaurants and bars down on the pier, and the occasional merrymaker—drunk, still in work clothes—headed home. You follow, by chance, one dressed-for-success couple for two long blocks. They hold hands and talk so quietly you cannot make out a single word. After a while the woman glances back, then murmurs something to her companion. They accelerate noticeably until, relieved, they reach the municipal lot where their car is parked. You watch them drive away, flip them the bird.

You keep on walking. Your left hand feels lighter than your right. You run your thumb over your ring finger, feeling its soft nakedness.

Could it have fallen in the lake somehow? Maybe it fell out somewhere at the university. No. You had it in the car afterwards. It's lost, that's all. Gone.

Up ahead, you see a familiar figure. The Writer, backpack and all, eyes focused on the sidewalk. You slow as he approaches. He does not look up. When he is just a few feet away you stop.

Hello, you say.

Hey, he replies, not pausing, his eyes still aimed at the ground.

Before he gets too far away you call out again. Are you—? and you mention the writer's name. He stops, turns. We met on the ferry, you tell him. Remember? You asked me about places to stay. I told you the Y. Remember?

He stares.

Am I right? you ask. Are you—?

His black eyes bore into you. Buy me a drink?

All right.

You take him to the Bulbous Nose and settle in a booth toward the rear. The place seems not to have changed one iota

193

from last night—same mustachioed barkeep, same sad customers, same music. You wouldn't at all be surprised to see Didi and her friends arrive.

From the barkeep you order a stout, the Writer orders a cosmopolitan.

Got hooked on them at a little place down in New Orleans, he tells you. No one makes them as well as they do down there, but I have a good feeling about this bartender.

It's the mustaches, you say.

Yes. That's it, I suppose.

The Writer removes his baseball cap, revealing a smooth, bald head. He keeps his eyes directed at the table top, mostly, with occasional furtive glances at your face.

I have to confess right up front, you say. I haven't read your books.

He smiles. That would put you in the vast majority.

I just never get around to reading all I want to read.

I'm the same, he shrugged.

Are you researching a project? A book about Seattle?

Not a book. A screenplay. For Boyd Hart. Have you heard of him?

Of course. *Shot in the Head.*

Good movie. We met in Bali. He read my last book, hired me on the spot.

That's great.

It's money. What're *you* doing here?

Oh, just traveling around. I needed a break from New York.

Manhattan?

Yeah.

That's a bad place. Bad for the soul.

You think so?

I know so. Too much hostility in the air.

You think so?

I can't breathe there.

The barkeep arrives with your drinks. The Writer lifts the candy-colored cosmopolitan and sips.

Not bad, he says. I had ten of these one night and ended up in the Mississippi with a transexual hooker.

Really?

That's what I wrote, anyway. What do you do? For a living?

You look away and say, I write, also. Then you quickly add, Press releases, mostly, for book publishers.

He laughs. Does anybody read those things?

Not many, you say, only slightly hurt. But surely you've been interviewed by people who haven't read the book itself—only the release.

I'm sure.

What's the screenplay about?

He smiles, as though he's about to reveal state secrets. Well, he says, I'm just taking notes so far, but it's more or less about a guy—Boyd Hart—who takes a trip to get out of a bad situation.

A trip to Seattle?

Among other places, yes.

What's the bad situation?

I haven't determined that yet, but something very personal, a tragedy of some kind. Perhaps a death.

A loved one?

That's possible.

What's his name?

Not sure yet. What's *your* name?

My name?

Maybe I'll use it.

Caleb.

That'll do.

And what happens to him? To Caleb?

The Writer shrugs. No details yet, but I know it involves more loss.

A loss of innocence?

Nah. That's old hat.

The Writer holds up his empty glass until the barkeep looks over and nods. How many of these will you have to pay for, you wonder.

I went kayaking today, you tell him.

Really? Now that's something my guy might do.

A pontoon plane nearly ran me over.

The Writer pulls out a small pocket notebook and begins to jot down notes with a stubby pencil. You mind if I use that?

I guess not.

The barkeep brings over another round.

Mmm, the Writer says as he takes a sip. Even better than the first one. How'd you find this place?

You tell him about last night, about Didi and her friends.

Did you sleep with her?

No.

Why not?

I don't know. It didn't seem to be in the cards.

Sounds to me like you could've slept with her.

Think so? You run last night over in your head—Didi's eyes, her smile, the way she lingered when the others were leaving. Maybe.

Definitely, the Writer says.

Then you tell him about the Eros and the noise leakage. He laughs, shakes his head, scribbles in his notebook.

Is this all going in your script?

Possibly. With your permission, of course.

Sure. Why not?

You begin to tell him more stories, and he fills in several pages of his notebook. You are flattered. You order another round. And another.

After four pints you are drunk. I better get going, you announce, before I tell you too much.

You pay the barkeep for all the drinks. The cosmopolitans were seven dollars each. The Writer, who seems unaffected by the alcohol, follows you outside. The stars are bright. You feel a little seasick.

Are you at the Y? you ask.

I have a room there, he answers cryptically. Tell me, how'd you get those scratches on your arms?

You laugh nervously. You sense the Writer's eyes as he walks alongside you.

Are you gonna put that in your movie too?

It depends on your answer.

So you tell him. Why not? It's only a movie. By the time you're done you are in front of the Eros. An iron gate has been lowered in front of the ticket booth.

Home sweet home, you say.

That's a hell of a story.

Think so?

Is it all true?

I honestly don't know, you say.

I'll use it, if you don't mind.

Feel free.

If not for the movie, then for something else.

No problemo.

Thanks for the drinks.

G'night.

Take care, Caleb.

Fumbling with the key, you unlock the front door. Before you enter, you take a look back, intending to wave goodbye to the Writer, but he's gone.

Chapter Fifteen: The Wedding

We were married in a civil ceremony attended by family and friends—about fifty guests in all. I wore an antique dress of off-white lace once worn by my maternal grandmother, Caleb wore a dark suit with a flaming red tie. An old college friend of mine played the piano as the guests arrived, then pounded out "Here Comes the Bride" as my father escorted me down the aisle. Caleb was scared stiff, but made a valiant effort to smile. Moments earlier, he'd been pacing the back room in a highly agitated state, cursing the judge who was to perform the ceremony, who happened to be late. We laughed about it later, how he was nearly in tears, Miles trying to calm him with a pint of whiskey. More than anything, he confessed, he was mad at his mother, who had refused to make the trip from Florida.

Then there was the strange weather. After an unseasonably warm afternoon, the sky had turned a technicolor green and, thirty minutes before the wedding was to begin, a thunderstorm unleashed torrents of rain. It's good luck, Corinne told me as I watched forlornly out the window.

Both wedding and reception took place in the same building, an old mansion in Brooklyn that had been converted into a club for hire. The place was once beautiful, you could tell, but the rugs were now a little shabby, the floorboards creaky, the windows dusty. It's like a haunted house, Caleb had remarked when we first visited the building, but the price was right, and we figured the affair would at least be memorable.

The ceremony itself went smoothly, all five minutes of it. Judge Harper—a former professor of mine at law school—made a brief speech about the enduring power of love. When I met these two a few weeks ago, he intoned in a deep bass voice, his hair still wet from the sudden downpour, I could tell they were meant for each other, and would stick by each other through thick and thin for the rest of their lives. It is written on their faces just as surely as it's written on the marriage certificate they will sign this evening.

For much of the speech I stared at Judge Harper's lips, thin and straight and stern. To look anywhere else would have been to cry buckets. As rain pelted the windows, we exchanged vows and rings, and before we knew what was happening, we were pronounced husband and wife. We kissed, and the guests applauded.

Directly afterwards, everyone gathered in the reception room for drinks and hor d'hourves. We dutifully circulated among the guests, smiling and numb, relieved to have the hard part behind us.

During dinner several toasts were made. My father welcomed Caleb to the family, and Miles, as best man, recounted the story of how, one drunken night, Caleb bet him one hundred dollars that he would never get married. With great fanfare Caleb paid off the bet, loudly insisting that it was his pleasure.

I felt so bad for him, though. His brother and sister were there, but it wasn't the same without Claire, who had claimed it would be too costly and inconvenient to leave Florida. He was heartbroken and embarrassed.

After dinner we danced to the tapes Caleb had made of all our favorite songs. During our first dance as husband and wife he asked if I was happy. I said I was. Very.

I'm going to do everything I can to keep you that way, he said, and I believed him.

We spent our wedding night at a bed and breakfast near Prospect Park. It was late when we arrived and we had to sneak up the stairs in the dark to our third floor room. Earlier in the day, when I had stopped by to pick up the key, I mentioned that I was to be married that very evening. The proprietress, a middle-aged woman with a pinched face, said, Oh, that's too bad, then regaled me with tales of her two divorces. Think twice, she'd said. I wish *I* had!

The room was cramped with antiques, including an old-fashioned four-poster bed. Caleb carried me over the threshold, then slowly removed my gown. It had been a long, tiring day, and in the middle of making love we both admitted that we were too exhausted to finish. He stretched out his arm and I lay my head on it. As I was falling asleep I heard him ask, again, Are you happy? I tried to wake up and answer, but the quicksand was pulling me in, and I drifted away to a deep, dark sleep.

Chapter Sixteen: Spirit Lake

The road up to Mount Rainier winds through lush, dense forest, left turn, right turn, left right, left right, with the occasional clearing that offers heart-stopping views of the snowy peak. You are relieved to be out of the city, even if you are but one of many tourists snaking up this road, leaving behind your exhaust fumes to choke these beautiful trees.

When you checked out of the Brentwood this morning you did not mention the disruptive noises from the Eros, nor did Ada remind you of the incident as she tallied your bill. Several strands of her hair hung loose over her face as she bent over the calculator, and you had to restrain yourself from reaching out to gently pull them aside. She thanked you when you paid in cash, and told you to come again, and you said you would, someday, be back.

Up up up you drive. On the steeper inclines you can feel the little car straining, you have to push the accelerator to the floor, and your stomach curls in on itself as you imagine the car breaking down on this narrow, two-lane road half way up the mountain.

As you were getting into the car this morning, Eddie approached and called out to you, Sir? Sir?

You turned on him. Yes?

Sorry, he said, but I think there might be something wrong with your car.

What do you mean, something wrong? Your heart was pumping furiously.

Well, do you smell that smell?

It was true. The stench seemed to pour from the trunk like water from an overfull tub.

What smell?

You don't smell that?

No. Sorry. I have to run now.

You started the engine and quickly pulled away as Eddie stood shouting and gesticulating in the rearview mirror.

You can hardly smell anything now. The cool mountain air helps.

You turn off at the Paradise Visitors Center and park at the far end of the huge lot. On the other side of the lot stands the lodge— a beautiful wooden hotel—and the visitors center, and above it all rises the massive, jagged peak of Mount Rainier. The air up here is crisp but the sun shines so strongly that no more than a t-shirt is necessary.

You head for the hiking trails, following signs warning hikers to remain on the paved areas so as not to disturb the fragile ecosystem of the mountain. You trudge up a fairly steep incline, passing children and overweight tourists, until you reach a section of trail covered by snow. The sky is a ferocious blue. Looking down you see the sloped roof of the lodge, the thick forest, and to the south, the stunted gray peak of Mount Saint Helens. At this level there are few trees on Rainier, just snow and rock all the way up to the top. To your right a small waterfall breaks the silence with its almost comical tinkle. A chubby groundhog frolics in the snow. You make a snowball, its chill a shock to your bare hands, and toss it at the animal. It falls short. The groundhog, amused, stands on its hind legs and chatters. You try again, this time nailing the groundhog on its pointy head. It squeals and disappears into a hole in the snow.

You continue on, following the footprints of those who came before. Your shoes are wet, but you don't mind for now. It is a kick to be in the snow like this, in a t-shirt, on the side of a mountain.

Around a bend you come across a young couple headed back down. They are red-cheeked, smiling, holding hands. When they see you they stop and wait for you to reach them.

Excuse me, the woman says. Would you mind very much taking our photo?

She has an accent. German? Scandinavian? She holds out a

small camera. Without a word, you take the camera and the two of them pose with the peak of Mount Rainier in the background. It's very simple, the woman says. Just point and shoot.

You stare through the lens for a long time. The woman wraps an arm around the man, pressing against him in a familiar, intimate manner.

Did you take it yet?

You do not answer. You look through the camera, as if deciding on the composition.

Is there a problem?

She looks confused, and pulls away from the man. That's when you snap the photo.

You hand back the camera without saying anything. The woman shrugs, takes the man's hand, and heads down the mountain, muttering something in another language.

You continue climbing until the footprints thin out. There is nothing but pure white snow between you and the peak. It doesn't seem so far away. How long would you last? You turn and look below, at the hikers at the foot of the trail, like insects in the snow.

On the way down you meet no one until you reach the waterfall, where a group of Japanese tourists watch the groundhog cavort. They snap photos in all directions, surely one or two of them catching you on film, sweaty and flushed, as you move quickly down the trail.

《《—》》

Have you talked to Leakey yet? Sara asked.

No, he said, but I will.

This was a lie, he knew, but he said it anyway.

That was lame-brained of me to forget like that.

Yes, it was.

They were at DeMeo's, downstairs from her apartment. When they'd arrived the waiters all nodded in recognition. They think we're still together, he thought.

Sara had called earlier that day. She wanted to get together, chat, catch up, she told him. What was she up to? he had wondered. Was she just trying to make up for missing the appointment with Dr. Leakey? Or was it possible that she missed him and wanted him back again? He couldn't stop himself from thinking it, and his heart beat faster from the moment he hung up until this very minute.

So what's new? she asked. She was on her second glass of wine, and her cheeks had taken on that flushed complexion that always turned him on.

Nothing, he answered. He had not told her of his travel plans, and was not sure he would. He liked the idea of her calling and calling, not knowing where he was. Perhaps she'd become so worried that she'd realize just how important he was to her.

I don't believe you, she said.

She could always read him. He was transparent.

My life is at a stand-still, he told her. Work is slow, and as you know, I have no personal life.

This is New York, sweetie, she said. There's loads to do and see. So many new people to meet.

I don't want to meet new people, he said. I want the old people.

You weren't happy with the old people.

True. But I'm even less happy now. I'll take unhappy over miserable any day.

I saw Miles the other night.

So?

He knows how to have a good time.

Miles didn't just get dumped, did he?

You have a point there.

He reached out and took her hand. I think we should get back together. No—don't say anything. Let me finish.

He had rehearsed this speech all afternoon, speaking loudly as he paced the apartment to drown out the incessant squeaking of the vent across the way.

I think we owe it to ourselves to give it another shot. I've said it before, Sara, but it bears repeating: you're giving up on us without a fight. And you *owe* us a fight. We've given each other six years of our lives—*six years*—and you talk about it as though we've dated for a few months. But it's just not that easy. Talk to anyone who's been married fifteen, twenty, twenty-five years.

Talk to your folks! They've been through this. They've had serious doubts. They've wanted to be alone, to give up, to walk away. But they've worked very hard to stay together. That's what I want to do. It's hard work. It's harder than your job, it's harder than anything. Maybe it won't work out. But how the fuck do we know unless we try? Huh? Why won't you try with me?

Throughout this speech Sara bravely kept her eyes level with his, but they were ice cold, dead. They held no light for him, not a glimmer. There was once something there, a spark—love, or whatever you want to call it—but it was gone now. How long had it been like this?

She said a few words but he barely heard her. Something about wishing things were different, wishing she felt the same. He couldn't listen. He wanted to get up and run, run far away from her dead eyes, but he could not think of where to go. He didn't think he could even make it to the door. When their food arrived he did not eat a bite. Sara told him to try, to please eat, but he couldn't. The thought of it made him sick. Sara toyed with her veal parmesan, but ate only a few bites herself. Mostly she sat looking at him the way one looks at an invalid, someone too far gone to reach with words. Eventually the thought of staying became more unbearable than the thought of leaving. He tossed a few dollars on the table, pushed back his chair, pulled himself to his feet.

Caleb, please, Sara said, but he was already gone, out the door, up the street, running, running.

《《—》》

The car really reeks now. You have to keep the windows down as you descend the mountain, stuck behind a Sunday driver who slows to a crawl at every bend in the road. You try to pass, but there is too much traffic coming from the other direction. Only toward the bottom, when the road starts to straighten, are you able to reach full speed.

As the sun is setting you reach a small town between Mount Rainier and Mount Saint Helens. Three blocks of stores and bars and a diner, and, at the edge of town, the Bailey Motel, a collection of ramshackle cabins. The old woman at the desk insists you see the room before committing. Cabin Two is dank, dark, with dirt brown carpet and a lumpy bed.

I'll take it, you tell her, handing over the cash.

Let me know if you need anything, Mr. Shepard, she says before running back to the game show she was watching.

After a quick bite at the diner, where the locals take to staring at you as if your picture had been in all the papers, you return to the motel and lie on the bed and watch television. At midnight you turn off the light and try to sleep, but the bedsprings dig into your back, the sheets smell like mold. Crickets rattle loudly outside the open windows. Every once in a while someone walks by the door. You hear voices, cars coming and going, but you see no one through the thick curtains. In the next cabin someone is playing music. You toss and turn, and eventually, gradually, fall asleep.

You check out early the next morning. Did you sleep okay? the old woman asks.

Tell you the truth, you say, your other customers kept me up a bit.

Her eyes narrow in concentration, as though she did not hear you properly. I'm sorry?

Especially those people in Cabin Three, you say. Sounded like they were having a party.

You head out the screen door with a wave.

We didn't have any other customers, the old woman says.

You stop half way out the door. No? Well then, who were—?

You follow the old woman to Cabin Three. The room is untouched, the bed made, the towels folded neatly on the bathroom racks.

Musta dreamed it, she says.

Yeah. Must've.

You climb into the car and start the engine.

Mister? the old woman says. What's that stink?

You wave goodbye and pull out of the lot, headed straight for Mount Saint Helens.

《《—》》

He ran home through the soggy twilight, threading among the clusters of sweating tourists and teenagers, holding back the tears. He passed the super's wife on the front stoop and kept his face from her when she called out hello. He took the stairs two at a time, all six flights, and struggled to find the right key through the tears that were flowing now down his cheeks.

The heat in the apartment hit him like a wall. Goddam rain storm last night hadn't helped a bit. The cramped living room was like a sauna. Hot air streamed in through the open window. He rolled on the sofa and cried out her name. He let the snot stream from his nose, mingling with the tears and sweat. He pounded a pillow, then tossed it at the portrait of Kate, knocking it cock-eyed. He ran to the window and shouted, FUCK YOU! *FUCK YOU!* The diners below stared up at him, waiting for something to happen. Their faces were so funny, he had to laugh. What're *you* looking at? They stared for another moment, then, a bit disappointed, they returned to their meals and conversations.

His back ached now, and his face stung from the salt of his tears, but he also felt lighter. He washed his face and looked at himself in the mirror. Fuck you, he said again, this time so softly he could barely hear it. Then he went into the living room and turned on the air conditioner.

«««—»»»

At such an early hour the road leading into the Mount Saint Helens National Monument is deserted—no cars, no rangers at the gates. You drive through lush forest, not yet at the point where the volcano wreaked its havoc back in 1980. Then, as if you've crossed an invisible line into another world, you find yourself in a vast desert. You check your rear view mirror and see vivid green, while up ahead lies nothing but brown and gray. Here, at the outer edge of the destruction, there remain a few dead trees standing, like ancient sign posts. On a craggy promontory stand three withered trees with outstretched arms. The farther you go, however, the greater the desolation. Tree trunks lie in great clusters up and down the hills, millions of them, like pick-up sticks tossed by the gods. Occasionally you catch sight of an oasis—a patch of grass, flowers, even—but mostly the landscape is dry and dull.

You pass your first car coming from the opposite direction. The people wave, but you ignore them. A few miles later another car passes, and again the people wave. Or were they pointing?

Worried now that something's wrong with the car, you pull into a small overlook area and inspect the wheels, look under the body. Nothing. You lean against the car, wipe your brow. Those people—they were just being friendly. A hiking trail starts here, you notice, and meanders a mile or so down into a valley to Spirit Lake, a refreshing half circle of deep blue. Though you are exhausted and have no water with you, you decide to hike down. Not far into the valley you notice that the lake is actually much larger than it appears—fully one third of its surface is covered with floating logs, driftwood created by trees torn from the ground in the eruption. Not long ago, you realize, this very trail wound through a dense forest filled with wildlife. You would not have been able to see the lake, or the sky, through the trees. Now, there is not one tree standing for as far as you can see, nor is there a bird to be heard singing.

When you reach the water's edge you sit on a log and stare at the deep, vibrant blue of the lake. The driftwood undulates hypnotically on the surface. (DRIFT LOGS CAN KILL!) Beyond the lake is what remains of Mount Saint Helens, still a formidable volcano, though one third of it evaporated in the eruption. According to your guidebook, it remains active and could erupt at any time.

A small plane buzzes by overhead. You check for pontoons, but it does not have any. You watch it shrink to the size of a pepper flake then disappear. There is no sign of life anywhere, from horizon to horizon. You turn toward the lake, your face directly in the wind, and scream. No words, just sounds, like a wild animal. You scream louder, pushing your voice to the limit, feeling your vocal cords grate. The sound is absorbed by the wind, the lake, the drift logs. For five full minutes you shout like this, until your throat is raw. Then you collapse on the ground and suck in the cold air blowing in off the water.

On the way back to the car you pass two small groups of

hikers, and are asked both times, How far to go? and both times you reply, Not far. Not far at all.

«« — »»

He lay in bed, unable to sleep. The apartment had cooled off, the air conditioner set at extra cold. Just one more day, he thought, and I'll be gone. How long since I've flown alone? He couldn't remember.

He rolled onto his side, then his back. His legs felt as though they needed to run, they were charged with electrical energy.

He climbed from bed and paced through the bedroom and living room and hallway and back again, all in the dark. When he reached the kitchen the third time a light switched on across the air shaft. Through the window he could see the super's wife in her kitchen. She wore just a t-shirt that fell to her upper thighs, barely covering the slope of her ass. Her legs were muscular, dark, smooth. She opened the refrigerator, pulled out a pitcher of water, and filled two tall glasses. She drank one entire glass then filled it again. As she filled it the hem of her shirt rose an inch to reveal a patch of dark hair. Then she shut the refrigerator door, turned out the light and disappeared in the darkness.

He was suddenly seized with panic. I have to call Sara! He picked up the phone and dialed. It rang two times before the answering machine picked up. Was she out? The clock read 2:34. She could be at a club. She could be asleep. He listened to her outgoing message, then hung up.

After pacing for another ten minutes he returned to bed, where he lay wide awake for an hour before finally drifting off to sleep.

«« — »»

The carry-on feels heavy in the thick black air of Ape Cave. At the bottom of the metal staircase it is forty degrees, half the outdoor temperature. Forewarned at the ranger's office, you have brought an extra shirt, but you are still chilled to the bone.

You could not resist Ape Cave. There is the name, of course, but also the promise of a deep black hole in the ground. The perfect place for a burial.

The kerosene lantern—rented at the ranger's office—shines a dull yellow light on the rocky cave floor. The walls are rough and shiny with moisture, the ceiling virtually invisible in the darkness. Ahead are patches of yellow—other tourists with their lanterns—but you cannot help but feel alone. If the lamp broke or ran out of fuel you would be enveloped in complete darkness. You would have to crawl like a child along the ground to the staircase. To calm yourself you whistle as you slowly and carefully step around rocks and over holes in the ground. With the carry-on in one hand and the lantern in the other you feel weighted down, lead-booted.

As a small family passes in the opposite direction, a little boy asks, Daddy, what's that bad smell? The father tells the boy he doesn't know what that smell is, but he gives you a dirty look that lingers long after they've gone. The cold air deadens the stench, you've found, but it is still noticeable, like that of a skunk that has had its glands removed.

After a hundred yards or so you've reached a point in the cave where there are no other hikers or lamp lights in sight. The cave is pitch black ahead of you and behind. You hold out the lantern, scanning the area for crevices. A drop of water lands on your head like a sharp fingertip.

You examine the wall more closely until you find the perfect hiding place. The bag fits nicely. You step back and shine the light on the wall—the carry-on cannot be seen unless you walk right up to the crevice and peer inside. It could be years before someone finds it, maybe never.

You remain there for what seems like a long time.

What are you thinking? Are you remembering?

Your teeth are chattering. When you move the lantern the shadows on the walls elongate and shorten, making shapes that resemble ghost-like animals or people. The air is perfectly still. There is no sense of the earth spinning. You are in a deep black hole breathing dead air.

Goodbye, you say.

Then you head back to the entrance, moving quickly and crouching low to the ground to better pick out the obstacles. You are shivering. You pass a family, several children and their parents. The kids say hello to you, one by one, five of them, but you do not answer. Near the staircase is a young couple, kissing against an outcrop of rock, faces lit a fluttery yellow by the lamp at their feet.

Looking up at the staircase you can see natural light dribbling down from the surface. You run up the stairs, nearly tripping on the condensation. As you climb, the temperature rises until, near the top, you finally stop shivering. When you step out onto the grass you have to shield your eyes from the sunlight. A bird sings. Trees swish. A group of tourists stare at you as they head toward the cave entrance. Only when you reach the car do you realize tears are streaming down your face.

CHAPTER SEVENTEEN: ILSE

Driving into Portland from the north, the city seems familiar to you, you know exactly where you're going, past several landmarks you recognize from last week. The bright bold sheen of newness is gone.

At the Orenthal Hotel you re-encounter GLORIA—the same double chins and the same baffled expression when you pay in cash. You request Room 231, for old times' sake, and it just happens to be available.

After a quick shower to wipe off the grime of Ape Cave you head out for a drink. You walk with a light step past the old red brick apartment buildings with their APT. FOR RENT signs, straight to Bubba's Sulky Lounge, where the barkeep greets you warmly.

What'll it be this evening, buddy? he asks. Not another grief beer, I hope.

You smile, shake your head no. How about just dog-tired?

Is it a pleasant tiredness, as after a hard day of work, or a weary tiredness, the result of sloth and/or depression?

Bubba's is not crowded, there are only two customers at the bar and a few others at a table. A Hank Williams tune drifts across the room from the jukebox, along with the satisfying crack of billiard balls.

The dog-tired beer goes down smooth, washing away the metallic taste that has coated the back of your throat ever since you left the cave.

How's it taste?

Perfect.

Bubba grins and walks the length of the bar to attend to another customer.

«《——》»

He spent the last day before the trip running errands. Laundry, housecleaning, withdrawing money from the bank. The heat wave had finally broken, and people were now moving at their usual quick pace on the sidewalks, shouting and laughing, their faces bright and visibly relieved. He took a long walk from Washington Square Park to the piers, and several times stopped at a public telephone to call Sara, but never went through with it. He would not tell her anything about the trip. Maybe he would send a post card.

Later that night, as he was finally completing the press release for *Rebound*, he realized he didn't have a suitcase. He had brought his clothes here in paper bags, like a vagrant. Now it was too late to buy a new bag. He would have to go over to Sara's and borrow one.

He called first, and no one answered. On the way out the door he imagined Sara discovering her bag missing. Maybe she would be preparing for a trip to Los Angeles, and would be angry that he had taken it. This made him smile.

«《——》»

Still dog-tired? Bubba inquires, gesturing toward your empty pint glass.

One more, you tell him.

Whatcha writing? Bubba asks as he scoops up the empty glass.

Just notes, you tell him. Ideas.

The barkeep shrugs and fills the glass with beer. The jukebox plays an old Elvis Costello tune. You hum along, having forgotten the words.

«《——》»

It felt strange to enter his old apartment building. The garlicky smell from DeMeo's tickled his nose as he ascended the stairs. He paused outside Apartment Two and listened—not a sound. He knocked, just in case. No answer. She was probably out at a party, or dancing with Corinne.

213

Hey!

Mia came bounding down the stairs.

Oh. Hey, Mia.

How are you doing? I'm so sorry to hear about you guys.

She told you?

Yeah. I was asking where you were. I came down a couple times and you weren't around, so…

He nodded. His heart racing.

So where are you staying?

Over on Tenth Street. A sublet.

Close by, then. That's good.

I guess.

Listen, if there's any way I can help, anything I can do. I feel really, really bad about this. You guys always seemed so—oh, I don't know—so in love.

Well, I guess not.

Anyway, I'm just on my way out. I got a date tonight.

What happened to Paul?

Oh, he's history. You were right about him. He was a jerk.

Caleb opened the door. Well, he said.

Good luck with everything, Mia said. Maybe it'll all work out.

Maybe.

I mean, if you want it to.

Right. Bye bye.

He unlocked the door and turned on the light. Dilsey immediately appeared at his feet. Good girl, he said, but when he bent over to pat her she darted through the kitchen into the bedroom. He followed her and switched on the overhead light. The dark blue bedspread, the photos on the walls, the books, Sara's bra thrown over the back of a chair. The room smelled of her.

Dilsey leapt up onto the bed and mewed, but, again, she ran away when he approached, hiding this time behind the bureau. Why are you hiding from me? he asked with a hurt voice. He missed Dilsey and often imagined seeing her black shape out of the corner of his eye at the other apartment. Come here, sweetie pie, he pleaded, but she ignored him.

«‹‹—››»

The saloon door opens and who should traipse in but ILSE, wearing her flight attendant uniform. Sighing dramatically, she sits two stools away at the bar. She looks exhausted. You turn the other way, hoping she won't recognize you.

Gimme an exasperated, will ya? she asks Bubba in the manner of a very regular customer. You turn your face three quarters away but roll your eyes far to the right to catch a glimpse of her in the mirror behind the bar. She looks straight ahead, watching her own reflection, pulling the hair off her face. When Bubba places a beer in front of her she gulps half of it down, then wipes her pouty, foamy lips with the back of her hand.

Much better, she announces.

What's got you down? Bubba asks.

She leans forward, elbows on bar, and stares deep into her beer. I'm just tired of flying, she says. It takes too much out of me.

Was it Tom Waits who said jet lag is the time it takes for your soul to catch up with your body?

Whoever said it knew what they were talking about, ILSE says. My soul never even has a chance of finding me. Right now it's over Canada somewhere.

Refill?

Yeah. Make it a lost beer this time, though. In honor of my soul.

Why on earth did you run away from her that time at the museum? You could have come here and shared a lost beer instead of—

Hey—don't I know you?

Go on. Drain your glass and slide from the stool. Head for the door.

Hey, ILSE says. Wait a second.

Keep on moving. The door, the door.

You're that guy from the museum!

As you near the door you cannot see her but you can actually feel her gaze—a well-thrown dagger between your shoulder blades.

You're that weird yoga guy!

215

Open the door.

Caleb Caleb!

Step outside.

Hey! What's your problem? *Hey!*

The door swings shut behind you. Run!

You make it around the corner, then slow to a fast walk. Your heart is thumping against your ribs. Keep walking, one block, two blocks. You want as much distance between you and Bubba's as is possible right now.

Then it hits you. Your notebook. You left it on the bar. Everything is in it. Everything. ILSE is probably looking through it right now. She's probably laughing out loud. She's reading passages to Bubba and the others. Everyone is howling.

You have to go back. You have to get it.

On your way there you rehearse your explanation. It's part of a novel, you'll tell her. An entirely made up story. It's about this guy whose wife leaves him and how he copes. It's all fabricated. It's in the third person, after all. You wonder how she'll react. Will she think you're crazy? Or will she be interested? Hmm. The more you think about it, the more you actually *want* to tell ILSE about it. She'll get it. She'll understand, you're sure of it. Yes— ILSE will understand. By the time you reach Bubba's, you're excited.

But ILSE is gone. An empty beer glass sits at the bar where she was sitting.

I thought you'd be back, Bubba says, holding up the notebook. You grab it and run out the door. She must be close by. The first side street is empty. On the second side street some children are playing hopscotch, but no ILSE. When you reach the third you think you spot her two blocks north. You run.

She turns a corner and you slow down to follow at a half block distance. You are beginning to think this is ridiculous. What will you say to her?

She must be a little drunk. She's zigzagging down the sidewalk, stepping a bit too high to avoid cracks and humming loudly to herself.

You could say, ILSE, listen—I have a story I want to share with you. Or, ILSE, I can see from your eyes that you're a decent person, you would understand. Or, ILSE, I'm sorry if I frightened you at the museum, it's just that I was afraid, please let me tell you why.

But you've never spoken to anyone like this in your entire life. You can't imagine any response other than bafflement and ridicule.

As she turns another corner she glances back and spots you. She freezes for a second, then continues, but at a faster clip, until she is nearly running. She glances back and starts to move even faster.

ILSE! you cry. Please stop! I need to talk to you.

She nearly stumbles on an uneven slab of sidewalk. You've closed the gap to within half a block.

ILSE, please!

She turns again. There are tears on her face. She runs.

I'm sorry! you shout. Please!

She stops, turns. She looks at you with big eyes.

I didn't mean to frighten you, you tell her. Please give me a chance to explain.

You tell her how, at the museum, you panicked, you thought she was someone else, you were confused, jetlagged, it was all a mistake, you feel terrible about it.

I've been going through a lot lately, you say. Can we talk?

She smiles.

Please?

She lives close by, she tells you, and you follow her home. Her apartment is small but cozy, with exposed brick walls and a fireplace. She brews some tea, and you sit with her in the kitchen reading long passages from the notebook. She listens without saying anything. You read everything, it takes a couple hours, and she does not complain. She makes dinner, and you eat it on the floor in the living room, in the near dark. She is quiet, thoughtful, you can tell she is processing all the information you've shared with her. It is incredible—she does not judge you.

I leave tomorrow, you say, and she nods sadly. While you are making love she tells you how much she admires you, how truthful and courageous you are, how she wishes she'd met you earlier, before any of this had happened—all this while she lowers and raises herself above you, grinds into you, until she comes, quietly, with a sneeze-like gasp, and drops her face onto your shoulder.

But that's not what happens, is it? That's all in your head as she stops and turns to face you.

Stay the fuck away from me, you sick fuck!

You stop in your tracks. Two small children, playing in their front yard, stare at you. ILSE starts running again.

Please! you shout after her.

She turns a corner, and by the time you reach it she is nowhere to be seen. There are trees and shrubs and wide front porches—plenty of hiding places. One of these homes may even be hers. She could be on the other side of one of these doors.

ILSE! I need to tell you something!

No answer. You could check behind every tree, every bush. You could ring every doorbell. You could do any number of things. But what you will tell people, if anyone bothers to ask, is that after making love you walked slowly along the path on which you came, careful not to get lost in the dark, all the way back to the Orenthal Hotel.

《《《—》》》

He opened the double closet. There, among all Sara's clothes, were the suitcases. Two large cases and a carry-on. He yanked out one of the larger ones and opened it up. Sara's winter clothes. He carefully piled them inside the closet. Would this bag be enough? Should he take the carry-on also?

As he was mulling this over he noticed a prescription bottle on the bedside table. He examined the label. SULFA, to be taken orally twice daily.

The phone rang, nearly giving him a heart attack. Should I pick it up? he thought. No. He let it ring, then listened to the message.

Hello, luv.

He recognized the voice. British. Or Scottish. Male. One of Sara's clients. A rock musician.

I've arrived and am all checked in here. A very lovely room you've booked for me, with a huge bloody bed on which I am lying at this very moment. I know you're coming at nine but since I'm a bit early I was hoping we could make it sooner. I'm, uh, eager to see you, I suppose. Oh—and I've ordered some bubbly. Ta.

Ta.

The tongue on the roof of the mouth, just behind the front teeth, and then the expulsion of air. Ta. He may as well have said, Come on over here, luv, and suck my cock.

Ta.

Francis Dunleavy lived in Los Angeles. It was starting to make sense.

He sank to the edge of the bed.

Dilsey leapt up beside him.

Dilsey, he said.

She moved to the other side of the bed, watching him.

Come on. Come over here, sweetie. Come to daddy.

He moved toward her but she leapt from the bed.

Dilsey, he said. Come on. Be nice.

She was under the bed now. He got on the floor and looked. She was crouched over near the wall, her green eyes aglow.

Here, girl. Come on, Dilsey. *Please.*

But she did not budge. When he crawled part way underneath the bed she scooted past him and stood over near the closet.

Dilsey, *come here.* I just want to *hold* you.

She ran and hid behind the bureau again.

Come on, Dilsey. Be a good girl.

He shut the bedroom door so she would not be able to escape.

Okay, Dilsey. You're trapped now. Just come over here for a minute. Please, Dilsey. *Please.*

When she sprang onto the bed again he lunged for her, and scooped her up into his arms. She wriggled madly to get free. He squeezed her tightly and tried to nuzzle his nose into her soft neck fur.

Come on, Dilsey, give me a hug, just like that first time.

She hissed and scratched his arm. He cried out and dropped her. Godammit!

There was a four inch long, bright red line of blood on his arm. It stung like hell.

Dilsey watched him with electric eyes from the top of the bureau.

219

C'mere, girl.

He could feel the blood pumping through his veins and slowly oozing from his arm.

C'mere, Dilsey. Come to daddy. Come on. I won't hurt you. I promise.

CHAPTER EIGHTEEN: HONEYMOON

Honeymoon: It was a custom in ancient times for a newly married couple to drink a special potion containing honey on each of the first thirty days—a *moon*—of their marriage... There is still another explanation of the use of *moon* in this phrase. According to the World Webster Dictionary, this referred "not to the period of a month, but to the mutual affection of newlyweds, regarded as *waning like the moon*."
— *Dictionary of Word and Phrase Origins*,
by William and Mary Morris

We spent our honeymoon on St. Barth's. We didn't belong there, we were pale Americans with a limited budget, but we went anyway, the thought being, This is our honeymoon, it happens once, let's splurge.

Upon our arrival, we were escorted from the airport to a nearby villa apartment, one that was so close to the runway that the buzz from the arriving and departing flights rattled the dishes in the cupboards. The rental agent informed us that this would go on every thirty minutes, from nine a.m. until sundown, and that, for an extra charge, we could rent a villa in a less noisy location. She was a fit, tan woman clearly torn between wanting a larger commission and the desire to leave us as soon as possible. I was in favor of changing—the rental company had vacant villas all over the island—but Caleb was perfectly content. Too expensive, he said. He was exhausted, and didn't want to go traipsing around the island searching for the perfect place. We'll just stay here, he declared, setting his bags on a table in the bedroom, It's good enough, and I had the distinct feeling he was not just speaking of the apartment, but also about *us*.

After the rental agent left, he undressed and lay on the bed. How about some nookie? he asked.

How about we go to the beach?

It was late afternoon, the sun was low in the sky, the water was a blanket of rippling diamonds. A gentle breeze rustled the leaves on the palm trees outside the villa. Fifty feet down the beach was an outdoor bar where we could sip rum drinks and watch the beginning of the world.

Me so horny, he said.

I thought you were exhausted.

Me so hooooorny, he said, the tip of his erect cock flopping against his belly.

Can't we just go down to the beach first and watch the sun go down? We've come all this way.

It's our honeymoon, he explained, the trace of a whine in his voice. Honeymoons are for nookie.

Look, I said. Let's make a deal. You'll get your nookie. I want nookie too. But we just flew a jillion miles, the last few on a *very* wobbly airplane, and I am tired and cranky and I feel dirty and I need to relax a little, okay?

In the middle of this short speech there came a loud buzz from the airport as a plane—the one we flew in on—took off for St. Maarten.

That's going to drive me crazy, I said.

Me so hooooorny.

«««—»»»

I still dream about the beaches. Golden vanilla sand, translucent water, craggy cliffs, tall, arching palm trees. Sometimes it was just the two of us, or else there were a few others, scattered at wide intervals, the women nude, often the men too. To lie completely naked in the hot sun—I felt giddy, like a child. But Caleb, he wouldn't remove his swim suit. I'm afraid I'll pop a stiffy, he said. And no doubt he would have. It was all he talked about:

222

How about we head back to the villa and play doctor?

What's say we ditch this boring place and go play hide the salami?

Hey. Hey. Wanna fool around?

Someone wants to *talk* to you.

Me so hoooorny.

One day, after an afternoon at Governor's Beach, we returned to the villa for a nap. I was sunburned and exhausted. He was red also, but it didn't seem to take anything out of him. After half an hour's sleep I woke up with his hand between my legs.

Hey!

Rise and shine, he said.

Cut it out!

Aw, c'mon.

I'm trying to sleep.

Well, don't mind me, he said, placing a hand on my breast.

Stop! I shouted, and rolled away.

What's *up* with you?

I'm tired, that's what's up.

Tired? All we do is lie around all day on the beach.

Lying in the sun makes me tired. Swimming makes me tired. Life makes me tired, and work makes me tired, and this is a vacation from all that.

Fine.

He stalked out of the bedroom and slammed the door. In between blasts from the air conditioner and the buzz of airplanes I heard him slapping the pages of a book out in the living room. I never did get back to sleep.

«««—»»»

For our stay on St. Barth's, we rented a small, convertible jeep. Unfortunately, my driver's license had expired, so Caleb had to do all the driving on the island's narrow, winding roads. Driving to and from the beaches, he was extra cautious, often holding up the more daring local drivers for miles at a time. I could see him getting upset when they honked their horns. Goddam French bastards, he muttered. When I suggested he drive a little faster, he said, What—and go plunging off the edge of the road? Is that your idea of a honeymoon? No, I thought, but then neither is this.

One night we had dinner at Trois Chevaux, a small restaurant at the highest point of the island. On the way there, he drove like an old lady, probably to annoy me. We'd argued earlier about the usual thing, and his lips had been turned in on themselves ever since. When another driver barreled past us with a long, loud honking of his horn, Caleb flashed him his middle finger. Soon the driver slowed and pulled off the road, and Caleb spent the rest of the ride looking nervously in the rearview mirror to check if he was following us.

Don't worry, I laughed, He's not after you.

What? You think I'm worried about *him*?

No, I said, smiling. You're not worried.

What? *What*?

Nothing, I said, not smiling anymore.

We were the only customers at the restaurant. The chef pampered us, promised a perfect meal, and I quickly drank two glasses of wine. Look, I said, you can see the ocean from here.

He nodded and ate some bread. There was an expression on his face I'd rarely seen, but would eventually come to know very well. A stony blankness, as though everything inside had frozen. I recognized it as his mother's face. It frightened me, but I didn't know what to say or do, so I remained silent also, choosing instead to pat the small, scrawny cat that had appeared at our feet.

His name is Dieu-Dieu, the chef told us. He is looking for scraps.

I hope Dilsey's okay, I said as I picked up Dieu-Dieu and rubbed his raggedy ears.

Don't do that, Sara, Caleb said. It probably has fleas.

But I continued patting Dieu-Dieu, who purred contentedly, and he remained on my lap through the entire meal. This was the first time I can remember ignoring Caleb.

«««—»»»

The day before we left St. Barth's, we went snorkeling with Pascal and Claude, a gay French couple who ran a tour service from the main harbor. I knew a little French and though they spoke rapidly to one another as we headed out to the reefs I managed to pick up that Pascal and Claude thought Caleb was cute. Claude, I think, sensed that I'd understood this, and he occasionally made amusing comments about *votre mari* that made me laugh.

I don't know why I didn't share this with Caleb. I suppose I wanted a secret. It was pure resentment. He was acting so distant and hostile that I didn't feel at all close to him. I was having my first misgivings about what we'd done—our marriage—but did not want to acknowledge them. Meanwhile, Pascal and Claude were being charming, and so I spent all my affection on them.

With a mischievous gleam in his eye Claude brought out the punch. When no one was looking I poured mine over the side, but Caleb, as he always did when perturbed, drank too much, too quickly, and soon became even more sullen. Normally this would have annoyed me, but I was continually amused by the Frenchmen's antics—it seemed that the less communicative Caleb became the more attractive they found him. At one point, just as we were slowing down near the reef, I told them in broken French that Caleb and I were on our honeymoon but that they could borrow him for a night if they wished. He has more love than I can handle, I explained, and they both laughed merrily.

The water was glorious. Calm, clear as glass, warm with refreshing little pockets of cool that made my skin tingle. Pascal jumped in with me to demonstrate how to use the snorkel while Claude remained on board to prepare our lunch. Caleb, meanwhile, flopped around in the water trying to keep his flippers on. Does your husband want some help? Pascal asked. I think he's fine, I said, and was amused by the look of disappointment on Pascal's face.

I immediately swam as far away as I could and still feel safe. It was wonderful to be alone. For a few moments it was just me and the magnificent fish swimming innocently below. They appeared so free and content, though I knew in fact they were basically scavenging for food and, were they to stop for even a little while to enjoy themselves, the way we sometimes do, they would either starve or be eaten by some larger fish.

I did not hear Caleb calling my name. I had no idea he was anywhere near me until I became aware of a splashing close by. Looking up, I saw a pair of flailing pink arms. Oh my God, I thought. And all of it passed before my eyes: the image of his lifeless, waterlogged body being pulled onto the boat, his skin slowly turning blue, the dark wood of a coffin, his mother's black dress. The next thing I knew Pascal was there, his impressive arms around Caleb, a look of amused calm on his face as Caleb resisted and shouted incomprehensible things. When Caleb was finally under control, I followed as Pascal towed him back to the boat, and somehow the French came to me, and I asked if my husband was going to be all right, and Pascal, pleased with himself for saving him, said, *Oui*.

CHAPTER NINETEEN: THE END

There is an announcement over the loudspeakers concerning your flight. The aircraft is late getting into Portland, but it has finally landed and will soon be at the gate.

Check-in went smoothly. The woman at the counter barely looked up from her computer monitor. Your name did not set off bells, she did not call for security. And she was very pretty.

There is a commotion over near the gate doorway. The flight crew has arrived and one of the attendants is gesticulating excitedly. Your fellow passengers then start mumbling and craning to look down the hallway. It's him! someone says excitedly, and you turn to see Boyd Hart, the film actor, hustle past a crowd and through the gate. He looks smaller in person than he does on screen.

《《——》》

He waited patiently at the gate, fidgeting in the hard plastic seat, rubbing at the barely scabbed scratches on his arms, periodically touching the carry-on bag at his feet to make sure it was still there.

He was so tired. He hadn't been able to sleep. Not with the carry-on in the apartment.

Everyone seemed to be watching him. He was sure he'd caught several people staring. When they saw him look they turned away.

He stood up, slung the bag over his shoulder, and paced the floor. He kept eyeing the bank of telephones nearby, wondering if he should call her apartment, leave a message.

Happy birthday, he muttered to himself.

«‹‹——››»

Another announcement—it's time to board. You rise, feeling light and carefree without the carry-on bag, and wait in line. You hand your ticket to a uniformed woman at the doorway. She smiles gaily, tears off the stub, hands the ticket back.

Have a nice flight.

Thanks. I will.

«‹‹——››»

He got in line to board. In front of him an old man struggled with a wheeled bag. Through the window the runway shimmered. Breathe. The gate attendant smiled, took his ticket, tore off the stub, handed it back. He stared down the long tunneled walkway. It looked like a cave. Breathe.

Sir? You can board now.

He could not move.

Sir?

The people behind him began to grumble.

Sir?

Sorry, he said.

The woman smiled in an official way. Take your time, sir.

He headed down the long walkway.

Breathe...

About the Author

Chris Belden is a graduate of the Fairfield University MFA program. His work has appeared in numerous publications, including *American Fiction, Skidrow Penthouse*, and *The Newtowner*. He is co-writer of the feature film *Amnesia* (starring Ally Sheedy and John Savage), and has released two albums of original music, *Songs About Anything* and *Camouflage* (SpankyTone Records). He has taught creative writing at Fairfield University and Garner Correctional Institution, a high-security men's prison. Chris Belden lives with his family in Connecticut. For more information, please visit at www.chrisbelden.com.